HER SECOND CHANCE

BETTE FORD

COPYRIGHT

Her Second Chance
Copyright © 2018 by Bette Ford
Print ISBN: 9781641970587

NYLA Publishing
121 W 27th St., Suite 1201, New York, NY 10001
http://www.nyliterary.com

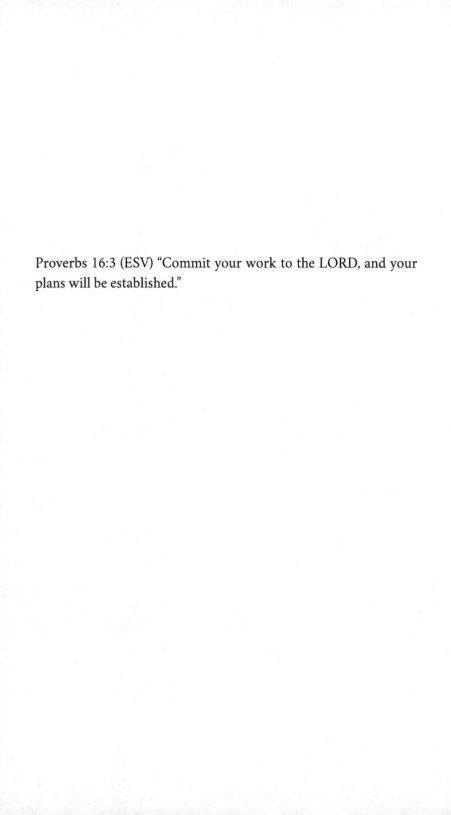

Proverbs 16:3 (ESV) "Commit your work to the LORD, and your plans will be established."

DEDICATION

Honor and glory to the heavenly Father,
To the dedicated readers who never gave up, who hung in there with me
and encouraged me. It has been a long rough road, but thanks to your
prayers and God's blessings I did it!
To Michelle Ray, whose friendship has come to mean the world to me.
To Johnna Lynn Johnson, thanks so much for running countless errands
so I could focus on writing.
And to Carla Fredd, Beverly Jenkins, Crystal Hammonds and Mary
Pittman, just because.

1

------

*W*hen Trenna McAdams stepped off the elevator, she ran smack into a hard male chest and bounced. The only thing that saved her from falling onto the thick carpeting was a pair of large hands that gripped her shoulders to steady her.

"What the…" she stopped, managing not to let loose a word her beloved, sweet mother would have never approved.

"Are you all right?"

Her petite body stiffened at the sound of the familiar deep, throaty voice. She had to lean back and tilt her chin up in order to look into a pair of twinkling, midnight-blue eyes. Darrin Morgan! She detested the prominent attorney and smooth-talking woman-izer. Fuming, she used both hands to push him away.

Unfortunately, she hadn't been able to push him out of her dreams at night or the wild fantasies that crept into her daydreams when she least expected it. Just the thought warmed her cheeks, causing her deep, coffee-bean skin to flush with embarrassment.

"Trenna, are…" Darrin repeated.

"I'm perfectly fine. Thank you," she said politely. "You can let go of me."

Darrin's generous lips curved upward. "Always the lady. Do you ever get flustered?" Before she could respond, he said, "Tell me, how may I help you, Ms. McAdams." She must have looked as baffled as she felt, judging by his next comment, "You came to me, remember."

Cognizant of his warm, ivory skin and startling good looks, she inhaled his clean, male scent. The waves in his thick, close-cut, black hair, his strong nose and generously curved mouth left no doubt of his African heritage.

Trenna didn't need to use her imagination to know there was no shortage of females in Darrin's life. The women in the Morgan-Green Building had nicknamed the Morgan twins the 'Ivory Princes'. Darrin was labeled Number One and Douglas was Number Two. Both were lawyers and business partners, but they were also good-looking, smart, with the advantage of having well-toned muscular bodies and wealth.

She could never forget their first meeting when she had just moved into the building. She and her BFF Maureen Hale Sheppard had been working hard to get her nursery school up and running. During a break for lunch they were seated in one of the building's most popular restaurants, Cheezy's Grill. The third floor sandwich shop was packed, with no empty tables. Douglas and Darrin came in together and helped themselves to the empty seats across from them. Maureen made the introductions.

When Darrin's dark blue eyes locked with Trenna's, she felt her heart pick up speed. Her breath seemed to be lodged in her throat at the jolt of awareness. The attraction was immediate and so unexpected that it scared her... No, he scared her.

Darrin Morgan was big, full of confidence, virile, and utterly male. He was too much...he unnerved her. His dark eyes missed nothing as they slowly moved over her. Normally when a man started flirting, she ignored it or laughed it off, but she couldn't with Darrin.

He was a strong, determined man, used to being in control and perfectly suited for his chosen career. She decided then and there she didn't like him. Evidently, he didn't get the message. At the first opportunity he asked her out. Unfortunately for her he saw her refusal as a challenge. Trenna had had her fill of controlling men. Following her instincts, she knew she had to stand firm. From that day to this, as far as she was concerned he was off limits.

Trenna knew about loss. First, she'd lost her parents and then later her husband, Martin. It had taken time to adjust to the change. The young widow valued her hard-won independence and had no interest in remarrying. Unfortunately for her, Darrin made it no secret that he found her attractive and persisted in asking her out. The nonsense had gone on for nearly three years now.

What annoyed her to no end was that the mere sight of him caused her heart to race with awareness and her temper to flare. No matter how many times she asked herself why, of all the men in the city, did the chemistry have be so strong with him. There was no answer that made sense her. Everything about him made her uncomfortably aware of his masculine appeal. It was grossly unfair considering how much she disliked the man.

Had he ever had to work for anything in his life? Judging by the way he'd stepped up to head the family-owned firm after his father passed, her answer was a decided no. Following in their father's footsteps, the twins attended Howard University in Washington, D.C. and practically flew through college and then law school. They finished in five years and graduated with honors.

Darrin certainly looked the part of being spoiled and rich, dressed in a custom-made, navy blue suit that he'd teamed with pale blue shirt, navy and white stripe tie with a matching pocket square. It disgusted her the way women of all ages chased after him as if he were the last man standing.

Samuel Morgan and Adam Green started the biracial law firm back in the fifties. The two had met in law school and became fast friends despite the racial climate of the country at the time. The firm was very successful handling many civil rights cases. It wasn't long before they expanded, buying a modern high-rise in downtown Detroit, Michigan near the waterfront. Morgan and Green were visionaries, taking the top floor for their offices, and then bringing in a top chef to open a first-class restaurant, and then trendy nightclub with live entertainment. Both had proven to be very successful.

The partners had passed their love of law onto their sons. Andrew Green, like the Morgan twins, was full partner and part owner.

After losing her husband, Martin, Trenna needed to put her life back together. She'd moved from her hometown of Charleston, N.C. cross-country to Michigan in order to be near her best friend, Maureen Hale Sheppard.

Maureen recommended the Morgan-Green Building because she certain it was perfect for the Little Hearts, Trenna's nursery school. The fact that the Morgans and Sheppards were longtime neighbors and friends had clearly swayed her friend. Plus, Trenna would be less than a mile from the Valerie Hale Sheppard Women's Crisis Center that Maureen owned and ran with her grandmother. The Center had been named after and honored Maureen's late mother.

One of Trenna and Maureen's friends, Sherri Ann Weber was a lawyer, who worked for Morgan-Green. Trenna rarely saw her during business hours. There was no doubt that Sherri Ann was a hard-worker and on the fast track to make partner.

"Well?" Darrin prompted, his dark eyes moving slowly up from her high-heeled black booties to the black pantsuit, which she'd teamed with a pink ruffled blouse.

"Well what?" Trenna blinked, lost in thought. It seemed that every time their paths crossed, the tension between them was palpable and her awareness of him soared. She decided early on to be sensible and stay as far away from him as she could. Why wouldn't he take the hint and leave her alone? She wasn't about to change her mind.

He pointed out, "You came to me."

"I did no such..." Trenna stopped so quickly her teeth clanked together. She only then noticed she stood in his firm's opulent lobby. The firm's name was mounted on the wall in large gold block letters behind the receptionist desk. Embarrassed, she said, "I pushed the wrong button. Instead of going down, it went up. Good day."

Spinning around, she headed back to the elevator. So annoyed when he kept pace with her, she broke a nail when she jabbed the call button. Swallowing a frustrating scream, she stared straight ahead, pretending he wasn't there.

The domineering, over-confident, arrogant jerk set her teeth on edge. He reminded her of a past mistake. Unwilling to get involved with a man she knew was wrong for her, she had become an expert at avoiding him. No doubt he saw her actions as a challenge. Unfortunately for her, he seemed to thrive on challenges.

"How much longer?" Darrin asked softly.

He tried, but he couldn't take his eyes off her petite beauty. She was tiny, barely five-one, and, at six-two, he towered over her curvy form. His mother had said she reminded her of true African beauty. To Darrin she was a queen...his beautiful queen. Although her delicate small, features and luscious full lips were gorgeous, it was her warmth and kindness that he found irresistible.

He wanted her, and that had not changed since the day he first saw her in the crowded sandwich shop. He had made the mistake of asking her out immediately. Her refusal was swift. It was his bad luck that the most desirable woman on the planet was not only a recent widow but had also taken an instant disliking to him.

He had tried to show her the proper respect. He had given it a year before he tried again. She'd refused and hadn't stopped saying no. Nothing he said or did since had managed to crack her protective bubble. And it had gone on too long. He needed answers and wanted them, now.

She snapped, "Excuse me?"

"Don't play games with me, Trenna McAdams. You're a very smart lady, an excellent educator and top-notch businesswoman. You've managed to keep your business thriving in spite of hard economic times. There're plenty of private nursery schools closing their doors all over the city, yet you have a waiting list of parents willing to pay through the nose to get their little ones in your school. How long do you plan on avoiding me?"

When she frowned, he reminded himself that she came to him. He was no saint and was not above using her mistake of getting off on the wrong floor to his advantage.

TRENNA SIGHED. Darrin was right about her work. She had been ecstatic the day Little Hearts Nursery School opened their doors. She liked the building, loved the space, from the big windows to the large airy rooms. The facility was perfect, located on the first floor in the east-corner and was both bright and sunny. They had converted the small parking lot on the side of the building into a gated playground.

She soon found out what it was like to be pursued by such a charming, smooth-talking male. The main thing she knew from having been married to an attorney was that they were skilled and determined to win at any cost. She was not flattered by his persistence. But she was determined to protect herself and not to let him get too close. Her instincts screamed for her to keep her distance. He was dangerous.

He repeated, "How long…"

"I heard you!" she snapped.

"Well, well." Chuckling, Darrin drawled, "I finally got a rise out of you. You forgot those lady-like manners your mama must have drilled into you. It's about time you slipped up, considering how easily you've gotten under my skin," he whispered close to her ear.

"Don't start with me."

"Start?" Darrin laughed without humor. "I've lost count of the number of times I've asked you out. Are you ever going to give me a reason? Or don't you date light skin brothers?"

"No you didn't go there!"

"Yeah, I did. The least you can do is tell me why."

Trenna glared at Darrin as if she had serious doubts about his sanity. "Now who's playing games? I said no."

A muscle jumped in his cheek, as if he were grinding his teeth. "Tell me why, Trenna."

She propped a fist on her hip and said tightly, "Maybe I'm sick of your inability to take no for an answer? Perhaps I think it's time you realized you are not irresistible to every female on the planet? You think I don't know that I'm nothing more than challenge to you? Darrin, you really need to deal with that huge ego of yours. And even if I could look beyond all that, I haven't forgotten you are responsible for getting the rapist who attacked my friend off free."

"You're wrong, Trenna. You're more than a challenge to me. My ego is not the problem. The last time I checked, there was nothing wrong with a man showing his interest in a beautiful woman. And my work…"

"Don't! Clearly, you're either spoiled rotten or ruthless."

"That's a bit harsh." He stared at her, then asked, "What are you afraid of?"

She stiffened, but before she could respond, the elevator bell chimed, signaling its arrival. It was a good thing that it was empty, because as soon as the doors slid open, Trenna dashed inside intent on reaching the control panel. As if anticipating the move, Darrin blocked the panel with his broad frame.

Frustrated by his antics, she hissed, "Move!" She jutted out her small chin and folded her arms beneath her breasts.

Then there was a shout, "Hold the elevator!"

Darrin's arm shot out, preventing the door from closing.

Thoroughly ticked, Trenna tapped a small, high-heeled foot on the floor. Pointing to her wristwatch, she said, "Some of us have to actually work for a living."

Darrin grinned as if she had told a joke.

Captivated, her heart picked up speed. "Why?" she muttered beneath her breath. Why couldn't he be ugly? "Why..." She clapped a hand over her mouth.

Good grief! What was her problem? No! It was his fault! He had her so flustered that she was not only talking to herself but doing it aloud too.

"Put a move on it, bro," Darrin called.

Douglas Morgan hurried inside the elevator with a briefcase in hand. He too, was dressed in a chocolate brown custom-made suit and a bronze silk tie and shirt.

"Sorry," Douglas said. "I thought you'd be halfway to the court-house by now." After he punched the unlit button marked "L" for lobby, he spotted Trenna hugging the back wall and grinned. "Hey, Trenna. How are you? Stopped in for a visit or business?"

"Hi Doug," Trenna relaxed, responding to his warm smile. She was able to laugh when she admitted, "I wasn't paying attention and hit the wrong button after leaving Trader's." She referred to the restaurant that was on the floor below. "When the doors opened I got off. I ended up in your lobby. Very nice, by the way, who's your decorator?"

The twins exchanged a look and then smiled.

Douglas admitted, "Our mother, she ...".

Darrin finished his twin's sentence, "...did our offices as well."

"I didn't realize."

Trenna liked Tina Morgan. They attended the same church and Bible study. Plus, they served on several of the same committees.

"I should have known," she laughed, unconsciously slipping into the charming,

lady-like demeanor she'd grown up with thanks to her southern mother. Although, she refused to glance his way, Trenna could almost feel the heat of Darrin's dark gaze. For a moment she was startled, surprised by what she had seen in his eyes. No, she must be mistaken. It couldn't be sadness. No, it had to be anger or frustration. She shivered, struggling to concentrate on the decreasing floor numbers. She broke the awkward silence by asking, "How is Megan?"

Douglas grinned, his dark blue eyes sparkled. "Great!"

"Wedding plans all set?"

Chuckling, he said, "Mine are. I plan to show up when and wherever she tells me."

Trenna giggled, "Good idea. I received my invitation to the bridal shower. I'm looking forward to it."

Douglas nodded happily.

Just then the elevator slowed to a stop and the doors slid open.

Stepping out first, Trenna said, "Good seeing you, Doug." Remembering her manners, she added, "... bye Darrin." She didn't wait for a response but quickly crossed the lobby to the glass double doors marked Little Hearts and hurried inside.

THEY FOLLOWED THE HALLWAY, passed the bakery and the card shop heading to the rear entrance. Douglas glanced back at his twin, then quizzed, "What's wrong?"

"Not a thing."

"Then why the scowl? You should be grinning like a fool. You had some time alone with your lady."

"My lady?" Darrin snapped. "Hardly! I can barely get her to speak to me. She couldn't get away from me fast enough. Believe me, there's nothing worth celebrating."

Douglas affectionately squeezed his twin's nape. "Come on, bro, talking is how you earn your bread and butter. According to Melissa, once you spot a lady, in less than two minutes you have her ready to follow you anywhere."

Darrin rolled his eyes skyward. "It's a shame that you and our assistant have nothing better to do than listen to the building's gossip mill and speculate on my love life."

Douglas hooted with laughter. "Why should you be exempt? Everyone in our office knew I had a thing for Megan long before she agreed to go out with me."

"I suppose."

"Suppose? As you well know, it was a big deal considering, Megan was the assistant prosecutor on the Kentfield-Benson case and on the Clark-Johnson case. We were constantly battling it out in court and were not supposed to be eyeing each other across the table. That didn't stop the sparks from flying. The woman made me sizzle."

They reached the parking lot and stood beside Douglas' bronze Lexus.

Glancing at his watch, Douglas urged, "Since we're both due in court, in ten words or less, tell me what happened."

"She said I can't take no for an answer, that I'm either spoiled rotten or ruthless. She even brought up that I took the Todd Marks case. Clearly, she resents me for it and believes he raped her friend Grace Brooks. She blames me for getting him off. "

"What? It has been awhile. Enough time for emotions to cool. She's a professional and should realize it wasn't personal. You were only doing your job. "

"Evidently it hasn't been long enough for Ms. McAdams. She really won't talk to me and it's making me nuts. "

Douglas chuckled. "If you tell Mom I said this, I'll deny it. But I swear females have no limit when it comes to holding a grudge."

Darrin didn't crack a smile when he muttered, "Me, ruthless? How would she know when she's never given us a real chance? Her defenses have been up since the day we met. "

"She's a widow. It has to be grief."

Darrin shook his head firmly. "No, that's not it. Her husband has been gone a few years. She's been dating." He grated bitterly, hating his jealousy and resentment. "According to Melissa, Trenna went to the Women's Halloween dinner-dance with John Dearing."

And there was one night that Darrin couldn't forget. Trenna had stopped by to see his mother. It was a few days after their father had passed. She had come with food, intent on spending time with them. Darrin wasn't hungry. He stayed in the den, away from the others. Although the television was on, he wasn't watching.

He hadn't welcomed her visit, not then. His grief had been too painful...raw. She hadn't insisted he eat, hadn't argued. Instead, she sat quietly with him, and then she told him about losing her parents, both at once. She had only been eighteen. There was no doubt she understood loss because she had lived it. Her warmth and compassion had touched him.

Although there had been lots of people there, his father's friends and colleagues, he was cognizant of her. Even though, he had been unable to shed any tears, seeing her at the funeral and burial, knowing she offered her support had gotten him through. She had shown him another side to her personality, shown him a sweetness that he still craved.

"Dearing? The accountant on the fourth floor?"

"Yeah."

"Have you talked to Maureen?" Douglas referred to their mutual friend and neighbor. "Or asked her why Trenna..."

"No!" Darrin interrupted, "Like Maureen would rat on her BFF?" He scowled. "It's embarrassing how many times I've asked her out since we met, and she always says no. She has to be nursing a major grudge against me. But why? When she relocated to Michigan four years ago she was obviously ready to move on with her life. And she has. She's clearly a gorgeous, smart and savvy business woman. She can have any man she wants."

Douglas grinned, "I may be getting married next summer, but I'm not claiming that I understand why women do what they do."

Scowling, Darrin muttered, "I have my pride. I shouldn't care that Trenna couldn't get away from me fast enough." A glance at his watch had him jogging toward his own car.

She believed he saw her as a challenge, but she was dead wrong. He could not admit it to anyone, not even to his twin, how much her rejection hurt. Nor could he reveal how deeply she had gotten to him. She was right when she said he had an ego. It felt as if she had crushed his manhood beyond repair. Yet, she possessed an incredible sweetness that was impossible to resist. He could no more stop the wanting than he could stop breathing.

His brother called, "So you're going to give up?"

"No way!" Darrin called back as he started the engine.

Douglas yelled as he drove past, "Morgan men never quit!"

"We're too damn stubborn or stupid," Darrin murmured aloud.

2

---

*T*he instant she was spotted inside the noise-proof facility, Trenna was bombarded by the welcoming sounds of children's voices ranging from squeals of delight to boisterous laughter, petulant whining and cries.

Her chest swelled with pride as she looked at the warm and bright learning environment that she had created for the children. It had taken years of planning and a tremendous amount of hard work to ensure that every child was safe, secure, loved, and confident enough to spread their little wings and soar.

"You're back!" Tasha Redman said, Trenna's assistant only worked part-time because she was taking a full schedule of classes at Wayne State University. The younger woman found that she enjoyed working with the little ones so much that she decided to major in Early Childhood Education.

"Most days I'm glad we met at the Women's Crisis Center. But today, not so much," Tasha teased.

"What happened?" Trenna had been volunteering in the Saturday afternoon mentoring program for close to two years. Like several of her friends, she enjoyed helping the teen girls in the foster care system's independent living program. When the founder of the mentoring program Laura Murdock Kramer moved to Chicago, Trenna had taken over mentoring Tasha and recently become her employer.

"Marjorie was sick after lunch and threw up all over both of us. I helped her change and then called her mother."

Before Trenna could respond, Tasha reported, "And Billy's in the time-out chair because he was upset when Lena knocked over his blocks, so he grabbed her doll and deliberately threw it on the floor as hard as he could. He put a big dent in the forehead. It was her favorite and she was inconsolable. Oh, and you had a call from Anna Prescott Gaines, the caterer. They're having a problem with the menu."

Trenna nodded but was close enough to Tasha to wrinkle her nose. She offered, "You're welcome to use my office bathroom to shower and change. There are clean tops in the closet."

Her office had all the comforts of home, including a sofa that let out into a queen-size bed, a private bath, fully stocked with fresh towels and toiletries. In a pinch, Trenna could spend the night in relative comfort. Once she had worked very late, finishing a report only to go out to the car and find her tire was flat. Another time she had hosted the Elegant Five, her book club, after hours at the school. After two glasses of wine, she didn't trusting her driving skills and ended up staying over.

Bad weather was the main reason she had outfitted the office like a studio apartment. Normally, she avoided driving in the snow or ice. She could never forget the time it had started to snow while she was more than halfway home. Although she was a nervous wreck, through much prayer she managed to get there in one piece. It was a miracle, considering how difficult it was for Trenna to drive in Michigan's harsh winters.

Suddenly, she realized she was shaking, still annoyed with herself for letting today's encounter with Darrin Morgan throw her. Having been on her own for nearly five years, she had thought she was prepared for almost anything.

Kaleea Prescott yelled, "Miss M! You came back!" the instant she spotted Trenna. The three-year-old wrapped her little arms around Trenna's hips and held on. Trenna worked with all the children in the school and it was not unusual for a child to become attached to her.

"Hi, Kaleea," Trenna smiled, before she squatted down to hug the little girl. Trenna silently mouthed the words, 'ten minutes,' to her assistant.

Since the arrival of her baby sister, Kaleea had become clingy and insecure. Kaleea's father, Wesley Prescott, played football for the Detroit Lions and traveled a great deal. Her mother, Kelli Prescott, although a stay-at-home mom, worked out of their home.

Her parents enrolled her in nursery school, hoping that being around other children would boost her confidence. It had taken several weeks, but Kaleea was starting to bloom. She enjoyed school and had become close friends with Nina Johnson. Unfortunately, Nina had the flu and wasn't in school today. Clearly, Kaleea was feeling the loss.

"Tired, hmm," Trenna surmised, smoothing a hand over Kaleea's back as the little girl rested her head on Trenna's shoulder.

Kaleea vigorously shook her head no, even though her eyelids were drooping.

"Come, I'll read you a story." Trenna led her over to the wooden rocking chairs. "Go pick out a book."

Kaleea smiled, heading over to the child-size bookcase.

Once she was settled on her lap, Trenna set the chair in motion, she read, "Brown bear, brown bear what do you see?" By the time, she reached the color green, other children joined had them, and were sitting on the colorful area rug, but Kaleea was asleep.

Trenna kept reading but signaled Connie Underwood, one of the teaching assistants, to take the sleeping child into slumber room where cots had been setup. Despite the administrative demands of her job, Trenna finished the picture story, and then read another before she sent the little ones off to the art room where Kathy Donavan was waiting to show them how to sponge paint leaves on the trees they had draw previously.

For Trenna, the nursery school was a dream come true. It was her special blessing, the one that had taken years to receive. In the meantime, she had prayed for and prepared for it. It was something she would never take for granted because it meant too much. And now, here they were, licensed to service children that ranged in age from six-weeks-old up to five years old.

Trenna hadn't taken time off between her undergraduate and graduate program. She had wanted to teach, but her husband objected. Martin didn't want her to work outside the home. She'd completed her Master's degree in Early Childhood Education and was working toward a doctorate in Administration when Martin passed. She worked hard and was confident in her abilities. She had planned every aspect of the nursery school long before she was able to make it happen.

She was thrilled that Little Hearts had succeeded far beyond her expectations. The school offered more than the basics, and they'd worked hard to insure all the children's needs were met. Because of that hard work, their first year was very successful. Word of mouth had done much toward filling their slots and creating a waiting list. The facility was privately owned, attracting the area's most affluent and wealthy.

She wanted the facility to be available to everyone, especially low-income families. It had become important to her, and she developed a scholarship program….so important that she used part of her inheritance to establish her foundation. This past fall, she had given away scholarships to two of her students. She took as much pleasure as their parents did that the children were flourishing.

The first thing she did when she reached her office was call their caterer. Anna Prescott Gaines and her team produced healthy, yet delicious meals that appealed to the children while staying within the school's budget.

Trenna gave the okay to substitute oranges for nectarines on Wednesday's menu. "Thanks Anna. I appreciate the call. Will there be a problem getting the bananas for the two children with citrus allergies?"

"None. We have the bananas ready to go. And no, I should be the one thanking you. You guys have done a remarkable job with my niece, Kaleea. She loves school and wants to go every single day. "

"Kaleea is a sweetheart."

Anna laughed. "We love her but that does not make us blind to the facts. She has been spoiled rotten by all of us. And for the first time since she had the new baby, my sister-in-law, Kelli, has been able to get some rest. As you know by now, Kaleea can be just as stubborn as her father. Since he was hurt and unable to play football, he has been impossible to be around. You have worked wonders with Kaleea and she loves you."

"Thank you. And we all love her."

As soon as she ended the call, her cell phone rang. Trenna said, "Hi, Maureen."

"Busy?"

"Always, just like you."

The best friends laughed. These days the two were business owners, responsible employers with specialty clientele, requiring them to put in long days. They'd met at Spellman College in Atlanta and were roommates their freshman year. By the end of that first year they were close friends. Over the years, they managed to remain close in spite of living in different parts of the country at the time.

Maureen was a counselor and in her element at the Valerie Hale Sheppard Women's Crisis Center, which she ran with Mrs.

Hale, her grandmother. The Center catered to the needs of sexually assaulted and abused women and children.

Trenna and Maureen had a lot in common. They were both only children of very successful parents and hated not having siblings. They loved to read and shared books. They had grown up attending their local AME church and shared a love for God. They agreed they were blessed and talked about someday being able to give back. Surprisingly, during their second year in college they had both been engaged.

Yet, Trenna was the loner and Maureen was an extravert. Trenna was comfortable at home or in company of close friends while Maureen made friends easily and loved dining out, concerts and dancing.

Over the years, they had shared much. Trenna had held Maureen and dried her tears when she found out the truth about her fiancé and had been forced to break off the engagement. Maureen had been Trenna's maid of honor, despite her belief that Trenna was making a huge mistake by rushing into marriage. Plus Maureen had been there for Trenna when she lost her husband.

They had encouraged each other to follow their dreams. Even though their interests varied, it was no surprise to them that they became business owners or that they were dedicated to their clients. They now also lived in the same neighborhood with their offices barely a mile apart. Because of their busy schedules they rarely found time to have lunch together.

"I'm calling to make sure we're still on for tonight...dinner and a movie?"

Trenna smiled, "Absolutely. I will meet you at seven. Will it be just the two of us?"

"Grace and Vanessa are joining us. That okay?"

"Of course. It's always good to see them both. How is Grace? She still volunteering at the Women's Center?"

"Yeah, she has done well considering what she has been

through. Because of her willingness to share her experience, she has been a true blessing to the other rape victims."

"She's a good person and shouldn't have to live in fear," Trenna said vehemently.

Maureen had been assigned to Grace's case at the hospital the night of her rape. And she took Grace on as a client at the Women's Crisis Center. As Grace progressed, she eventually agreed to take part in group counseling.

After completing counseling, Maureen had introduced Grace into their circle of friends. Like their? other friends, Grace began to volunteered at the Women's Center, mentoring the teen girls who were in foster care.

Maureen said, "I can't argue with that. We both know Grace is a wonderful person."

Both Trenna and Maureen had been in the courtroom to support Grace during the difficult trial, along with Darrin who played a decidedly different role. Trenna refused to let her mind remain on that dark thought for long. "Tell me how you managed to convince Vanessa to join us tonight? Normally she and that gorgeous husband of hers are practically joined at the hip."

Maureen laughed, "I didn't have to do any convincing. Ralph recently had a late night out with the guys—a Piston's game I believe. It's Vanessa's turn to have an evening out. It has been a while since we've spent time with her."

Trenna sighed. "I can't remember the last time. I must I sound like a broken record but, the three of us haven't talked books since our last book club meeting, which was right before Laura married and moved to Chicago."

Maureen admitted, "Yeah. I know what you mean. We aren't the Elegant Five anymore, not with both Laura and Brynne living out of the state."

Trenna reminisced, "It was a blast. Laura could really pull a book apart. And the five of us really had a good time together.

When we selected the name we were all single, sassy and some serious reading sisters."

"Of course," Maureen laughed. "It was Brynne, who started our downfall when she fell for her ex, Devin Prescott, and then married him."

"For heaven sake's, they made a baby together! You make it sound as if we blame her."

"No, I didn't mean to. Brynne and Devin had been apart for years. I just hate that he plays for the St. Louis Rams and not the Lions. I miss Brynne and sweet Shanna."

"Those Prescott men must be irresistible because Vanessa was next. She fell hard and married Devin's cousin, Ralph. With that love bug going around, we should not have been surprised last year when Laura succumbed while on vacation and married her hotel mogul, Wilham Kramer."

"And he wasn't even a Prescott!" They laughed.

Maureen admitted, "I am glad Laura and Wil are relatively close in Chicago."

"Which leaves only you, me and Vanessa in the book club. We've turned into the Pitiful Three," Trenna quipped.

"I tried to talk Sherri Ann into joining but she turned me down."

"As an attorney, Sherri Ann doesn't have much time to read for pleasure. Plus she works for Darrin Morgan. That can't be a picnic." Trenna revealed, "I thought about asking Grace to join our club but decided against it. Since the trial, she has had a hard time dealing with that awful man's release." She paused, and then asked, "How's Mrs. Hale?"

"My grandmother is fine. Why did you change the subject? What aren't you telling me?"

"Nothing important."

"You know I'm going to find out sooner or later, so you might as well tell me."

"I ran into Darrin Morgan today. And I mean literally. I bounced off his chest like a Ping-Pong ball."

"What? Were you hurt?"

"No, I'm fine. He caught me before I landed on my behind. Evidently, I pushed the wrong button and got off the elevator on the wrong floor." When Trenna heard her friend's snicker, she snapped, "It's not funny!"

Maureen grew up playing with the twins and had attended the same schools. The Hales and Morgans were long-time friends and neighbors.

Laughing, Maureen said, "I wish I could have seen your face."

"It's not funny."

'It's hilarious!"

"Goodbye, Maureen."

"Don't hang up! I was only teasing. Okay, okay, I'll stop. Tell me why you're upset?"

"You know why." Trenna shivered recalling Darrin's intense masculine charm. "He asked me out. Again. Why can't he get it through his thick skull that I'm not interested and leave me alone?"

"You sound so angry. Why? What terrible thing has he done besides ask you out?" Maureen didn't wait for a response, instead rushed ahead, saying, "Come on, Trenna. Darrin has been interested in you since you opened the nursery school. Why don't you go out on one date with him and get it over with? Then, the two of you will realize there's no chemistry between you and we can all move on."

"Absolutely not!" Trenna frowned. If only it were that simple. "How many times do I have to say, I don't like him?"

Sighing, Maureen said, "But why? You haven't given yourself a chance to get to know him."

"Why bother? He has enough women running after him, he doesn't need me."

"That may be true, but he's still interested in you."

"Maureen, I don't like him!"

"Careful. Have you forgotten, 'Thou shall love thy neighbor as thy self'?"

"That was low, Maureen Sheppard!"

"Nope, my friend. That was from the Most High."

They couldn't help but laugh, they attended the same bible study class. "Well?" Maureen prompted.

"I'll try," that was as far as Trenna was prepared to go.

"Fair enough. The Morgan twins are not afraid to go after what they want. They've brought in millions since their father passed and Darrin's been at the helm. You and Darrin should go out to lunch and talk. It could be a good thing, right?"

"Maureen, are you listening to me?"

"Trenna, are you listening to yourself? You're interested in Darrin. Only, you're just too stubborn to admit it. I've seen the way your eyes light up and sparkle whenever you hear his name."

"Don't you mean sparks fly? He makes me see red. Why are you trying to fix me up with him? Never mind! I'm hanging up. I will see you at seven-thirty."

"Wait! Before you go, ask yourself why you're protesting so strongly. After all, we're talking about spending one evening with a sane, single, and gainfully employed male, who openly admits to finding you attractive. There's no harm in that."

"Be that as it may, we're talking about Darrin Morgan. I can't forget the way he tore into Grace on the witness stand. It still makes me shudder. He was ruthless! And because of him, Grace's rapist has been walking around free."

"No!" Maureen said sharply, "We both know Todd Marks raped Grace. And Marks had enough money to hire the best. Darrin's the best."

"I get that, but I'm not you. Logically, I know that Darrin was not responsible for what Todd Marks did to Grace. Emotionally, I can't help resenting him."

"Are you sure you're not using this case as an excuse to keep Darrin at a safe distance? He makes you feel things."

"You're wrong."

"Well, there's enough blame to go around. The prosecutor lost her case. She didn't do enough."

"You're wrong."

"Trenna, I'm sorry but I have to run. My client is here..."

Trenna quickly hung up. She didn't have the answer. She certainly did not feel things for Darrin Morgan, but Maureen was right about one thing. There was enough blame to spread around. But that didn't change the fact that the female prosecutor didn't raise Trenna's blood pressure just by walking into a room.

It was close to eleven when the four friends walked out of the movie theater together. They had loved the movie and were discussing *Hidden Figures* until they reached Vanessa's car. She and Grace had driven together. They hugged each other and waved goodbye.

Maureen and Trenna linked arms as they continued on across the parking lot.

"That was fun," Maureen said. "I really enjoyed the movie. I haven't seen a really good one, not since *Belle*. And you know how much I loved that one."

"I agree. Did you download the book?"

"Not yet. Have you read it?" Maureen quizzed.

Trenna nodded. "Loved it."

"What's the title again?

"*Belle: The Slave Daughter and the Lord Chief Justice* by Paula Byrne."

"Thanks. Grace mentioned a new author that she has been reading, but I can't remember the name. Everyone knows it's always better to read the book first…" Maureen stopped suddenly, "Are you listening to me?"

Since Maureen was taller with a long stride, Trenna had no choice but to stop. Not only had she not been listening, she had also been oblivious to their surroundings. Her cheeks were hot with embarrassment when she said, "Sorry. You caught me."

"On top of not listening, you weren't looking around either! Coach says"—Maureen referred to the self-defense instructor, Michael Jameson, who taught at the Women's Crisis Center—"a woman walking at night, talking on the phone or unaware of her surroundings has set herself up for disaster."

"I said I was sorry. What? Are you gonna sue me because I was lost in thought?"

"It's Friday night and the parking lot is well lit and busy or your behind would be toast." Tugging her along, Maureen warned, "Beside, if I was going to sue you, it wouldn't take you three guesses to figure out whom I would hire…the best, Darrin Morgan."

"Don't start!"

"Trenna, admit it! You're still annoyed with me for pointing out the truth."

"The truth? That's not how I see it."

Maureen quirked a beautifully arched brow before she said, "It's not nice to hang up on your very best friend."

"Stop! I said goodbye before I hung up."

"No, you didn't."

"Uh-oh. Are you having problems with that 'having the last word' thing again?"

"Again?"

They both laughed. They reached Trenna's car first. Maureen's was parked several rows over.

"Get in. I'll drive you over," Trenna said as she activated the keyless entry. When she eased the car to a stop, instead of getting out, Maureen caught Trenna's arm. "I'll follow you home."

"Why?"

Maureen said, "It's time to talk."

Trenna instantly understood. Firmly, shaking her head, she said, "There's nothing to discuss. We made a pact to leave the mistakes we made in the past. Why bring it up now? And why don't you admit, you're no more comfortable talking about this than I am?"

"True," Maureen acknowledged, "But if it will help you recognize that all men are not cut from the same cloth, then I'm willing to go there."

"I'm not! Look, I will say this and then we're done with this subject. It happened when we were young and foolish. We fell in love for the first time with the wrong guys. Just be grateful that you realized it was a mistake and you didn't compound the matter by marrying, like I did."

"I am grateful." Maureen was worrying her bottom lip when she asked, "Why can't we talk? What are you afraid of? There's nothing wrong with me telling you that I think Darrin is a decent man. Who knows? He might be good for you. Please, I might be able to help you work through..."

"I'm not one of your clients!"

"Martin may be gone but that doesn't mean..."

"Stop!" Trenna shouted. She had been over this hundreds of times in her head and couldn't bear to talk about it. From the first, it was a mistake. Martin had been a family friend and their attorney. When her parents passed Martin had been appointed as her legal guardian. She was eighteen. He had gone from being her guardian, to her friend, and then her husband and tormentor.

"Trenna..."

She took a deep, calming breath. "I don't want to talk about Martin anymore than you want to talk about ..."

"Okay! Okay! I get it. But you need to remember that Darrin is not like either of them. You must see that Darrin ..."

Trenna finished the sentence, "...is a good-looking womanizer, who has never had to work for anything in his entire life. It's disgusting the way the women in the building practically fall at his feet when he looks their way. Even the married ones don't attempt to hide their fascination with him. They act as if he's God's gift to womankind. Why would I want to join that group?"

"You should ignore the rumors. They don't matter. But what if he really cares for you? Can you ignore that?"

"Maureen, I get it. He's an old family friend. You and your grandmother adore him and his whole family. I agree they are wonderful people, but that does not mean Darrin Morgan is right for me. He's not! What about our pact?"

"Trenna, you have always wanted babies. You would make a wonderful mother. This may be your chance."

"At one time I wanted a family," Trenna said candidly. "But so did

you. It's not going to happen for me, not unless it's a miracle birth like the baby Jesus, or I adopted a couple of the foster care teen girls from the mentoring program."

3

---

*T*he late autumn air was crisp, and the temperature had dropped sharply at night. The sun had not yet risen in the cloud-covered sky when Trenna parked her car. After dinner with her friends and brain-storming ideas to raise money for her foundation, she had been restless and unable to sleep.

The foundation was a scholarship fund she had developed for low-income children, who could not otherwise afford the high cost of her school. It was her pet project. Having learned the value and rewards of giving back from her parents, she'd heavily invested in both time and money.

Around four, she gave up trying and got ready for work. After a quick stop at a nearby drive-through for breakfast, she parked in a slot close to the back entrance of the Morgan Building. Maureen would probably classify it as nothing more than a crisp morning, but Trenna shivered from the bitter cold as she hurried along. Even after four years, she had not gotten used to the harsh Michigan climate. It was barely November and she was freezing.

Juggling a heavy briefcase and her shoulder bag while balancing a cardboard tray that held her breakfast sandwich and a cup of steaming hot chocolate, she struggled to get to the keys deep in her coat pocket.

"Morning! Let me get that door for you," Darrin said from over her right shoulder.

Although startled, she refused show how much he rattled her. She said calmly, "Good morning." Despite the pre-dawn gloom, she would recognize him anywhere.

He reached past her to insert a key into the door's brass tumbler. For a moment, she was cocooned by his large frame. Immaculate in a navy blue suit, his only concession to the weather was the scarf around his neck. The clean, male scent of his skin was mixed with the citrus fragrance of his aftershave. Keenly aware of the warmth of his breath on her nape, she tried valiantly to control the tremors but failed. Her senses were on high alert.

"You're shivering," Darrin said huskily.

Even though they weren't actually touching, he was too close for her to ignore. She asked impatiently, "Did you get it?"

"Nope, I dropped my keys."

"Use mine!" she volunteered, desperate to make it inside quickly and put some distance between them. "They're in my right coat pocket."

Even through the layers of a long, wool coat, pantsuit, and turtleneck sweater, she felt the heat of his hand near her hip. Feeling light-headed, as if she couldn't get enough air into her lungs, she was relieved when he said, "Got them!" He cupped her elbow to steady her. "You okay?"

She quickly nodded. Flustered, she nearly asked what he was doing here, but it was a silly question. Like her, he worked in the building and put in long hours. It was just her bad luck to come in early, only to run into him.

"You're early today. Trouble sleeping?" He was close, so close that his big body provided a barrier that blocked the wind coming off the river.

She lied, "I slept fine, thank you. What's taking so long?"

"The lock's stiff, must be frozen. You're shaking."

She didn't know whether she was shivering from the cold or nerves. He was too darn close. "It's freezing. Evidently four years hasn't been long enough to adjust to your Michigan winters. It's not even November. Darrin, hurry!"

"Thank you," his voice was deep, gravelly and incredibly sexy.

Although unsure why he was thanking her, the instant he held the door open, she hurried into the dimly lit interior. She passed the empty reception desk, aware that the security team could be anywhere in the building. Even though it took a moment to retrieve his own keys, Darrin had no trouble keeping up with her.

They passed the bakeshop, which had not yet opened for business, but the scent of vanilla and cinnamon filled the air. They were approaching the doors to Little Hearts Nursery School when curiosity got the better of her.

"Why did you thank me?" After glancing at him, she accused, "You're grinning."

His lips were full, almost lush, making her curious about things she had no business considering, such as how his lips might feel...how they tasted. Tingles raced up and down her spine. Goodness! What was wrong with her?

Darrin explained, "You used my name," then shrugged his incredibly broad shoulders. "I like the way you say it."

"What do you mean by that?"

He smiled, "Southern belle, you have a charming accent." Before she could protest, Darrin took her heavy leather briefcase and the food carrier, then dropped her keys into her small gloved palm.

"Thank you." The good manners that had been drummed into her since childhood were impossible to ignore. Unlocking the heavy glass double doors, she hurried to the covered panel on the wall and punched in the numbers to the alarm's security code. When she turned back he was still there.

Looking around, he admired the bulletin board covered with

children's paintings of fall trees and jack-o'-lanterns. "You show be proud of what you've done here, I like how warm and welcoming it is, even to adults. The kids seem to love you and love coming here."

She was shocked that he had noticed and by the warmth that stole over her from his compliment. She managed to repeat, "Thank you." But this time, she actually meant it.

Before she could ask why he was still there, Darrin said, "One of my fraternity brothers Jackson Murray and his wife are in town. He's a real estate developer and investor. He's here on business for a few days, looking for new investments. He's contributed handsomely to several charter schools in Baltimore, two in Boston and one in D.C. All are very successful. I told him about your school and foundation."

"Really?" Her eyes went wide, and she couldn't contain her smile.

Darrin stared at her mouth but then looked away. "Yes."

"But why would you..." her voice trailed away.

"Help you?" he finished for her.

Trenna nodded.

"Because I hope we can start over, as friends."

She frowned wondering what kind of game he was playing this time. Friends! Did he think that she hadn't heard that one before? "Don't you think it's a bit late for that?"

"No, I don't." After a glance at the wall clock, he said, "I'd better get moving. There's plenty to do before I'm due in court." He placed her things on top of one of the child-size tables. "Trenna, I admit I can be aggressive, even ruthless in the courtroom, but that has nothing to do with my personal life. You made an immediate impression on me. Maybe I came on a bit strong? I can admit when I've made a mistake."

It was a struggle not to respond to the warmth in his voice. Made a mistake? Was this some kind of maneuver to disguise his true agenda? The man was a master at seduction.

He was really lathering on that smoothly male charm this morning. How easy it would be to weaken toward him. She would be foolish to underestimate him. She must not confuse his so-called interest in her foundation with a true willingness to help. They could be tools to get what he wanted from her. Would he sink that low?

With her hands balled at her sides, Trenna said, "Please, don't let me keep you."

Careful to keep her emotions in check, she reminded herself that he had admitted to being aggressive, even ruthless, and possibly controlling. Were those the prerequisite in order to pass the bar? Certainly they were the reasons Darrin excelled in his practice.

To her, aggression, ruthlessness, and control issues were red flags, reasons to stay clear of involvement. She knew all too well, since her late husband had been an attorney. And Trenna prided herself on being a woman who learned from her mistakes. There was no doubt in her mind that she was never going to get close enough to Darrin Morgan to allow him to hurt her.

His mouth tightened. "I'll call when I have news. Bye."

She said nothing as she watched him leave.

"Call with news?" she mumbled aloud, suddenly she realized this was no maneuver. He was serious! He expected his friend, the investor to get back to him. Trenna started to shake at the very real possibility. She was forced to take a deep breath to steady herself. It was alright. He said he wanted to help. That was a good thing. Only last night she had been struggling to find ways to fund her foundation. And now this?

If he was serious, then she needed to be extremely cautious. After all, she would have to deal with Darrin Morgan. Talk about a wolf in sheep's clothing!

He said he had made a mistake. That he wanted to be friends. Now that was highly unlikely. His offer to help with her founda-tion didn't mean he hadn't set out to seduce her. Not for one minute did she believe him. She was a challenge to him and nothing more.

Trenna watched until Darrin reached the bank of elevators. That was when she recognized she had been staring at him as if she couldn't get enough of his tall, muscular length. She bristled, suddenly angry with herself.

Hadn't she come in early to work? Why was she focused on him when she needed to get a handle on her paperwork? The man collected women like she collected designer handbags and shoes, and she shouldn't spare him another thought.

She went from classroom to classroom turning on lights, making sure everything was clean, tidy, and ready to go. She checked the supplies in the art and music rooms and then the computer room, which included the children's main computer, a twenty-six inch, all-in-one desktop. It was bolted, for safety reasons, to a sturdy child-size table.

Each child had access to the tablets that were stored in locked cabinets. There were small tables where the children worked in groups or individually on their assignments. All the children were exposed to the appropriate digital material, including the toddlers. Their progress was amazing. For them it was fun, play. Unlike adults, the children didn't fear the electronic devices; there was nothing to unlearn.

Trenna loved children and, at one time, wanted a house-full. Sadly, she had married a man who had already fathered two children and didn't want more. She had put the thoughts of having babies behind her and had focused on her graduate studies and her dreams of some day opening her school.

It was amazing how quickly she had learned to adapt, learned to ignore what she could not change. Martin didn't want her to work outside of their home, but she refused to let him stop her from getting her Master's degree or working toward her doctorate.

Trenna lingered in the nursery, her favorite room. She adored spending time with the babies. She loved holding them close, enjoyed their warmth and sweet scents. Being in the nursery always soothed away the stress of the day and eased her tension.

She lovingly ran her hand over the smooth wood surface of one of the cribs, and then gazed fondly at the row of changing tables. Murals of familiar animated movies and nursery rhyme characters had been painted on the walls.

There were shelves for baby toys and labeled drawers where each baby's bedding, diapers, and changes of clothing were stored. Wooden rocking chairs with cushioned seats were spaced conveniently around the room and the floor was covered by a colorful area rug done in pinks and blues.

One entire wall was lined with shelves, the bottom portion displayed an array of picture books. Everything was bright and colorful. The closet held extras: diapers, linens cubby toys and baby clothes. Nothing had been overlooked.

Trenna stopped in the children's restrooms before moving on to the large kitchen that was equipped with the top-of-the-line stove, two refrigerators, and dishwasher. One of the refrigerators was used exclusively for the children's meals, plus there was a warmer to keep the children's meals at the proper temperature.

Although the children's lunches were catered, Trenna hired a cook for all other preparations. One cupboard was stocked with emerging food supplies, in case of a power outage. All was spotlessly clean and ready to go.

Normally business hours were from seven-thirty AM to six-thirty PM, but the staff generally arrived at seven. Because of the staff meetings that morning, the children were not scheduled until one.

In her office, Trenna hung up her coat and nearly reached for the phone, but stopped herself in time. It was too early, a little after six. Maureen was probably still in bed and wouldn't care about the possibility of an investor. Besides, she already knew what her best friend was going to say about Darrin's offer of friendship. Maureen would scold her. Nope. It was better to keep her mouth shut. Anyway, Trenna had much better things to do than second guess herself about what she had said to Darrin Morgan. The man had already taken up too much of her time this morning.

Pulling her laptop out of her briefcase, she got right to work. She was hungry by the time Amber arrived. After making use of the office microwave, Trenna bowed her head and said a quick prayer of thanks before she bit into her sandwich. Sipping her hot chocolate, she gazed out the window and smiled. There was much to be grateful for. Each day she made it a point to give thanks to the God who created her and blessed her with the skills to love, to learn, and to teach.

Trenna thrived on the challenge of making Little Hearts warm and inviting for all the children. Many viewed their rapid growth as success, but not Trenna. She believed in a hands-on approach to learning, with the focus on each child's needs. That was the key to their success. And in order to continue doing that, they needed to remain small, and insure that the nothing was overlooked or left to chance.

She had hand-picked the staff. She knew their strengths and weaknesses. Her teachers were experts in early childhood. Everyone who worked for her had undergone a complete background check. Most important, they loved the children and worked hard to make the school successful. But it was Trenna who put in the longest hours, a necessity, in order to maintain the highest standards.

Less than a month after their grand opening, they had reached full capacity. The first indicator of that her plans had worked beyond her wildest dreams was the waiting list. Each year their waiting list had grown, but this year had been simply incredible. Trenna was thrilled, but she hadn't been tempted to expand or open a new facility. Excellence was her primary goal, not money. Although, early on, she learned that being the best was costly.

Because Little Hearts was a private school, it was expensive to run it well and to maintain. By necessity, their fees had to be hefty.

There was much to be grateful for and she was determined not to take her blessings for granted. She had drawn from the trust fund she had inherited from her maternal grandmother to start the school and from the funds her parents had left her to start the scholarship fund. She knew she was fortunate to have the profits from her family's business fall back on.

Pleased by the morning's progress, she had finished the state licensing report, the agenda for the staff meeting, and had printed the handouts. Around nine, she realized she was having trouble concentrating on the lesson plans the teachers had turned in for the following week.

Her thoughts kept going back to her run-in with Darrin. She trembled, recalling the heat of his hand near her hip as he searched her coat pocket. His closeness had rattled her. She had been overwhelmed by his size, cognizant of his warmth, and keenly aware of the smell of his clean male skin and citrus after-shave. Again and again, she had tried and failed to push thoughts of him away. What was it about the shape of his mouth that so fascinated her? It was pointless to speculate on how his lips might feel or taste. She was never going to know. Goodness! Why did he have to be so attractive?

She found herself wondering if she would feel differently about him if he hadn't taken the Todd Marks case. Only, she had no answer. Would it help her to talk to Grace? They hadn't really spoken about the trial since it ended so badly. And the last thing she wanted to do was upset Grace.

Trenna didn't need any reminders that some things were too painful to discuss, even with her best friend. She and Maureen couldn't be closer. They had shared much over the years, but long ago they agreed there were a few choice topics that were best avoided. Maureen had pushed that boundary to the limit the other night, and at the time Trenna had not taken it well. Because they loved each other, neither of them had ever aimed to hurt the other. They had moved on.

Because she had been so busy with her school, she hadn't realized how much time had passed since she talked to Grace. She was glad that Maureen had invited Grace to join them. Grace didn't realize it, but the two of them had something in common. Trenna had never been raped, but she knew what it felt like to dominated and controlled by a ruthless man.

Trenna and Maureen had made an effort to be there for Grace. It had been a hardship to offer their support during the trial. She couldn't help wondering if volunteering at the Woman's Crisis Center was enough for Grace? Did Grace still have trouble sleeping? Did she still have to fight her fears every single day just to go out her front door?

Trenna frowned. She didn't know the answers. Lately, she had been so self-absorbed, caught up with her own issues that she had not reached out Grace. Feeling guilty, Trenna picked up the telephone and punch in a familiar number and waited.

"Sheppard Women's Crisis Center. Maureen speaking, how may I help you?"

"Hi. Got a minute?"

"For you, maybe five. You sound tired."

"I didn't sleep well last night. I gave up trying around four and got ready for work," she blurted out. "It was barely six when I got here. I can't believe I ran into you-know-who again."

"Darrin?"

"Yes."

"You don't mean literally, do you?"

"No, but it wasn't comfortable."

"Normal animosity?"

"Not exactly."

If only it were that simple. She was struggling to accept that Darrin had offered to help with her foundation. A wealthy investor would be the answer to her prayers. What a blessing! Her head was still spinning at the possibility. Excitement bubbled deep inside as she kept thinking of the things she would be able to accomplish. A solid investor would allow her to expand the foundation much faster than she'd dare hoped.

This autumn she launched her foundation by giving away two scholarships. And she was thrilled that both children were doing very well. It validated that she was moving in the right direction. Only Maureen knew that Trenna had used her own funds to jumpstart the foundation and that she purposefully kept her salary low. The profits had gone back into the school.

At dinner last night with Maureen and Mrs. Hale, Maureen's grandmother, they had wracked their brains to come up with ways to raise money for Trenna's foundation. And then their neighbor Tina Morgan, Douglas and Darrin's mother, stopped by for dessert. Trenna liked Mrs. Morgan and was surprised when she came up with some novel ideas for funding the foundation. She suspected Mrs. Morgan spoken to Darrin.

Did it matter? Trenna had to be practical. Next year, she'd hoped to maintain the present scholarships and expand to include two additional low-income children. But at this point it was just that...a hope.

Trenna revealed, "Darrin offered to introduce me to one of his wealthy friends, a possible investor. But he ruined it because in the next breath he asked if we could start over and become friends."

"Investor? Did he say who?"

"Jackson Murray. Do you know him?"

"I've never met him but he's a well-known philanthropist."

"Really?"

"Yes, when you have a free moment, type his name into your search engine. I don't know about you, but I'm excited!"

Darrin hadn't? been joking around. Trenna didn't know what to think. Suddenly, her knees were wobbly, and she was forced to sit back down.

"Trenna, this could be a tremendous opportunity for your foundation to grow. Darrin's a good person. It seems to me that he's already acting like your friend. You're the hold out."

"But…"

"What can it hurt to be nice?"

As the question seemed to echo in her mind, Trenna barely suppressed a scream of frustration. Had Maureen forgotten that the last man who asked for her friendship hadn't stopped pushing until they were married and she was under his control? Plus, there was Grace. Trenna couldn't dismiss Grace's trial.

"I appreciate his offer to help, but I'm not naïve. That offer comes attached with strings. I'm not getting involved with Darrin Morgan."

"Friends, Trenna." Maureen said with a laugh, "A girl can't have too many."

"Not funny."

"Think, Trenna. Can you afford to ignore a potential investor? Just last night we were brainstorming ideas to expand your scholarship program." Before Trenna could respond, Maureen advised, "Before you cut off your nose to spite your face, consider this—" Then she paused.

"What?" Trenna prompted.

"If Darrin hadn't taken Todd Mark's case, and if you had never seen him at work in the court room, would you accept his friendship or date him?"

"No. He asked me out the day we met and I declined."

"How much of a difference do you think it would have made if he hadn't defended Todd Marks?"

Trenna had asked herself that same question. "He makes me uncomfortable. Maureen, our history with men stinks. Have you forgotten our vow not to repeat past mistakes? I haven't changed my mind. Have you?"

"No, but Darrin…"

"Another attorney, no thanks. I will pass."

"Trenna! Where did that come from? If you gave Darrin half a chance, you'd know by now that he is nothing like Martin."

Trenna silently groaned. She should have known better than to voice her fears by linking the two men together. She didn't want to think or talk about either one of them. Martin was gone and Darrin was a complication she couldn't afford. The mere thought of being intimate again was disturbing.

Maureen barely paused long enough to catch her breath. She hurried on to say, "Clearly, you're still upset about the other day. Once you have time to calm down and think I'm sure that….. "

"Maureen! Stop grilling me. This isn't one of your counseling sessions."

"Grilling you? My, my, aren't we defensive. Missy, you called me, not the other way around."

"I know, but not to rehash the past or talk about men. I just realized I've been so busy with my school that I have neglected Grace. It has been months since we really talked. Can you tell me how she's doing?"

"Fine.

"Maureen, you know what I'm mean. "

"And you know I can't talk about Grace and why. I won't betray her confidence."

"Maureen! I'm not trying to pry, I'm concerned. She seemed a bit too quiet the other night after the movie. I was wondering if something changed."

"I can't! Now if you have a general question, ask away."

"Okay, okay. On Saturday, when I talked to Laura we talked about forgiveness. Laura mentioned it's not unusual for a victim to forgive her rapist. Do you think it's possible?"

"Anything's possible. Do you remember what Pastor Graham said on the subject? That God wasn't playing around when he made that law. We are to love everyone, even those not so love-able…no exceptions."

"I remember," Trenna added, "But it seems to me that rape

goes beyond the ordinary forgiveness. It's such a cruel, hateful crime that I'm not sure that anyone can manage it. I'm sure I couldn't. How about you?"

"I don't know. It's a tough one and would require a boatload of prayers to get there."

"You're right. Jesus died for all us sinners, not just people we approve of." Trenna swallowed a heavy sigh. She didn't add the likelihood of her forgiving her husband was right up there with Maureen forgiving her ex. It wasn't happening.

"About Grace. Is she still having trouble sleeping? How about leaving her ..."

Maureen said, "Trenna, call her. Talk to her."

"I can't. It would be cruel to upset her and remind her of such a very painful time." Before she would say more there was a knock on her open door and her assistant Tasha came in carrying a crystal vase filled with flowers. Trenna gasped.

"What is it?" Maureen asked.

4

"Hold on, Maureen," Trenna said into the phone as Tasha placed a beautiful floral arrangement in the center of her desk. "Thanks."

"Well?" Maureen prompted.

"I'm staring at the most beautiful bouquet of pink and white tulips, surrounded by yellow and pink Gerber daises. Are you sure you didn't ..."

"Yes... "

"Excuse me, but ..." Tasha said.

"Maureen, hold for another minute." She looked at her assistant, "Yes?"

"Everyone has started gathering in the conference room for the staff meeting. When should I tell the kitchen staff to bring in the cheese and fruit trays?"

"Now," Trenna said but she couldn't stop staring at the flowers.

Smiling, Tasha said, "There's a card."

"Hey!" Maureen called out.

"I'm back," Trenna blushed, having forgotten she was still on the telephone.

Maureen demanded, "What's going on?"

"Let me get the door…" After closing it, she quizzed, "It's not my birthday, did you by any chance send…"

"They are not from me. There has to be a card. Hurry up! Find it!"

"Okay, okay." Trenna didn't realize her hands were shaking as she pulled out the small envelope tucked into the blooms.

"Well?"

Trenna read aloud, "'I'm meeting with the Murrays, the investors, I told you about. Dinner at Antonio's. I'll pick you up in the lobby at seven.' It's signed, D. M."

"Darrin Morgan," they said at the same time.

"I remember now. He's that former NBA star that played with Ralph Prescott. And he has become one of the most successful developers on the east coast." Maureen exclaimed and then revealed, "His wife's a well-known singer and actress. She performed in the *Wiz* on Broadway. She was nominated for a Tony award a few years back. Tall and very beautiful, don't you remember her? Jennifer Adams?"

"That Jennifer Adams!"

"The same. Her family is from Detroit. And her father wrote several of Motown's biggest hits. I remember Darrin talking about him. They own properties all over the country." Maureen demanded, "You are going, aren't you?"

Dazed, Trenna nodded and then realized her friend couldn't see her. "Of course, I am going."

"What are you wearing?"

"A black dress, what else? It's business. Look, I've got to go. I'm going to be late for my meeting."

"Wear the pink!" Maureen advised before she said, "Didn't I tell you that Darrin was serious? Why else would he go out of his way to help your foundation?"

"It's spelled s-e-x," Trenna snapped. "He won't give up until I sleep with him."

"So what? You've had no problem telling him no in the past. Has something changed?"

"Of course not!"

"Then why are you acting as if you're scared to go out with him?"

Trenna had plenty of male friends. But when it came to Darrin, she knew he wanted a whole lot more than friendship. As far as she was concerned, intimacy was no longer an option, nor was it open for discussion. From the beginning, Trenna's instincts screamed at her to stay clear of him.

"I'm not!"

"You know you can tell me anything."

She wanted to scream, 'Not this!' but the words couldn't get past the constriction in her throat.

"Trenna?" Maureen prompted.

"I'm here."

"Remember that just because Darrin finds you attractive doesn't mean he doesn't respect you or expects sexual favors from you. Go in there and wow them with your brains and, while you're doing that, make Darrin drool. So wear your pink dress. Good luck," she said before hanging up.

Trenna was running late and didn't take the time to go home. She showered

in her office's private bath and hastily re-did her hair and makeup. In the hopes of boosting her confidence, she changed into a black, lace dress with a pale-pink under-sheath and long sheer-sleeves. The knit fabric skimmed her lush curves without clinging and stopped above the knee. The dress was a classic style, and like most of her clothes, had been designed by her talented mother.

Over the dress, she wore a black, suede trench coat, her feet were in pink high heel pumps, and she carried her small, black evening purse embroidered with pink sequined butterflies.

DARRIN WAS WAITING in the lobby. His heart began to race the instant he saw Trenna. She was too lovely for words, he decided, as he watched her tuck her keys into her tiny evening bag. His hands balled into fists as his body began to ache with need. The wanting was back with a vengeance.

"Hi. You look nice." He said before he quizzed, "Ready?"

She was breathtaking. She had brushed her short, thick, wavy black curls until the strands hugged the beautiful curve of her scalp. Nice was too mild of a word to describe her exquisite beauty. She had chosen a dark pink lip stain and added a sheer gloss that drew his hungry gaze to the lush beauty of her full mouth.

"Yes. Thank you for the flowers and the invitation."

He nodded. "You're welcome. Let's go, our driver is waiting.

"Driver?"

Darrin nodded and smiled, taking her brief case. "There's no half stepping for Jackson Murray. I hope you're not upset, but when he called I didn't wait to get your okay and accepted for both of us," he said as he ushered her to the limousine parked in the front of the building.

Seated in the back of the luxury car, he could see the dismay in her eyes. He knew she questioned his motives. She was certain he wanted something from her. He doubted that there was anything he could say or do that would relieve her doubts.

She had no idea that when he looked at her, he remembered her kindness. He automatically went back to the night she had come to pay her respects to his family. He had been encased in such incredible despair and grief that he was unable to share his emotions with anyone. The pain was lodged deep inside. Even though his twin brother and their mother were also suffering after the loss, he felt isolated. That night Trenna came and sat with him in the den. Her willingness to open up and share the loss of both her parents had profoundly touched him.

Trenna had stayed, yet had not asked or expected anything in return. To him, surrounded by darkness, her smile had been like a ray of sunshine. When his mother told him about the brainstorming session to jumpstart her foundation, immediately, he wanted to help.

She surprised him when she touched his sleeve. Determined not to read anything into a simple touch, he refrained from curling his fingers around her small hand. "Yes?"

"Is there anything I should know…about your friend?"

"Friends. Jackson's wife, Jennifer, will be joining us."

"You mentioned it this morning that he was an investor. You said nothing about his wife being Jennifer Adams! Why didn't you tell me?"

"I didn't think of it." Darrin shrugged. "Trenna, you have no reason to be nervous. Jennifer's good people."

"All of this feels crazy. I'm out with you, going to meet and have dinner with strangers. And on top of that, I'm sitting here with my heart pounding like a drum inside my chest, praying they will like me and give me money."

Darrin chuckled. He couldn't help it. "The money's for your foundation." He covered her hand with his. "Relax. You are going to like the Murrays and they are going to like you. Wealth and fame are relative. It doesn't mean the Murrays aren't down to earth or earnest about giving back. Besides, pretty lady, when you put your mind to something it gets done."

He smiled at her, and she returned his smile.

"Thank you."

~

TRENNA GENUINELY LIKED Darrin's friends. Jennifer and Jackson Murray were both warm and engaging. The evening was a delight.

They dined on a wonderful meal of lobster tails and prime rib, with creamy twice-baked potatoes covered in butter and cheese, and mixed green salad followed by decadent chocolate lava cake.

Even though Jackson hadn't pulled out his checkbook and written a check tonight, Trenna was pleased and very encouraged that the couple hoped to visit the school before they left the city.

"You look lovely tonight, Trenna," Darrin said softy.

Surprised by the compliment, she said, "Thank you," then quickly changed the subject. "The evening went well. I'm looking forward to showing them the school."

"It's a good sign. You should be pleased."

"I'm more than pleased, I feel blessed that they are considering Little Hearts. We have only been open a few years. Thank again for your help."

While resting her hand on the plush, luxurious armrest of the sleek gray limousine, she realized she was shaking like a leaf. The evening was nearly over and now she started to shake.

The further away they traveled from the restaurant the greater her unease. No, that wasn't exactly true. Her nerves had been on edge the second she greeted Darrin. He was freshly shaved and handsome in a pale blue shirt and tie. He looked good in blue; it brought out his deep blue eyes.

She'd lost count of the number of times throughout the evening she had had to remind herself that this wasn't a date. It was a business meeting and the sole purpose was to strengthen her foundation. Her heart had no business picking up speed whenever he looked her way or smiled. What was her problem? Most of the time, she was unsure if she even liked the man.

Darrin nodded. "You're welcome. And yes, it did go well."

Glancing at his strong profile in the car's dim interior, she finally voiced what had been upmost in her mind. "I still don't understand why you went out of your way to help me."

"It's not complicated. Friends help friends. I admire what you've accomplished in such a short time. You are not only smart but also willing to work hard to reach your goals. I'm impressed that you want to give back, and that alone made me want to help. Jackson called to let me know he was coming into town. We usually get together, just to catch up. But this time I jumped on it. "

Surprisingly, she was touched by his compliment and said, "I still don't get it. Expanding my foundation was something I've prayed for, but you had no way of knowing that. Most of the time, we barely speak. Yet tonight, you've gone out of your way to smooth the way for me. Why?"

How could she make him understand that this wasn't a game to her? Her school was her life. She didn't want any unwelcome surprises or a misunderstanding between them. Her heart pounded in her ear as she waited for his response.

"Why shouldn't I help, Trenna? We're friends."

She clenched her teeth. She was beginning to hate that word. Who was he trying to fool? He didn't want her friendship—he wanted what all men want... Sex.

"Come on, Darrin! We are not friends."

"I've made no secret that I have been trying to get you to go out with me for what seems like forever. But I am your friend, Trenna. That's why when I heard from Jackson, I thought of you. I want to help. It was the right thing to do."

"I do appreciate your willingness to help me, and I enjoyed myself. Dinner was great and so are your friends."

He nodded "Let's do it again, dinner and a play this weekend. Have you seen the play currently running at Fox Theater? I've heard..."

"No."

"You've seen..."

"No and no."

There was a long uncomfortable silence before he asked, "Why? And don't tell me it's because you're still in mourning. Men talk. And you, lady, have a reputation for dropping poor guys after only a few dates. Last month you went to the charity dinner-dance with that accountant on the fourth floor."

She gasped aloud. "His name…"

"The name doesn't matter," he grated harshly. "What matters is you went out with him and not me. Why?"

"Isn't it obvious? You're not my type. I thought you knew that I've sworn off womanizers. Why do you want me? Don't you have enough women running you down?"

"There's no explaining why two people are attracted to each other. Now answer my question."

"Aren't you forgetting something? Tonight was a business dinner."

"I enjoyed spending time with you, Trenna. I haven't given up on us. I'm a Morgan—we're stubborn and not afraid to go after what we want."

Trenna couldn't see his eyes in the dim interior, but she could smell his aftershave. She could also feel the heat of his gaze on her skin. Goodness! Her senses went on high alert as if he was caressing her, and her body ached.

"That's a pity because you're wasting your time."

He chuckled, "It's my time to waste. There's no explaining what attracts a male to a female or vice versa."

Rather than call him a mule-headed fool, she changed the subject. "Jennifer and Jackson don't have children. Yet, they are very much involved in investing in children and educational projects."

"There's nothing wrong with wanting to give back. For them it's not a hardship."

"And I am so grateful!" She laughed, then added, "Now I have to make sure there are no slip-ups on my end."

"Will you please will keep me in the loop?"

"Of course."

"And let me know if you need me to look at the contract."

"You are confident," she gushed.

"I have confidence in you and your abilities."

Although flattered, she dared not let it show. Staring out the window, she reminded herself to be careful. His compliments made her uneasy; they came too easily to him and meant nothing. They were part of his charm.

And now here she was caught in traffic jam, trapped in this luxurious car with a man who practically oozed sex appeal. Smooth, sophisticated, and far too close for her peace of mind. He had probably forgotten more about women than she'd ever known about men.

Trenna had only slept with one man, her husband. Darrin Morgan was way out of her league. And he had come out and admitted he was attracted to her. Uncomfortable, she struggled to keep a lid on her awareness of him.

The most disturbing to her was that as the evening progressed, her awareness escalated. All evening her heightened senses had her zeroing in on his husky voice, the heat radiating from his muscular frame, and enjoying his clean male scent.

She was weak with relief when they were finally moving. In the glare of passing headlights, her eyes lingered on the shape of his mouth. His lips were generous, firm. She couldn't help wondering how they felt. When she glanced up, she met his gaze. She blushed in embarrassment and then looked away.

When the car turned onto the Morgan property, her entire body was taut with tension. Finally, the car slowed to a stop.

'Almost over,' she silently repeated as she picked up her purse. She jumped when her door opened and the lights came on. They weren't blinding but bright enough to cause her to blink rapidly. How had he gotten out and around car without her noticing? Goodness! She had to keep her wits about her.

"Ready?" Darrin held out his hand.

Ignoring the gesture, Trenna said "Just a minute, I need my keys." Taking off her gloves, she searched the bottom of her small bag, retrieving a tube of lip-gloss, her compact, cell phone, and packet of tissues, but no keys.

But Darrin was too close. When Trenna felt the brush of his sleeve, she dropped the purse, spilling the contents over the dark carpet.

"Oh no!" She exclaimed.

"Let me help." Before she could protest, he pulled out a pencil-slim flashlight from his pocket and leaned in to gather up her things and dropped them in her lap.

"Thanks."

"Makes no sense why females carry around such expensive designer luggage they call handbags when a pocket can serve the same purpose."

She quirked a brow. "Right. And you know this how?"

He gave her a cocky grin, causing her heart to pick up speed.

"Just an observation."

Realizing she was staring, she quickly looked away. She searched her coat pockets and ran her hand between the seat cushions. Mumbling she said, "I was sure that I put them in my purse. Oh!"

"Find them?"

She nodded, the keys were inside the zipped compartment. She hands shook from nerves. For heaven's sake, she had certainly had her share of key issues that day, enough to last a lifetime.

Cupping her elbow, he helped her out of the car. "Do you need to go into the building?"

She was so rattled it took her a moment to say, "No."

"What about your briefcase? Laptop?" he asked as he laced his fingers with hers.

Already struggling to ignore his warmth, she was now forced to contend with his long length as well as his delicious scent. It wasn't fair. Goodness, why did he have to be so darn attractive? He seemed to radiate with a heat that sizzled along her nerve-endings. The sensations were intense, sharper than any she'd ever recalled experiencing.

She didn't want the unwelcome reminder of what happened this morning, when he had slid his hand into her pocket. And now he was doing it again, invading her space. This had to stop.

Trenna pulled her hand free. He was a danger to her peace of mind. This recent claim for friendship was only a ploy to get under her skin. Underestimating her intelligence was a pet peeve of hers. One she refused to overlook.

Even if she wanted to, she couldn't say that he had not been honest. He asked her out the day they met. He wanted her and she wanted no part of him. There had been no pretense. They knew were they stood with each other, until now.

But his offer to help her foundation had thrown her off-balance. It was an unexpected complication…a complication that she had no choice but to take seriously. The Murrays' sponsorship could make a major difference not only to her but also to the low-income children in the neighborhood. Everything would be just perfect, if she believed he sincerely wanted to be friends. But she didn't.

Darrin Morgan wanted more than a few dates. He wanted involvement. Plus, he was a normal, healthy, virile male, who eventually expected to have sex with his partner. It was a shame she wasn't bold enough to tell him why he was wasting his time trying to romance her. The memories were too painful to talk about. The past was better left where it was: in the past.

She didn't want to think about him, didn't want to care about him. She would never tell him her secrets. What was the point? They were barely friends, hardly candidates to be romantically involved.

Besides, she had been married long enough to know what men expected. Once involved, sex became an obligation, one she was unwilling to revisit. Those days were behind her. She could happily live the rest of her life without sex.

She had never discussed the intimacy problems in her marriage with anyone, not even her best friend. It was humiliating. She'd rather forget and then pretend it had never happened. She'd lost count of the times she had blamed herself for failing to satisfy her husband. It wasn't that she hadn't tried to make him happy, to be a perfect wife, but she failed over and over again. Blame and shame became daily companions. No matter what she had tried, it was never enough.

When she relocated to Michigan she had made a promise to never look back. Never again would she have to see that kind of disappointment in a man's eyes or ever have to endure another tongue lashing because of her shortcomings.

"Trenna, do you need..."

"No, both are safely locked in my office."

After unlocking her car door, she waited for him to put her small case on the floor behind her seat. He was full of surprises, clicking her seatbelt in place.

"Thanks for everything. I didn't expect..."

"Glad to be of service. Be careful on the road. It's late and the fools are probably out. Give me a second and I'll follow you home."

"I'm fine."

He nodded. "I'll be right behind you."

5

――――――

*S*he watched him go over to the limousine and tip the driver, before jogging to his SUV. He flicked his lights to let her know he was ready.

Trenna wasn't sure who she was more annoyed with: him or herself. Instead of being halfway home, she was waiting for him. What happened to her resolve to keep her distance? Was it buried under all those compliments he'd been dishing out?

It had been over four years since Martin had passed. During that time, she hadn't had any difficulty resisting other men. What was it about Darrin? So what if her awareness of him was keen? It didn't matter.

No wonder women found him so irresistible. All evening he'd been thoughtful, considerate. He was not only as smooth as silk but also easy on the eyes. But if he thought for even a second he could hop into her bed, then he was in for a rude awakening.

Her temper simmered as she headed west on Interstate 96 toward Southfield. By the time she exited the freeway on Twelve Mile Road she had her emotions under control. She slowed at the entranced to the gated community and smiled at the guard on duty. "Evening, Mark."

"Hello Mrs. McAdam."

As the gate lifted Trenna giggled, giving Darrin a wave as she sped through. She followed the curved to the right and made a left at the corner. Her small home was on a corner lot. She turned into her driveway and activated the garage door opener. As she pulled inside she spotted Darrin's late model SUV, turning in and easing a stop behind her.

If she had been a swearing woman, she would have turned the air a brilliant shade of blue. Instead, she pounded the steering wheel with a small fist. Thoroughly annoyed, she grabbed her case and slammed her car door. Instead of hurrying inside through the garage, she closed the garage door and came down the drive.

She asked evenly, "How did you do it?" She was proud of herself for not yelling.

"Do what?"

"How did you get past the guards and inside the gate without a residence sticker?" she demanded.

Thanks to the row of sun lamps that lined her walk way and drive, she had no trouble making out his features. He didn't smile, but she sensed his amusement.

"I have a pass." He stood beside his SUV. "My brother lives three miles away and our mother's next door to Mrs. Hale and Maureen."

"Right." Why was he still here? Good grief! He had her so rattled she was muttering to herself as she passed him.

Knowing what was expected, that she do the polite thing and invited him in, didn't make it any easier. She battled her conscious, struggling to execute the good manners her mother and grandmother had hammered into her. After climbing the three steps up to the front porch, she slowly turned to face him.

"I really appreciate all you've done to help…"

Darrin interrupted, "I hope it works out with the Murrays."

"We'll know soon," they said at the same time, and then stopped abruptly. They looked at each other.

She politely asked, "Would you care to come in for a nightcap?"

"You're shaking," he observed, and then surprised her by lightly brushing his lips against her forehead before he took a step back. "No worries, sweet Trenna. Don't you know that nothing that you don't want will ever happen between us?"

"But you said…"

"What? That I want you? It's true, but I'm looking for someone special. Someone who wants me just as much as I want her. Night, Trenna. "

TRENNA WAS TIPTOEING out of the nursery where the babies were napping when little Johnnie Bornstein came hurling into her.

"Make 'em stop! Make 'em stop!" His small face was pale, tears filled his big blue eyes and ran down his cheeks.

Trenna dropped down to take the child into her arms. He rested his blond head on her shoulder as he sobbed as if his heart was breaking. And it very may well be, considering his parents were in the middle of a very nasty divorce. Plus, he hadn't seen his father in weeks.

"It's okay, it's okay," she soothed, rubbing his back. Once he was calm, she took him into art room to paint a picture for Mommy.

Although Trenna was aware that something had been going on between Brenda Hampton, one of the teachers, and Yvette McKnight, her teaching assistant, she hadn't interfered. As long as they keep the problem outside of the school, it wasn't her concern. But if a disagreement altered the climate of the school and upset one of their students it became Trenna's business.

When the school opened, she had laid out a set of rules and put them in writing. And she had never deviated from them. There were no excuses for exposing the children to anything less than a warm, loving, encouraging environment.

Being firm had not come naturally to her. She had learned from cold, hard experience that being soft and loving signaled weakness to her controlling husband. It had taken her years to regain the ground she had lost trying to be the perfect wife.

She arranged for Amber to take over the class while she met with the two. When they were all seated in the office with the door closed, Trenna could feel their animosity as they stared at each other.

There was no hesitation when she asked, "What's going on?" The meeting went downhill from there.

Brenda accused, "It's all her fault! Just because she's beautiful with all that long pretty hair she thinks she can have any man she wants. Well, she's wrong. I'm willing to fight for what's mine!"

Before Trenna could respond, Yvette jumped to her feet and said, "Have you lost your mind? I've had enough of you yelling at me because you're jealous of that broke, half-ass man! You're taking care of him."

"Who you calling broke?"

"He doesn't have a job! You told me couple of weeks ago."

Trenna would have laughed if the situation was not serious.

Brenda accused, "Look who's talking! Last time I looked, you didn't have two pennies to rub together."

They were both standing nearly toe-to-toe, glaring at each other.

Yvette snapped, "Just because you're a teacher, doesn't make you better than me. I may not have finished college yet, but I'm not desperate! And I have enough common sense to know the difference between love and being used!"

"Enough!" Trenna interjected. Refusing to raise her voice, she said firmly, "If you value your jobs you'll sit down and listen." She waited until they complied, and then she said, "Little Hearts is not the place for this kind of discussion. I don't care how you two feel about each other or who you are involved with but, arguing in front of students will not be tolerated. Since you two brought this here to Little Hearts, we will deal with it. Tell me how this started?"

"It's her fault." Brenda pointed at her assistant. "She started this mess."

Yvette ignored the other woman and said, "Mrs. McAdams, I'm really sorry about all this. I was upset, but really didn't mean to scare the children."

"Thanks, Yvette. I'm glad that you realize... "

"I knew you were going to side with her. You don't understand because you're pretty like her. Neither of you have any problems getting a man. Everyone knows, Mrs. McAdams that you can have anyone you want. Look at Darrin Morgan! He not only owns the building but's the best looking man in it. He stares at you. He wants you."

Trenna stiffened and pressed her lips together, to hold in a sharp retort. Although annoyed at having her name linked to Darrin, she was determined to remain calm. She took a slow, deep breath.

No, this was not about her or Darrin. Nor was it about the fact that she hadn't seen the man in more than a week. He'd said that he wanted her and then walked away. Clearly, he regretted what had been said because he was avoiding her.

"Ms. McAdams," Yvette rushed to say, "this isn't my doing! I'm having enough trouble trying to manage my student loans, finishing out this semester while trying to make sure I keep my grade-point-average up. I don't know about her, but I really need this job."

"I need mine, too!" Brenda added.

Trenna repeated her earlier question, "How did this start?"

Yvette said, "On Friday, when I went out to my car her boyfriend was waiting for her. He came onto me, not the other way around. By the time she came out he had gotten out of her car and followed me to mine, all the while talking trash. She assumed I was in the wrong."

Trenna stared at them in disbelief. They were risking their jobs because of some man! This was crazy. While the discussion was unpleasant, it was not something she could avoid. This matter was too important to ignore. For Trenna, the children always came first.

Brenda interrupted, "That's because you were wrong. I saw you flirting with my man! Don't try to deny it. He and I have no secrets. He told me everything."

"I doubt he told you that he asked me to go to the club with him on Saturday night. But I assure you that you have nothing to fear from me. I'd rather be alone forever than be with a man who can't be trusted. I don't need that headache. If you ask me, that's not love."

Even though Trenna agreed whole-heartedly, she said firmly, "If the two of you want to continue working here, then you will find a way to resolve this problem, away from Little Hearts and the children. Another incident like this one and both of you will be out of a job. Are we clear?"

The women nodded.

"Good. The children are waiting. "

Trenna felt bad for Brenda. She clearly had fallen for the wrong man, someone who didn't value her and she couldn't trust. In addition, she was making the mistake of blaming someone else for his weaknesses.

Once she was alone Trenna silently fumed. "Men!"

So many of them cannot be trusted. They ruined things for the few good men out there. It would be easy to assume that all men were users. But Trenna knew better. She'd been fortunate enough to have a good father. If Trenna had not grown up around such a strong, honest man she might not know that truth.

She hadn't asked, but she suspected Brenda's man was very

attractive, someone that women flock to. But she seriously doubted that he was as good to look at as Darrin Morgan.

Trenna frowned, annoyed that her thoughts kept returning to him. It was so aggravating! Brenda bringing his name up didn't help. She didn't want to think of Darrin, didn't want to remember his warmth or husky laugh as he joked with his friends. The entire time he'd been a perfect gentlemen, even made sure she got home safely.

Enough about Darrin, she thought as she paced her office. She especially didn't want to recall that he had gone out of his way to help with her foundation. Plus, he hadn't expected anything in return. It was true that she had enjoyed herself that night. She genuinely liked his friends. The Murrays were warm and generous, a lovely couple.

For heaven's sake! She needed to get over it. It was a single night. One evening in his company did not mean she'd lost touch with reality. Or, that she was at risk of letting her guard down enough to get involved with him. That was never going to happen.

Although she hadn't seen Darrin, Trenna had had a visit from his friends. The Murrays had toured the school, and the visit had gone amazingly well. Several times she had reached for the phone to thank Darrin again but always found a reason not to make the call.

No matter how many times she told herself that it was for the best that she hadn't seen him, she was upset. There was no doubt that he was avoiding her. She should consider it a gift. He was doing her a huge favor by leaving her alone. His absence should give her time to regroup and keep her defenses firmly in place.

She was no longer like Brenda Hamilton. She didn't have to have a man in her life to be happy. She was no longer the girl who had married for the wrong reasons. She had grown up. She was strong and could stand squarely in her own three-inch heels. She took care of herself both financially and emotionally. For her spiritual needs she turned to the Creator, her heavenly Father who continually strengthened her.

Finally, Trenna was in a good place and had developed genuine friendships with both men and women. If given a choice between friendship and sex, she would pick friendship every time. It was true that a few of her male friends believed the physical side of her nature had been badly neglected, but she could not care less. She didn't crave the physical pleasure that filled romantic movies and novels and love songs. Four years of marriage had proven to her that the sexual side of a relationship was grossly overrated.

Why Darrin Morgan? Surely, she couldn't be thinking of getting involved with him? Could she? But even as she shook her head no, she accepted it didn't seem as far-fetched as it had even a few days ago. After one dinner? Ridiculous! She had no business even thinking about intimacy with anyone, and certainly not with him.

Even if for some crazy reason, say she temporarily lost her mind and forgot her own history, it wouldn't be long before he discovered her secret. Darrin was an experienced man. One time would be all it would take. Once with her and he would throw her out faster than yesterday's dishwater. She had learned the hard way that she would never be enough for any other man.

She would not allow Darrin to tempt her into doing something that was completely wrong for her. Nor would she allow Darrin to raise her hopes that things between them could be different. Just because he was younger and better looking than Martin, didn't mean it would be better with him. She must not forget that the common denominator wasn't Martin…it was her. She had not changed.

Besides, Darrin was sophisticated, charming, a connoisseur of women. The only thing average about him was his male beliefs. For him, sex was a requirement, not an option in a relationship. When he told her he wanted her she should have been honest.

Why hadn't she come clean? Why hadn't she admitted that to her sex was about as exciting as having a root canal? He had the correct attitude. Keeping distance between them was the perfect solution.

Trenna didn't have a single doubt that if he knew, he would make a beeline for the closest door. Who was she kidding? Had she forgotten that she didn't have the best judgment when it came to men? She only had to look at the huge mistake she had made when she had married. Both she and Martin had suffered because of that error.

But there was something she craved...something she hadn't experienced in a very long time. She longed to be held. Hugs by friends were important, but not quite the same. Perhaps the longing was something leftover from her childhood? Her father made her feel safe and secure. She had come to him when she had been afraid or felt alone. She would snuggle up close to her father's side. In fact, she hadn't been held and felt loved since her father passed.

She sighed heavily. Being held was the one thing she couldn't do for herself.

WITH THANKSGIVING BEING LESS than two weeks away and the Christmas holiday in a little over a month, the excitement levels at the school was off the charts. Anticipation of Santa had both the three- and four-year-olds delirious with expectation while the two-and-under crowd were just happy, soaking up the festive atmosphere. The children's colorful paintings of turkeys and fall leaves covered the walls.

Despite the bright morning sun pouring in, Trenna frowned as she stared out at the snow. This was crazy, much too early in the season for snow. Nonetheless, the ground was covered in a light blanket of it and it wasn't showing any signs of letting up. The snow only added to the little ones' excitement. It was pure fun for them. They were not inconvenienced by it since they didn't have shovel it or to drive in it. Trenna didn't share their enthusiasm.

Although she had learned to tolerate the northern winter's bitter cold, she detested snow and ice. Nibbling on the corner of her bottom lip, she glanced at the clouds overhead before returning to stare anxiously at the white covering the ground. She had turned on the small, flat screen television on the shelf in her office. She changed the station to the weather channel.

"Don't do this," she chided unhappily, as she struggled to deal with a combination of fear and worry while a large dose of dread formed a knot in her stomach. With her hands balled at her sides, she blinked away tears as she read the forecast on the screen.

Although anticipating the worst, she had prayed that the snow would stop and the sun could come out. Sighing heavily, she reached for the telephone in order to put her 'back-up' plan into motion.

Just then three-year-old Carmen Meadows raced past the open door into the office, calling, "Miss M! Miss M!" She wrapped her small arms around Trenna's waist. Her small brown face and pretty black eyes danced with excitement. "Please come play "Tommy-Tom-Tom" for us! We want to sing!"

Trenna smiled. She leaned down to hug the little girl. Carmen was a delight. Her mother was single, with three other mouths to feed while struggling to make ends meet. Carmen was one of the children whose fees were paid by the foundation.

"P-p-pleeease!"

Trenna teased, "Tommy who? Does he come to our school?" She had started taking piano lessons when she was six and continued until she was in college. She played well. Love of music was something she shared with her parents who had also played instruments.

Laughing, Carmen couldn't control her giggles. "He's a turkey!"

"Oh! Who wants to sing?" Trenna asked, allowing Carmen to tug her out the door and down the hall to the music room.

Every time Trenna went to make her call she was interrupted. It was after one when her assistant let her know the public schools were closing. Despite her own increasing dread, Trenna asked the assistants to start calling parents to let them know they would close at three. She pushed her own problem aside to join in calling the students' parents. The majority of the children's parents came as soon as they were notified. By three-thirty all of the children had been picked up, and the staff had left. Finally, Trenna was free to make her call.

"Hi, Margaret, it's Trenna. Is Maureen free? Or is she busy with a client?"

"Hi, Mrs. McAdams. No, she had a family emergency. Mrs. Hale took sick and she took her to the doctor. "

"Oh no! How is she? I'm surprised she didn't text me. Is there any news?"

"Not yet. But she asked me cancel all her appointments for the rest of the day."

"Let's hope no news is a good sign. Which hospital?"

"Henry Ford."

"Okay, I'll start praying."

"Good idea. Is there anything I can do for you?"

Trenna was touched by the older woman's thoughtfulness. Margaret Hardwick had worked for Maureen since she and her grandmother started the Women's Crisis Center.

"No, I'm fine."

"If you need a ride home…"

"Thank you for the offer but it's too much of an inconvenience."

"But I don't mind."

"I know. Not to worry. I will be fine." The older woman lived only a block away from the Women's Center. It didn't made sense for her to battle the snow when she didn't have to. "Margaret, you take care. And I'll check with Maureen later. Bye."

True to her word, after she hung up, Trenna prayed for Maureen's grandmother. She was a lovely person who was both elegant and incredibly kind.

Around five Trenna received a text from Maureen, telling her that Mrs. Hale had pneumonia and they decided to hospitalize her. Then Maureen asked if she had a ride home. She text back that she was fine where she was and would stay overnight. She told Maureen to concentrate on her grandmother.

When the telephone rang a few minutes later, Trenna grabbed it on the first ring, "Hello, Maureen. I'm fine. I don't mind staying..."

"It's Darrin."

6

"*D*arrin?"

"Yes. I understand you need a lift home. I should be ready to leave in..." There was a pause before he said, "...fifteen minutes. That okay with you?

"Maureen called you?"

"Yeah. Look, I'm heading out now to clean off and warm up the Jeep."

"That's very kind of you but..."

He interrupted, "It's not a problem," then added, "meet me in the lot in...twenty minutes," before he hung-up the telephone.

Telling herself she had no right to be upset, she took several deep, calming breaths. She should be thankful, full of relief that Maureen had arranged a ride home for her and grateful to Darrin for agreeing to help her out. Maureen knew that she would rather be at home than being forced to spend the night at her office. All because she wasn't brave enough to tackle driving in the snow and possibly ice on her own.

She sighed resolutely then tucked her laptop and the early childhood professional journals she wanted to read into her briefcase. She pulled on the knee-length boots and a black down-filled calf-length coat. After wrapping a thick, pink wool scarf around her neck, she pulled on the matching knit hat and gloves.

After quickly checking the classrooms, kitchen, and bathrooms, she dimmed the overhead lights. The alarm was set and the doors locked when Trenna hurried to the rear entrance. As soon as she stepped out, blowing snow hit her in the face. It was cold, heavy, and she could barely see where to put one foot in front of the other.

"All set?" Darrin was dressed in a thick sheepskin coat. A navy wool cap covered his head and a navy scarf was wrapped around his throat.

"Yes." Darrin took her briefcase. Cupping her elbow, he guided her around a hump of snow to the Jeep parked at the curb. The parking lot was nearly empty, as only the security team on duty.

There was no point in wishing she had worn slacks that morning. So she began to shimmy, easing her ankle-length, straight wool skirt up to her knees. Trenna gasped aloud when Darrin encircled her waist and lifted her. She was forced to encircle his neck to steady herself. He placed her inside on the high seat.

Before she could thank him, he had slammed the door and was rounding the hood. She had her seatbelt fastened by the time he climbed into the driver's seat. Trenna shivered, but not from the cold.

"I'm sorry. Maureen shouldn't have gotten you involved. You had to have better things to do than chauffeur me home in a blizzard."

Darrin clicked his own seatbelt into place before he said, "Don't apologize. Glad to be able to help."

"I'm not your problem. Maureen meant well. She has a heart of gold, but she went too far. She has this silly idea that…" Trenna stopped abruptly.

"What?"

"Doesn't matter." Her hands tightly clasped in her lap. It was her problem, not his. She hated having to ask for help. Above all, she hated the paralyzing fear that gripped her whenever she got behind the wheel when the roads were slick.

She stared out the window. The snow was thick, like a heavy blanket covering the city. Darrin kept his eyes on the road and both hands on the steering wheel. The snow kept falling and had paced traffic to a crawl. They were following one of the salt trucks on the road. They joined the single passable lane and were barely moving.

Suddenly Trenna looked on in horror as a red sports car tried to speed passed them and quickly lost control. It went spinning nearly hitting the salt truck only to plow into a pile of snow on the side of the freeway. With her heart in her throat, she pressed down with both feet as if applying the brakes.

"What's wrong with him? Look what he caused! "

Rather than engaging the brakes, Darrin had smoothly steered them around the collision. Once they were back in their lane and the danger had passed, he said, "Relax, Trenna." He patted her hand. "We're fine. Do you have your cell? Good, call 911," then he gave her the number to the closest exit.

Although her hands were shaking Trenna quickly made the call.

"Thanks. I hope everyone is okay."

"Me too." She quizzed, "What was he thinking? He was going too fast for the road conditions. Even I know that much. If not for your quick reaction we'd be in that pileup!"

She was still trembling when she glanced back at the mess the reckless driver had caused. Two more cars had nearly rear-ended each other trying to avoid the sports car.

She shook her head, determined not to be a basket case. She was not letting old fears get the best of her. She and Darrin were fine, and were not going to crash. She wasn't behind the wheel, wasn't sliding on the ice off the road. She took a deep breath, trying to calm down.

What had she gotten herself into by accepting a ride from

him? Wasn't it bad enough that every time it snowed she had to inconvenience Maureen? Now Darrin was involved. She might need his help, but she certainly didn't welcome it. The last thing she wanted was to be dependent on any man...especially Darrin Morgan.

"Breathe," Trenna silently whispered. She could not afford to let this upset her. She must remain calm. She needed to think, to figure out a way to get past this.

After all, this was Darrin Morgan she was dealing with. She couldn't afford for him to so much as suspect she was aware of him, might be vulnerable in anyway. He could be ruthless and was not above using any weakness to his advantage. She'd seen him in the courtroom. No, no, no, he didn't need to know how much the near crash had bothered her.

She didn't want to be obligated to him. Darrin was Maureen's friend, not hers. Maureen was the one who had grown up with the Morgan twins. She hadn't any qualms about calling either Douglas or Darrin to ask a favor. If only it ended there.

Trenna wouldn't be surprised if her best friend was up to something. Maureen had called Darrin, not his twin. And Darrin had made no secret of his interest in her. Maureen had to be playing matchmaker. Right about now, if she was here, Trenna would have tried to shake some sense into her best friend. What was Maureen thinking? Maureen knew she still blamed him for getting Grace's attacker off. He was the reason that Todd Marks was a free man.

To make matters worse, Trenna knew she had a problem. Her awareness of Darrin seemed to be mushrooming. He was too darn close. She could smell his clean male scent. She trembled, alarmed because she was not just softening toward him, but she was also attracted to the man. Attraction led to desire and, as far as she was concerned, desire was a slippery slope to disaster. To say she was not upset would be a gross understatement. She didn't need this!

She had no idea when or even how it happened. It was as

unexpected and about as welcome as this blizzard! Maybe she was letting her emotions get the best of her? Yes! That was it! She was overreacting. There was no denying he was attractive man. So what? He was no threat to her.

"You okay?"

"I'm fine." Clearly, she had let her imagination go wild and it had gotten the best of her. She should be focused on being grateful that Darrin had been willing to help her out. Trenna couldn't believe she had gone so far as to blame Maureen. Her best friend wasn't the villain. She had only tried to help.

Beside, the two shared a common history. They both had a lousy track record when it came to men. Thank goodness they had both recovered and moved on with their lives. They had vowed not to repeat past mistakes.

Trenna wasn't ready to admit that between the two of them, Maureen had been the lucky one. She was grateful that her best friend had not experienced lingering heartache and pain. Maureen may not realize she was better off breaking her engagement before the wedding ceremony or that Trenna hadn't been that fortunate.

After her husband passed, Trenna had no family ties to hold her back. She moved to Michigan to be close to her best friend Maureen and her grandmother, Mrs. Hale. Her adopted family was all she had left.

Maureen was a beautiful woman with an active social life. She made sure Trenna felt welcome. She had introduced her to her friends. She went so far as to arrange double dates. They went to charity dinner-dances, jazz concerts, the theater, bowling alleys, and the movies.

For the first time in years, Trenna was able to enjoy herself, have fun. She didn't see the harm in her having male friends. Although she started dating in earnest, it was lighthearted, pure entertainment, nothing remotely heavy or serious.

Trenna was so thankful for their friendship. There was no

doubt that Maureen had always had her back. They shared nearly everything. Back in college, Maureen tried to convince her to wait, not to rush into marrying Martin. But Trenna had gone ahead. Although there was no doubt in her mind that Maureen wanted the best for her, Trenna had been so afraid of losing Martin that she kept telling herself they were in love. It had to work out!

No, Maureen was not the problem. She didn't have a malicious bone in her body. Trenna's problem was over six feet tall and too handsome for his own good. Suddenly, her eyes went wide. For the first time in her adult life, Trenna was attracted to a man. And it was not just any man, but the indisputably virile and sinfully sexy Darrin Morgan.

Her reaction to him was unnerving, so intense it scared her. No, he scared her. Trenna's response to something as non-threatening as a kiss on the forehead was crazy! How many times had she berated herself for acting like a teenager? A meaningless caress made her heart race like she was sprinting for a gold medal. He'd volunteered to take her home...not to bed.

She was overreacting. She should be laughing her head off. But the strength of her response to Darrin was far from amusing. If only she could dismiss his kindness, and pretend that he hadn't gone out of his way to help her and the foundation.

But he had taken her out to dinner. He had introduced her to his friends and potential investors. During dinner he had high praise for her accomplishments, boasted about school and her talent. Most importantly, at the end of the evening, he hadn't taken advantage of her in any way.

Since that night she had been unable to get him out of her thoughts. Nor had she been able to forget how it felt to be close to him. Had she started to trust him? Unfortunately, Trenna did not have an answer.

To make matters worse, she was unsure she trusted herself to be alone with him. He made her tingle, all over. Goodness! She didn't want to think about what it would be like to be held in his arms or feel his lips on hers.

SHIFTING IN HIS SEAT, Darrin did not allow himself more than a glance at Trenna. He did not enjoy her being so quiet and tense that she barely moved. Her hands gripped the sides of the seat. He could see she was clearly terrified of the road conditions. What he wanted to know was why.

When Maureen called to ask for a favor, hoping he could help her friend, he had jumped at the chance. Longing to see Trenna, he was not about to let pride get in the way. One dinner in her company had left him hungry for more. The last week and a half had been brutal, and his ego had certainly taken a beating. Darrin wasn't used to a woman putting so many roadblocks in his way. But then Trenna was nothing like the women in his circle of friends. She was unique, one-of-a-kind.

The wind had picked up, sending blowing snow straight into the windshield while the temperature dropped. The sun was setting, and road conditions were rapidly deteriorating. They were inching along in the only barely passable lane.

Hoping to distract her, Darrin asked, "Any news since the Murrays toured your school?"

"Not yet, but I am very hopeful. They seemed very impressed with the school."

"I'm not surprised. Like you, your school is first class."

Warmed by the compliments, she smiled. "Thank you. But I'm trying not to get ahead of myself. It's going to take time to decide, especially with so much money involved."

"True. Jackson and I have been friends for a long time. He is not impulsive, nor is he likely to run for the hills at the first sign of trouble. From what I understand, his accountant has gone over your books, and the Murrays have a copy of your goals and your long-range objectives. And all was good."

"Yes, but it's a lot to consider. He's not interested in taking over the scholarship fund, but in expanding the number of children per class. He talked about following the children from nursery school, elementary, middle, high school, and through college. That will take millions."

Darrin nodded. "It will be a life changing project that will affect the children and their families."

"If the Murrays says yes, I will owe you for…"

"You owe me nothing."

"I appreciate the introduction." She laughed. "It's very exciting. It has been a struggle to remain patient."

He swallowed a groan, realizing how much he enjoyed her laughter. She rarely showed any amusement around him. Unfortunately for him, her defenses always seemed to be in place. He was far from being a novice with women, but when it came to Trenna, he had no clue how to get close to her.

"You're taking the expressway?"

"They clear the freeways first." He reached over and squeezed her hand. "I know what I'm doing, Trenna. It's better to take our time and get there safe and sound. Besides, I promised Maureen I'd get you home. I keep my promises."

With the heavy, wet snow pelting the car, it was slow going, even in an SUV designed for rough terrain.

'Oh, yeah,' he smiled. Neither one of them were going anywhere in a hurry. He had to remember to send Maureen flowers. He owed her.

"It's getting dark."

He heard the anxiety in her voice. "We're fine. I'm curious. Do you remember the night that you came by to pay your respects to my family after my father passed?"

"Of course. What about it?"

"You and I were at odds, yet you went out of your way to help me. I don't understand why?"

"It was a difficult time for all of you. I'd lost family also. I knew what it was like. Besides, I'm a child of God so, of course, I'd do the right thing."

He nodded before he asked, "Have you ever been skiing?"

"You're kidding, right? I was raised in Charleston and went to college in Atlanta. I rarely saw snow and nothing like what you have here."

"You don't know what you're missing." Darrin began telling her about his first ski trip with his parents. The twins were seven. On the first day the twins were horsing around on the chairlift, and Darrin fell and broke his left arm. Their mom wanted to go home, but their dad said it wouldn't be fair to Douglas. The next morning on his first real hill Douglas fell and broke his right leg."

Laughing, Trenna said, "Both of you with broken bones, your poor parents. Evidently they couldn't take the two of you anywhere."

He chuckled. "Exactly what our folks said."

"Did that stop you?"

"Are you kidding? We loved it! We couldn't wait to get back on the slopes!" Darrin explained that by the time they were in middle school they were competing, and in college they were both on the ski team.

"Wow," she exclaimed.

He said with a straight face, "Does that mean I can't convince you to go ice fishing with me in late January? By then the ice on the lake should be thick enough to build a shanty."

Trenna stared at him in disbelief.

"I'm serious," he fibbed.

"No, you're not." Her giggle soon gave way to bubbling laughter that shook her petite frame.

Thoroughly charmed, he grinned. "It will be fun. Once we

deck you out in a couple layers of long johns and three or four pairs of socks, we will drill a hole in the ice..."

"Stop teasing!" By this time, she was nearly doubled in half with laughter, holding her side.

They were still smiling when he prompted, "Your turn. What trouble did you get into as a kid?"

Laughing, she shook her head.

"Come on. What were your hobbies?"

"I enjoyed swimming, not competitively. I took ballet lessons and started playing the piano when I was six. Both my parents played instruments. Speaking of music, Doug sang a solo with the choir on First Sunday and nailed it." She paused before saying, "I remember when the two of you used to sing together in church. You have a great voice. I have been told that you two even won several local gospel competitions. Is that true?"

"It's true."

Darrin knew Trenna was studying him. But as much as he has longed to have her attention directed his way, he didn't elaborate. He couldn't.

"Your brother and mother attend church regularly, but not you."

7

----

*H*is throat tightened as he heard the unspoken question in her voice. How many times had his family asked him why? What could he say? That he was angry at God? That he blamed Him for taking his dad? It was so sudden. His father was there, seemingly in perfect health one day and gone the next. There had been no time to prepare...no time to say a proper goodbye.

He knew that his refusal to explain frustrated his mother and twin. There was nothing he could say that would help. Filled with resentment and anger, the pain of his loss went so deep it was impossible to share with anyone.

Her continued silence brought him back to the evening she had come to offer her condolences. She hadn't been intrusive, but had sat quietly with him and was kind enough to share her own loss with him.

He surprised himself when he admitted, "I haven't been able to go inside any church since my father's funeral." She was silent so long that he cautiously took his eyes off the road long enough to glance at her.

Trenna said candidly, "I've been through grief counseling. I understand there are stages of grief. But I don't care what the experts say. There is no understanding loss. We're not all the same. And we grieve in different ways."

Darrin nodded. "You should know. You've had to deal with a great deal of loss in your life: first your parents and then your husband."

"Are you changing the subject because it's hard to talk about?"

"Yes—I mean no. "

She volunteered, "Losing my parents was especially devastating because I lost both of them at once, and it happened so quickly. There was no warning. Like me, you were raised in church. You don't need me to remind you that during difficulty it's easy to forget God's love is unconditional. He hasn't stopped loving you."

Darrin blinked, feeling as if he had been hit by a two-by-four. Uncomfortable, he asked, "Was your husband the reason you no longer wanted to stay in Charleston?"

"Maureen was the reason I moved to Michigan. Maintaining our friendship was important to both of us. Over the years she and Mrs. Hale had become family to me." Trenna confessed, "I've been praying for Mrs. Hale and trying not to worry. Do you think it's serious since they are admitting her?"

"Not necessarily. Maureen didn't sound as if she was alarmed. At Mrs. Hale's age I'm glad the doctor was cautious and sent her to the hospital. "

"I agree," she said softy, tucking a leg beneath her.

He was pleased that she was starting to relax, even leaned back against the seat.

"I asked if she needed me to sit with her, but she said no." Trenna surmised, "Having to make the hard decisions and facing them on your own are major disadvantages to being an only child."

"I disagree. Maureen's not alone. And neither are you."

The salt on the roadway finally seemed to be working. The traffic started picking up speed. She released a heavy sigh as they approached her exit.

"Darlin', you can let go of the door-handle," Darrin teased, "We're nearly there."

"Sorry. My nerves have nothing to do with your driving skills. I'm amazed at how comfortable you are behind the wheel. Even after living here for nearly five years, I'm not fond of driving in the snow or ice."

"Fond? That is a huge understatement. You've got more than a healthy dose of reluctance."

"Maureen didn't explain?"

"She didn't say more than that you needed a ride home. Why don't you tell me?"

"I appreciate the lift. Despite what you said earlier, this has to be a huge inconvenience."

Although disappointed that she was unwilling to talk to him, Darrin didn't comment. He shifted to ease the tightness in his neck and shoulders. Unfortunately, the snow was not letting up. "Looks like we have a blizzard."

"You think? Do you have far to go?"

"Nope, I'm only a couple of miles from my family. No need to say thank you again. I don't mind helping you out."

"But I appreciate your help. I had planned to stay in the building."

Frustrated, Darrin said, "Trenna, you've already told me. Once was enough."

He was relieved when she said, "Well, the little ones were thrilled." She smiled when she explained, "Santa's sled won't glide without snow, plus the fun in making snowmen and snow angels."

Darrin howled with laughter. "There's never a dull moment at Little Hearts."

"You've got that right."

When they slowed at the security gate, the guard recognized them and waved them through. The road conditions were not improving.

He said, "It looks as if the plow has come through here earlier, but it wasn't enough. Your driveway and walk haven't been touched."

"Aren't you worried about getting stuck?"

"Not likely with four-wheel drive and snow tires."

He eased the Jeep to a stop in front of her place. Stretching taut muscles, he said, "As promised, I got you home safe and sound."

"You did." She surprised him when she said, "You might as well come inside and warm up."

Before she could reach for the door handle, Darrin said, "Hold on. Let me get you down." Grabbing his coat from the backseat, he pulled it on, then came around to her side to open her door. He picked her up and kept going, cautiously mounting her front steps. They shivered from the brisk wind by the time she got the door open and switched off the alarm.

Just then his stomach grumbled, loudly. They both laughed.

"I hope you don't mind leftovers. I made chili last night."

"I love chill. But I'd better move the Jeep into the drive, just in case the snowplow comes through. Be right back. Where's your shovel?"

"The garage. But you don't..."

"Not a problem. Which way?"

She pointed to the side door.

Whistling softly, Darrin couldn't believe his good luck. His good-natured teasing seemed to have done the trick. The petite beauty had a gorgeous smile. He was grateful to finally have her smiles directed his way.

As he cleared the porch and steps, he realized he still had no idea what it was about Trenna that had fascinated him. From the first, he had been drawn do her. She was quiet, but her attitude and direct manner of speech was refreshing. No false flattery, or no pretense or attempts to stroke his ego.

She was beautiful. But his interest went deeper than the way she looked. By the time he finished with the sidewalk and was attacking the drive, he still had no clear answer. He would be lying if he failed to acknowledge that her smooth, flawless dark brown skin was driving him nuts, wondering if every inch of her was as soft as she looked. And her luscious mouth begged for his kisses. Talk about a moth fascinated by the flame. She was so classy, no wishy-washy high-low hems for her, or skintight skirts and leggings.

He meant it when he said he didn't mind clearing the snow. After being cooped up in the car, he relished the physical activity.

When he stepped inside he was relieved to be out of the blowing snow. He hung his coat beside hers on the coat rack in the entranceway and left his wet boots next to

hers on a rubber tray, beneath the long, cushioned bench against the wall. He padded in sock-covered feet into a great room.

Lamps illuminated walls covered in warm beige. The large, dark green L–shaped sectional sofa was positioned in front of a huge fireplace. Above the mantle was a large, wall-mounted flat screen TV.

"Very nice."

He admired the open floor plan. The galley kitchen was on the back wall; the mahogany and glass dining table with green and white leaf-patterned padded chairs were in the center of the room. Forest green and cream area rugs defined the space between the living and dining rooms.

"You must be freezing." She smiled. "Make yourself comfortable. Would you care for tea, coffee, or hot cider?"

"Cider?"

"I have a single brewer."

He nodded. "Coffee...please."

She flicked a switch and the electric flames instantly danced in the grate. She laughed. "Be right back."

He sat down, careful to keep his eyes on the flames.

Placing the steaming mug on the coffee table, she said, "I wasn't kidding when I said I'm not an outdoor girl. I can't imagine sleeping outside on the ground without indoor plumbing."

"There's nothing like a campfire beside the lake." He grinned. "Even my mother tried it, once."

Her mouth dropped open. "Your classy, beautiful mother slept in a tent?"

He nodded. "Dad talked her into going camping with us. We had a great time." Chuckling, he admitted, "Mom hated every second and swore she was never coming back. Dad enjoyed teasing her about it."

Trenna smiled before she surmised, "Love."

"Exactly."

"So that's where you got this outdoor enthusiasm from, your dad. Do you warm weather fish or hunt during deer season?"

"I've done both. Love any kind of fishing, but I've been deer hunting only a few times. It's not my thing." He chuckled, "Darlin', I'd really like to take you up to the cabin. I guarantee you will love it."

"No thank you."

They both laughed.

"I'm guessing that your parents were like mine...deeply in love."

"That's correct. Were your parents both teachers? Was that why you decided to go into education?"

She giggled. "Absolutely not. My mother was a very talented clothing designer. My dad was a corporate lawyer. She worked as a seamstress in a small boutique. The owner, Miss Elaine, was an older woman who knew fashion. When she saw some of Mom's designs Miss Elaine was impressed and encouraged her.

"They started with a few dresses and it quickly turned into a whirlwind. Then Miss Elaine hired two more seamstresses to keep up with the demand. Soon she signed an exclusive contract with the shop owner and shared in the profits. It worked out better than either of them had expected. They hired five seamstresses and my mother was finally able to design full time. When the owner needed to retire she offered to sell the shop to Mom.

"Dad was her biggest supporter and handled the deal. We were in a tourist town. Women on vacation came in and bought clothes. Soon Mom was getting orders from around the country. The boutique was always crowded, the phone was constantly ringing, and they couldn't keep up with the orders. When Mom needed help she turned to Dad.

"He took over the business part and allowed her to concentrate on her designs. Before Dad was done he'd opened several boutiques across the south, plus hired a manufacturing company to make the clothes and, eventually, we also bought the manufacturing company."

"No wonder you always look good."

She smiled. "Many of Mother's designs are classics and will never go out of style. She did asymmetrical hems first."

"I'm impressed."

Trenna nodded. "I feel blessed to have had such wonderful parents. Most important to me was they were so loving, always there for me. I couldn't ask for more."

He grinned. "Loving parents! Who would believe that we actually have something in common?"

She laughed. "Stop teasing me. Your family enjoyed sports while mine were huge music fans. During the summer, Dad used to drag us to open air concerts and jazz festivals around the country. Although my mom believed in healthy meals, she turned a blind eye when Dad stuffed me with cotton-candy, foot-long chili dogs, deep-fried onion rings, and mile-high ice cream cones dipped in chocolate and nuts."

He adored the way her pretty eyes danced with humor. He watched as she picked up the remote, turned the television to the local evening news channel, keeping the sound muted. The local weather map filled the screen with blizzard warnings, and school closings scrolled across the bottom of the screen.

"Do you want the volume up?"

Acutely aware that what he truly wanted was off-limits, he shrugged, "I already know that since I've come inside my SUV's covered. It's not letting up."

She shivered and went over to the picture window and closed the drapes. "Make yourself at home. The guest bath's there." She pointed to a closed door, tucked in a narrow hallway between the kitchen and dining room. "Excuse me, I'm going up to change."

Darrin's heart picked up speed. Unable to look away, he watched the delectable sway of her shapely hips as Trenna climbed the staircase that led to a loft. He watched until she reached the top of the landing and then was disappointed when she went behind the fabric-covered privacy screen.

He turned and went into her small pale green and yellow half-bathroom. When he closed the door he realized his hands were shaking. He took several slow deep breaths.

He stared at his image in the gold-framed mirror, determined to forget the way his senses had heated and his body had instantly hardened when he'd picked her up and carried her to the door. He took another long breath while telling himself that he couldn't give in to this overwhelming need.

Sure, he wanted her. So what? She was unavailable, a fact she was not about to let him forget. There was no doubt that she hadn't left any options open for them. First thing on her agenda was to let him know he wasn't her type.

He had to man up and deal with it. So what if he suspected she was afraid, running from something? Besides, it was her place and her show—he had no choice but to play this game her way. She didn't want or need him. Her secrets were safe.

He should be concentrating on giving thanks that she had invited him in. He must not forget that he was only in her home because he'd done her a favor and given her a lift home. His father had raised the twins to respect women. She invited him to dinner. He would clean his plate, help clean up, and then he'd say thank you politely and go home alone.

Trenna was what his parents called a good girl. She was special, the kind of female a man didn't fool around with. Plus, his mother liked Trenna. Unfortunately for him, Trenna had told him that she wasn't interested. It hurt knowing she did not want him the way he wanted her.

Unfortunately, his need for her was not going away. It was unrelenting, testing his control. He had never had a problem with accepting no from a woman. He had a healthy ego, and would simply move onto the next willing female. He was aware that a single phone call to any of the females in his past could solve his sexual issue.

Since the night she had come to their home to pay her respects to his family, he had gone without. His reason wasn't complicated. He didn't want another woman—he only wanted Trenna McAdams. The wanting started the day they met. Smart, brilliant, and so beautiful, she fascinated him.

It was crazy, and so was he for letting this thing drag on and on. When it came to Trenna it was long past the time he accepted she was not going to change her mind. With her he had no pride.

After using the facilities, he washed his hands, determined to ignore the too familiar ache in his groin. He swore beneath his breath because his body was not listening. About now, he could use an ice-cold shower. And then what? It would be nothing more than a temporary reprieve at best.

He tried everything he could think of to get her out of his system, and nothing worked. It didn't make sense. He asked himself a thousand and one times how he could continue to want someone who didn't want him and still had no logical answer. Just how big of a fool was he planning to be over this woman? He needed to get over her and move on.

8

_____

_W_ith both of them helping it didn't take long to get the food on the table.

"You look comfortable," he said as he poured the red wine.

"Just trying to stay warm." Trenna had changed into black fleece leggings and a pink tunic-length sweater and, on her feet, a pair of thick pink slipper-socks. She smiled, secretly pleased at the way Darrin wolfed down his meal. "Another slice of corn bread?"

He grinned. "You won't ever hear me say no to hot, homemade bread with butter and honey. And the chili and salad were delicious. You certainly know your way around the kitchen." His compliments had her beaming. Then he surprised her when he asked, "Are you afraid of snow because you grew up in Carolina?"

She jerked, nearly dropping her spoon full of chili topped with cheese. She stalled, smoothing the green cotton napkin covering her lap. "I'm surprised Maureen didn't explain. But you are wrong. I'm not afraid of snow, but I don't like driving in snow or ice."

"No one does. But we're talking about more than dread. Why?"

Trenna shuttered, taking a sip of water before she said, "It's a long story. My husband and I were in a terrible car crash during an ice storm. I was bruised but not badly hurt because I was wearing a seatbelt. Martin wasn't wearing one and died at the scene."

"I'm…" he hesitated.

"Sorry you asked?"

"I'm sorry for your loss. I had no idea."

She nodded, picking up her spoon.

"I upset you."

"It's okay. Martin has been gone almost five years but it has not been long enough for me to forget. I'm left with this fear. I've always been independent and I detest having to bother others when the weather is bad."

"Sounds like you are lucky to be alive."

She said candidly, "I don't believe in luck. I was blessed to come out of it okay."

He reached out and briefly squeezed her hand. "Your fears are understandable."

She confessed, "Since I was driving that night his twin daughters hold me responsible for the accident. My husband was older than I was."

"Are you saying they blamed you?"

"Yes. Losing him was hard. But when I came away with only a concussion and a few injuries, it was too much for them. Plus, they were upset that I was in his will and would be receiving the bulk of his insurance policy. All of it was enough to convince them I never loved him and was after his money."

"Sounds like his girls never bothered to get to know you. Trenna, tell me something. How did you manage it? How did you get beyond your losses without being bitter?"

She sighed. "It wasn't easy. But acceptance came for me when I remembered two things. God is the one who determines the day we are born and the day we die. Instead of focusing on my parents' death, I decided to celebrate their life by being grateful every day for them and giving thanks to God for the time I had with them."

He made no response. He looked stunned as if he hadn't been expecting her answer.

She hesitated before saying, "I really thought I had gotten past the accident or at least that I was doing better, until one of our good friends, Jenna Gaines, was in a serious car accident. It was New Year's Eve. My girlfriends and I got together to celebrate. The weather was terrible. Jenna never arrived because her car was hit and sent crashing into a telephone pole. It was bad. We nearly lost her."

Trenna shuttered. "It brought everything back for me. I nearly lost the nerve to drive at all. But I'm much better now, except in the ice or snow. And I've been fortunate that Maureen has been so understanding." Trenna shrugged. "But life happens. Mrs. Hale needed her. I don't expect her to drop everything for me. That's one of the reasons why I designed my office to double as a studio apartment with a full bath, sofa-bed, and spare closet for emergencies."

"Smart," Darrin said. "How's Jenna now?"

"She's fine and happily married to the man of her dreams, Scott Hendricks." Trenna smiled. Taking a sip of wine, she surprised them both when she said, "Now, it's my turn to pick your brain, counselor. Why Detroit? You can practice law anywhere. Why not move someplace warm and sunny?"

Chuckling, Darrin leaned back in his chair, unwittingly drawing her eyes to his strong, handsome features. She was used to seeing him dressed formally in expensive custom-tailored suits and silk shirts and ties. Tonight his jacket was tossed over the back of her sofa, the top two buttons of his pale blue silk shirt had been left open, revealing the strong lines of his ivory throat. The color brought out the dark blue depths of his eyes while the cloth was pulled taut against his broad chest and lean mid-section. Gorgeous!

Why did he have to be so darn attractive? So sexy? More importantly, why couldn't she keep her eyes off him? His lips were lush, the bottom one fuller than the top. He was downright dangerous, especially to someone like her who had sworn off sex.

Hoping to distract herself, she prodded, "Well? Why not Vegas? Miami or L.A.?"

"That's easy. Detroit's home and my family was here. Dad, along with his friend and business partner, started the firm. Both men passed along their love of the law to their sons. It wasn't until Dad passed that we learned he wanted me to head the firm. I was reluctant. I would have rather shared the responsibility with Douglas but he wasn't interested. He's comfortable being a full partner."

"Why were you reluctant?"

"I'm not sure. Perhaps the grief? Or maybe I was busy wondering if I could fill his shoes?"

His hand rested on the table. She surprised them both when she placed her hand on his.

"You truly believe what you said about God determining the day of our birth and day we die?"

"I do."

Judging by his frown, she suspected he had his doubts. In hope of changing the subject and lightening the mood, she asked, "More chili? Salad?"

"No, but thank you. I ate like a pig. I can't eat another bite." He leaned back and laced his long fingers over his flat stomach. "You are full of surprises, Trenna McAdams. You're not only smart and talented. You're a darn good cook. I bet you can do anything you set your mind to. "

Smiling, she said, "Stop flattering me."

His gazed lingered on hers, before he said, "Have you spent the day watching the snow and dreading going out in it?"

Embarrassed, she hedged, "Some days are better than others."

"And today reminded you of the devastation of losing your

husband." He surmised. "I'm glad Maureen thought of me and I was able to help you out tonight."

Stunned by his kindness, she couldn't seem to pull her eyes from his dark gaze. Trenna couldn't name what she was feeling. Her heart felt as if it were doing somersaults in her chest. What was happening to her?

She managed to say, "Me too."

Genuinely flattered by the compliments, Trenna mumbled her thanks then jumped to her feet. She began collecting and stacking dishes and utensils. When she reached for his bowl and salad plate. He surprised her when he caught her hand. Her eyes were wide, questioning him. He surprised her even more, moving a caressing thumb over her knuckles. He leaned forward to lightly brush her mouth with his.

"Thanks," he said softy, "...for dinner. Now you sit while I'll clean up."

Deep chocolate-brown eyes locked with his dark blue ones. Feeling as if she'd been scorched by a flame, her face heated, and she blushed.

When she didn't reply he spoke again, "Trenna?"

She struggled to contain the shivers of awareness that rushed over her body. "Yes?"

Rolling up his sleeves over his muscular arms, he asked, "Do you wash them by hand or use the dishwasher?"

"Dishwasher." Gauging the way her heart was racing it was a wonder she could formulate a response. Goodness! She was a mess. The instant he'd touched her her brain had ceased working.

Trenna sat and watched him scrape and rinse the bowls and plates before he filled the dishwasher. She felt as if one of her silly fantasies about Darrin was real. He was here, in her home...so close she could touch him...could almost feel the warmth of his skin. She blinked in shock, realizing she'd been staring at his firm buttocks as he leaned over. She was rattled, in need of a diversion...and she needed it now!

"Cobber?" she blurted out, then clarified, "I made apple and pear cobbler last night. Would you care for some?"

Straightening, his eyes twinkled as he teased, "I've had apple and I've had pear, but I don't believe I've ever had them together." Rubbing his hands, he flashed that sexy grin. "I'm game."

"It won't take long heat it up. Why don't you relax on the sofa?"

Trenna was putting the deep-dish stoneware in the oven when the telephone rang. She caught it on the second ring, "Hi, how's your grandmother? Pneumonia? Okay, yes, we got in a little while ago. We just finished dinner and I'm heating the cobbler."

She saw that Darrin was flipping through the channels, then stopped to listen to the all-news channel. "Sorry, repeat that please." She listened as Maureen explained that she was staying overnight with his grandmother. "Are you sure you don't need me to come? No, are you sure? Okay." When she hung up she realized Darrin was watching her.

"How serious?" he asked.

"Maureen's concerned but not worried. The doctor wanted Mrs. Hale to stay in the hospital as a precaution because of her age. Maureen's staying with her tonight."

After switching on the coffeemaker, she prepared the dessert tray including scoops of vanilla ice cream.

"Smells wonderful," he said, coming over to carry in the tray. He placed the tray on the middle sofa cushion rather than on the ottoman.

Darrin moaned, savoring the dessert. "Delicious. Someone taught you well, darlin'. You're a great cook,"

"My mom," she said with a smile. "I'm glad you like it. It's nothing fancy. I've gotten a lot of my culinary ideas from Anna Prescott Mathis. Her catering company supplies the children's lunch."

"I know her husband, Gavin. He plays for the Detroit Lions. Have you taken lessons from her?"

"No! We talk, discuss menus over the phone. Both Anna's mother and grandmother were southern cooks." Trenna laughed, curling her legs beneath her. "She claims she developed the perfect menu that appeals to men."

"Say what?"

"It's true. It worked for Gavin." She explained that Anna had catered meals for some of the bachelors on the team.

She told him about growing up in Charleston and vacations at Hilton Head. She shared happy memories that she hadn't thought about in years while they finished up.

Sipping his coffee, he surprised her when he demanded, "Pictures!"

She laughed, "You want to look at old family photos?"

"I do."

Shaking her head in disbelief, she reached into end-table drawer and pulled out a thick photo album. Cradling it against her chest, she warned, "It's not too late to change your mind and save yourself from boredom."

Chuckling, Darrin moved the tray to the end table then patted the middle cushion. "Sit here, so we can both see. You can tell me who is who."

Time flew as Trenna shared childhood and high school memories. There was laughter and even a few tears by the time she closed the album. Surprisingly, she wasn't uneasy about how much private history she had revealed. She had let down her guard and been able to relax with Darrin. She felt no judgment coming from him, only acceptance.

He teased, "You come from good stock. Your father was able to take your mother's creative designs for clothing, turn them into very successful clothing boutiques and then expand into manufacturing the clothes. I'm impressed."

Trenna smiled. "Not much gets by you. You're an excellent listener."

"Thanks, an advantage in my profession." He grinned. "It's no surprise that you've made a success of your school. Brains, beauty, and talent are part of your DNA."

"Goodness! It sounds like a mutual admiration committee meeting in here."

"Something wrong with that?"

Flustered, she blushed. "Evidently not."

"Good." He caressed her check with the light brush of his knuckle.

Determined to ignore the quivers of sensation that ran down her spine, she needed a distraction. "More coffee?"

"I should go while I can. The last time I looked the snow hadn't stopped."

She had been enjoying herself, so much so that she'd forgotten the reason why he was here. She was disappointed, didn't want him to leave. She rose when he did telling herself it was better this way.

"Thanks for dinner, Trenna. If you tell my mom I will have to deny it, but that was the best cobbler I've ever had. If you ever get bored with running the nursery school, you can always sell pies. You'd make a fortune."

Laughing so hard her side hurt, she managed to say, "I'm glad you enjoyed the cobbler, but I think I'll stick with Little Hearts."

Nodding, he led the way into entrance hall. As he put on his suit coat, he said, "I can swing by in the morning and pick you up so you have a car this weekend."

Warmed by his thoughtfulness, she actually considered taking him up on the offer. But her keen awareness of his clean scent, his masculinity, his rock-hard body, was too much. She couldn't think!

Evidently, she had been silent too long because he prompted, "Trenna?" He placed a finger beneath her chin and lifted her face toward his. Their eyes met.

"Would you like me to…"

"No!" she said sharply but quickly amended, "I mean, I'm sure you have plans for the weekend. Maureen won't mind dropping me by the office, so I can pick up my car."

Studying her small, dark features, he said, "There is no need for either you or Maureen to go out in the cold. If you give me your keys, Doug can follow me and we will drop your car off for you. And you can stay warm and dry inside."

Unable to look away, she stared up into the heat in his eyes. She couldn't help being mesmerized by his handsome features, his dark lashes or his thick, close-cut, wavy black hair. Even his lips were well-shaped...enticing.

"I've inconvenienced you enough." Reaching up, she smoothed his shirt collar.

Darrin dropped to his head until he could say into her ear, "That's impossible, darlin'. Don't you know, Trenna, there's nothing you can ask that would inconvenience me?" His voice was deep, huskier than before.

An instant later he covered her mouth with his. She was surprised because he was gentle as he softly brushed his lips against hers. His touch was whisper-light and electric. Trenna quivered from the contract, her senses alive in sweet anticipation. Darrin? did it again and again until she released a sigh. She was completely awed by his tenderness. The kiss, while incredibly warm, was also gentle.

Using the tip of his tongue, Darrin teased the closed seam of her lips. Slowly he tantalized first the right side and then the left corner of her mouth. He repeated each caress again and again. Unsure if it was him or the kiss, she found it impossible to resist. She released a throaty moan as shivers of delight raced along her nerve endings. Her defenses quickly crumbled and she gave into her longing and curiosity. Eager for more, Trenna opened for Darrin, allowing him complete access.

Caught in a sensual haze, she silently vowed, 'Only one taste... just one.' She, tentatively sponged his lips with the tip of her tongue. Goodness, his lips were soft, yet firm. She sighed while he moaned as she caressed him, marveling over the velvety texture of his tongue. He relaxed, returning the favor and giving her access to him.

She was shocked that there was no pressure, no demands, and no force on his part. She always thought of Darrin as being macho, very male, but he was so tender with her.

This was so new that Trenna felt like a teenager. Almost as if she had never been kissed. She hadn't experienced such tenderness. She sighed in pleasure, thoroughly enchanted as she wrapped her arms around his neck, eagerly pulling him down to her.

Consumed with desire, Trenna became the aggressor. She explored Darrin's mouth, boldly taking his tongue deep into her mouth and sucked. He tasted of coffee, apple, pear mixed with a hint of cinnamon, but there was something more. Something she could not describe but was uniquely his. Cushioned against his long body, her petite frame shook with pleasure.

"Mmm," she moaned. With her eyes closed, she absorbed the pleasure of being cradled. He held her close. For the first time in a very long time, she felt safe.

How had she lived without the simple luxury of being held? She hadn't even realized how much she wanted this until Darrin had cradled her body against him.

Floored by his care, she was unprepared when he pressed her full length against him. His body was firm, his chest taut and his shoulders incredibly wide as he took her bottom lip his into his mouth and suckled. She trembled from the contact.

Amazed by how good it felt to be cradled against him, desire whirled around her, shooting sparks of need directly into her bloodstream. Goodness! He was confident and so assured of his masculinity that he had no trouble tempering his strength. He held her in his muscular arms as if she were made of spun glass. Slowly, he tantalized her senses, giving her the freedom to taste him and relish in his velvet heat. The kiss grew so hot it practically sizzled, sending ribbons of desire so deep inside that they reached her core.

It didn't occur to her to protest, not even when Darrin moved his hands up and down her back, following the soft lines from her shoulders to her spine. When he touched her hips they both moaned at the warmth of his caress. She sighed when he cupped her lush curves before he pressed her into his hard angles.

"So sweet, Trenna, you are so beautiful," Darrin hushed into her ear, "...pure perfection."

He kissed her again and again, hungry with need. The hot wash of his tongue on hers was mesmerizing, leaving her eager for more.

Passion sped along her body, spread like wildfire from skin to bone to muscle, encompassing soft tissue to every cell of her body. No part of her was unaffected. Suddenly her breasts felt heavy, so heavy they ached. The tips were hard and ultra sensitive, like twin beads of longing, piercing her resolve and attacking her entire system. She sighed, wondering why she was fighting it. Why was she even trying to control the urge to rub her breasts against his hard chest?

"Darrin..." she moaned.

He crooned in her ear, "Whatever you want, darlin'."

Her eyes went wide as she stared at him disbelief.

"Whatever..." he repeated.

She shivered from the mere thought of more of his kisses. They were better than potato chips and she didn't want to stop.

"Kisses...please."

"Yes, madam..." he crooned as he brought his mouth down to hers. The kisses were so incredible.…

"Yes..." she breathed in his scent.

Impatient to touch him, she quickly unbuttoned his heavy coat, pushed it off his shoulders along with his sport coat. But, she didn't stop there. She undid his tie and unbuttoned his shirt collar. She didn't slow until Darrin's warm chest was bare. Going up on tiptoe, she brushed her lips against his throat. His skin was supple, warm. They both trembled as she licked the scented hollow at the base of his throat.

She inhaled the heady combination, relished in his aftershave mixed with his male scent. Darrin's throaty groan thrilled her. She closed her eyes, moving her hand over his chest and savoring his strength and heat. Inhaling, she rested her face against him.

"Trenna..." he whispered, brushing his lips over her forehead.

His kisses were like him, exquisite and unbelievably sexy. Goodness, she didn't want it to stop! She couldn't seem to get enough. She was disappointed when the need for breath forced their lips to part. She didn't want him to stop...not ever. That realization frightened her.

9

_____

renna was shaking, unable to think. She couldn't recall ever feeling this way. Her reaction to him was intense, more so than ever before. Why was this happening to her? She had learned to be cautious, to always think things through.

But tonight was different. She was filled with such intense longing, with overwhelming feelings, all because of him. The instant he kissed her, her brain stopped working. One part of her warned her to be careful while another part urged her on.

She could have resisted, if he hadn't been so unbelievably gentle and caring. It was weird! Did he have a sixth-sense? How did he know that she craved his kisses? Or that she adored the way he cradled her body against his big frame? He made her feel safe.

Those things alone were enough to send alarm into her system. Goodness! His caresses were a major distraction and his kisses more decadent than the richest chocolate truffle. The man was dangerous. No! No! Things like this happened to other people, not her!

Peering at him through the thickness of her lashes, she watched him drop his arms and take a step back. She frowned, baffled by conflicting emotions. But what stood out in Trenna's mind was that she was not afraid of Darrin and did not want him to leave. Lost in thought, she was not conscious of reaching out and wrapping a hand around one of his wrists. "Darrin?" she said, unaware that she was caressing him.

Flames of desire seem to spark in his dark eyes and his nostrils flared as if he were inhaling her scent. Gazing down at her, he asked, "Talk to me. I need to know if you want me as much as I want you."

Her eyes widened and her heart picked up speed as she stared at him. Realizing he expected an answer, embarrassed, she dropped her lids. The instant she looked away he tugged free and bent to reach for his boots.

She said his name sharply.

"No games, Trenna, just tell me what you want."

"Please don't go," she whispered. This time when she touched him she slid her hands up his chest, until they came to rest on his wide, wool-covered shoulders.

"Why?"

She worried her bottom lip, then she said in a quick whisper, "I want you to stay and make love to me."

There wasn't any hesitation when Darrin feathered light kisses over each of her brows before placing kisses down her cheeks. He brushed her mouth with his before he raised his head.

He said, "Be sure."

She preferred to show him rather than to verbally admit that she hungered for more of his slow, drugging kisses. She longed to be cradled in his arms, skin to bare skin. Goodness! She had no idea how he had done it, but he made her feel both safe and utterly desirable. It was such a heady combination. And it was foreign to her. Even though she had been married, she had never experienced such heat, such tenderness.

"Trenna?"

It was not that easy to admit she wanted him. Nor could she

ignore the way her heartbeat drummed in her ears as she stretched up onto her tiptoes. But he did not drop his head so their lips could meet. Instead, Darrin encircled her waist and lifted her until their lips touched. They exchanged one sweet but brief kiss.

"Mmmm," she moaned, and then surprised them both when she took the initiative. Cupping his jaw, she sponged his bottom lip and then suckled. Wanting another taste of the rough, velvet heat of his tongue, she slid her tongue into his mouth. She sighed from pleasure.

Trenna was thrilled when she heard Darrin's deep groan as he tightened his hold until her breasts were pressed against him. She was glad he was holding her because her legs were shaking so badly she feared her legs would give out and she'd end up in a heap at his feet. The pleasure was intense, beyond anything she'd ever experienced.

"So good...." she whispered aloud.

Yet, the sensible side of her demanded she stop and think this through, that she use logic to evaluate what was happening between them. Her feminine side was hungry, though, focused on one thing alone: the pleasure she suspected he could give.

When their lips parted, she kept her eyes closed, struggling to be sensible, to think, but she couldn't! He was too close and so attractive that he tantalized her senses. Where their bodies touched, she quivered. She couldn't stop marveling over the way his strong, hard body felt against hers. Like a bee seeking nectar, her senses homed in on him, hungry for more of this gentle giant.

She adored his kisses, amazed at the way he teased and inflamed her senses. Shouldn't she be alarmed? Darrin's kisses were seductive, created need deep inside of her. His hands were incredible, almost hypnotic, and his touch was pure magic against her skin.

She lifted her chin to study his features but his head came down and covered her lips. There was no hesitation as he deepened the kiss, taking it from enticingly sweet to raw, and hungry. Trenna lost track of time and place as he sucked her tongue, taking it deep into his mouth.

Shocked, a small part of her wondered if she should tell him to stop, but she didn't...she couldn't! How, when he was slowly driving her out of her mind? Nothing had ever felt so good. The texture and taste of his mouth was headier than the most expensive champagne. He was sheer intoxication.

They were both breathing hard when he allowed her body to slide down his. Although her feet were on the ground, Trenna was so far from feeling stable. She felt as if she were still floating, her entire body seeming to hum from the pleasure of his kisses and closeness. He didn't help calm her racing heart when he smoothed his hands over her back to her spine. She was surprised by her disappointment when his hands dropped to his sides.

"Please, don't stop."

"We have to stop."

If not for the smoldering, dark blue flames of desire she saw in his eyes she would have been devastated by his rejection.

"Why?" she forced herself to ask. She needed to know if the problem was with her, if she wasn't enough. "I'm not involved with anyone else. Are you? Is that why you stopped?" Suddenly, Trenna was embarrassed. She felt like a lovesick teenager, longing for the most popular boy to pay attention to her. She quickly added, "Never mind, forget ..."

HE CUT her off with a hard kiss that quickly softened, making her want him even more. Had she ever been so responsive? Without a doubt the answer was no. Nor had she ever imagined finding such pleasure in kissing. Incredible!

What was it about him that made her feel special, desirable? Being in his arms had been incredible, so much so that she hadn't wanted it to end. She trembled, shocked that she wanted more. She wanted him.

Chuckling, Darrin stopped when he saw her face. Instantly sobered, he cupped her face as he whispered, "I am not laughing at you, Trenna. I'm laughing at the absurdity of the question. You're the only woman I want, darlin'. It's been that way for some time. And frankly, I'm thrilled that after all this time, you want me, almost as much as I want you."

Trenna's heart pounded with a combination of desire and fear. Was it true? Did he want her so badly? But what if she failed to plea... No! She wouldn't go back in time. She was with Darrin. She could see and feel his desire for her.

"Finally, you in my arms," he said as he kissed her temple and smoothed a hand over her hair. "The male part of me has already said yes to whatever you're offering. You fed me. I'm grateful. But, I don't want you to feel obligated. I don't want to rush you, Trenna, into something you might regret later. I should go."

That was the last thing Trenna wanted. She was so tired of being alone—tired of going without. She was sick of doing what was right and being the good girl that her parents raised her to be. Just this once, she wanted to feel like a woman. She couldn't remember the last time she had been impulsive, taken a risk.

"No..." Wrapping her arms around his waist, she hugged him close. "...please stay." She didn't wait for a response but finished undoing his shirt buttons and then stroked him.

He moaned, "You're not making this easy for me. I'm no saint. I want to make love to—"

"Good," she interrupted. "Because that's what I want."

"Are you sure?"

"Yes..."

She had barely gotten the word out when he swung her off feet and up into his arms and gave her a hungry kiss, using his tongue to glide inside and stroke her own tongue. The exchange was hot and needy, leaving her trembling, her entire body aching. Trenna was beyond thought as Darrin carried her up to the loft.

WHEN THEY'D REACHED the landing Darrin paused, gazing into her eyes. He cradled her against his chest as if she weighed nothing.

His voice was deep and throaty when he whispered, "This time, kiss me."

Brushing her lips against the base of his throat, she inhaled his sandalwood aftershave. She followed the line of his jaw, kissing his hair-roughed cheeks, enjoying the contrast. She tasted the sexy cleft in his chin.

When she licked his lips, he released a heavy sigh. Delighted by the sound of his pleasure, she took his lip into her mouth and suckled as if he were one of the all-day suckers she adored as a child.

Darrin didn't seem to mind, for he groaned huskily. When she parted her lips to take a deep breath, he boldly stroked the silky moist, lining of her right cheek and then the left. He took his time before stroking her tongue with his. The erotic caress sent chills up and down her spine. Soon they were both moaning from pleasure. When the kiss ended Trenna ached all over, feeling as if she were a huge mass of raw nerves. Her breathing was uneven.

When Darrin let Trenna's petite body glide down his full length. Her hips were snug against his hard, long muscled thighs. He held her shoulders, and she was glad because she doubted her legs would hold her. She closed her eyes, savoring their closeness. It was all she could do not to rub the aching peaks of her breasts against him.

When he shifted, there was no doubt he was aroused. The hard length of his sex was unmistakable. She was shocked by the strength of his desire. Maybe she should she warn him now?

She was also shocked by the deep, pulsating ache in her core.

Goodness! She couldn't stop shaking. But why? She was far from a virgin. She had been married for years to a man she had never been able to please. She had lost count of the times she had tried and failed to please him, and had finally she stopped trying. She hadn't been with another man since Martin passed. She hadn't been tempted.

With Darrin she didn't know what to expect. She had no frame of reference. It wasn't the same because he wasn't like Martin. She felt foolish, like a beginning swimmer about to jump into ocean without a life vest. What if she couldn't plea…

Just then Darrin gave her one of his slow, drugging kisses. As her lips melded with his, Trenna forgot her doubts and fears, forgot everything but how he made her feel.

He didn't stop with one. His mesmerizing kisses went on and on, assuring her, as nothing else could, that he wanted her. He kissed her the same way he held her and touched her: with such care. His thoughtfulness caused her heart to fill with warmth and race with sweet anticipation.

They laughed as they fumbled with their buttons and zippers, both eager to touch and be touched. She called out his name when he tongued the side of her throat, before his mouth lingered in the scented valley between her plump breasts. He inhaled her scent.

"Sweet," he whispered, and then he licked the top curve of her breasts. "Beautiful," he mumbled as he licked her again.

She gasped aloud, quivering from head to toe. When Trenna looked into his eyes there was no mistaking the hunger that burned in their dark blue depths. In spite of the fear, she wanted him. She longed to feel him…all of him, deep inside of her.

Before the shock of that thought could register, Darrin caught her around the waist and lifted her until he could feast on her soft mouth. When he cupped her bottom she automatically wrapped her legs around his waist. He gifted her with one exquisitely slow, erotic kiss after another until goose pimples peppered her skin and perspiration dotted her forehead.

Trenna was panting for breath by the time he freed her mouth. It took all her self-control not to demand to know why he stopped. The wanting was unbearably sharp. She took deep breaths, hoping to gain some measure of control, fighting to block the emptiness and the yearning for more. Her breasts felt heavy, the hard tips highly sensitive as she pressed into him. The most embarrassing was the moisture that dampened her panties and her longing to please him.

This moment in time was about only one thing: mutual pleasure. She didn't want him to guess that she hadn't been able to satisfy her husband in bed or that she hadn't been sexually active since his death. Her secrets were hers alone.

"What's wrong?"

"Nothing." Although there was a question in his dark blue eyes, she knew it was true. He wanted her and she wanted him. She might have refused to go out with him but that hadn't stopped her from fantasizing about him. His kisses were far better than what she had imagined. That was all that mattered. "Everything is fine. Make love to me," Trenna whispered.

Chuckling, he confessed, "I like you like this."

A low light on the end table had been left on. He set her down beside the bed. She blinked in surprised when he used his teeth to drag the strap of her lace camisole off one shoulder. Soon the camisole was tossed to the carpet and quickly followed by her black tights, pink lace bra and panties. Pushing the straps away he kissed each of her shoulders before he unhooked her bra.

As his gaze moved leisurely over her lush curves, she had to fight the urge to cover herself because she had never been comfortable in the nude. Martin often compared her unfavorably to his first wife, the mother of his twins. She had died suddenly from cancer. Trenna's breasts were too small and her hips not full enough.

She was thankful that her dark skin, hid her embarrassed blush. But her stomach was tight with nerves while her limbs trembled as she held her breath as she waited, preparing for a critical response.

"Beautiful," he said with awe in his voice. "Your skin is so rich and dark like chocolate. You are gorgeous, luscious, and sweet."

She swallowed a shocked gasp. Beautiful? Gorgeous?

He kissed her throat before he took her earlobe into his mouth to suckle. The tidal wave of emotions and raw need was overwhelming. He wanted her. She sensed his need. But was even more surprising, she wanted him...and she wanted him now.

"You're trembling." He ran his hands over her arms. "You must be freezing. I'm sorry, darlin', for standing here and staring at you, as if you were a painting hanging in one of the galleries in the art institute."

Grabbing the lush, faux fur throw from the padded bench at the foot of the queen-size bed, he wrapped her in it. Silently, she watched as he moved to the electric, flame- heater across from the bed and turned it on.

The flame shimmered, but she was too embarrassed to admit that she was not cold. She shaking from nervous.

"Better?" Darrin asked, as he came up and pressed his lips to the side of her throat, causing her to quiver from the contact. She turned, stretching up to bring his mouth back down to hers.

"Mmm..." she moaned, longing for more of his kisses. When he kissed her she couldn't think, couldn't worry that she might fall short yet again. Briefly she brushed her mouth against the base of his throat, hoping to tell him without words how much she wanted him.

While trailing kisses across Darrin's shoulder, she smiled, pleased by the way he groaned. She grew bold enough to tongue the place where his neck and shoulder joined, and was thrilled when his large frame shook in response. Next, she worried his flat, nipples until they beaded.

"Good?" she asked.

"Nearly perfect. It feels like I've waited forever to have your soft hands on my body."

He leaned down, kissing her hungrily. He soon had her weak with anticipation, her body suddenly hot, tingling with excitement. When Darrin finally lifted his head, she was breathing hard and her head was spinning.

Darrin placed her in the center of her bed that was covered by the colorful, handmade quilt. Her head rested on an array of white lace-edged pillows.

Blushing, she whispered, "You're staring."

He grinned. "Because you're beautiful."

10

Darrin was not exaggerating. He meant every word. She was gorgeous and had captured his attention from the instant he had laid eyes on her in the restaurant where she had been having lunch with Maureen. She had been stunning, poised, and absolutely gorgeous, so much so that he couldn't take his eyes off her. That was the moment the wanting had started.

Bold and confident, he asked her out, not taking into account that she was a widow and grieving. Trenna's defenses were being firmly in place when she had politely said no thank you. Unfortunately for him, though, the waiting and wanting had been relentless. Her ever-ready refusals nor his pride hadn't stopped him from asking her out again and again.

So what if it had taken a near blizzard to be invited into her home? She had welcomed him. He wasn't about to question his good fortune. Frankly, he didn't care what had changed. All that mattered to him was that tonight was special.

Even though he was beyond ready to make love to her, he was no fool. Now that they were finally together, he was not about to rush and risk messing this up. He had waited too long to kiss her, to hold her, to touch her, to have her.

"Trenna..." he whispered in her ear. He had to make it special for her. There was no doubt that she was worth the wait. His biggest hurdle would be to control his own needs. He took a slow, deep calming breath, inhaled her scent. Yes, he would take his time and ensure she would not be disappointed. He wanted her to enjoy every moment of this magical night.

He stood beside the bed, his heart galloping inside his chest and his fingers far from steady as he unzipped, then removed his slacks before moving to his boxers. His eyes slowly moved over her, as he tried to memorize every detail of her dark beauty. To say she was beautiful was an understatement. She took his breath away.

"So lovely," he whispered, as he came down beside her to kiss her soft lips before moving to her throat. He lingered relishing her feminine scent. She was flawless, her dark skin incredibly smooth, soft, and luscious.

Although petite, Trenna was all woman and incredibly sexy. Placing a series of kisses along her jaw line, Darrin discovered the sensitive spot behind her ear. He lingered when he felt her shiver. Smiling, he laved the sweet-scented valley between her small, plumb breasts. He sighed. Everything about Trenna was exquisite. She was warm, responsive, perfect for him.

When she trembled, so did he. And when she stroked his body, the physical combined with the emotional need to be with her was so powerful that it took every bit of his resolve to remain in control. He paused to take slow, deep, even breaths.

He adored her response to him. He stroked her and she nearly purred like a kitten. She showed him without words that she preferred a slow hand. She was so sweet that he was willing to give her whatever she needed...however she needed it. He followed instincts as old as time; he just knew to give her time to adjust to him and their intimacy. What they had was, although intense, also brand new and untried. He forced himself to ignore the urgent demands of his pulsating sex to hurry and finish.

Instead, he concentrated on pleasing her. As he tongued the soft skin between her breasts, he swallowed a groan. He lingered on a tender spot that made her gasp. He slowed even? more, learning where she was most sensitive.

"Mmm," he hummed deep in his throat. "...you're delicious, like a sun-ripened peach, so sweet and meant to be savored."

He took her engorged, ebony peak into his mouth. He laved the hardened tip, teasing until she whimpered with pleasure as he luxuriated in her sweetness. Cupping her, he took the nipple deep into his mouth while gradually increasing the suction. He didn't slow until she cried out her enjoyment.

Although hard and aching as his need to be inside of her intensified, he focused on her. When he shifted his attention to the other breast, he was thrilled when her moans turned into throaty feminine whimpers of need. Knowing she wanted him ratcheted up his own excitement.

He marveled at how good she felt in his arms, so right, as if God had created her just for him. Her earthy, feminine scent filled his nostrils and inflamed his senses as he cupped and then squeezed her unbelievably, soft mounds. She was slick and deliciously damp. Suspecting she might be close to completion, he increased the suction. Trenna's petite frame tensed an instant before her small body began to shake from the force of her climax.

He held her close as if she were a rare treasure, thoroughly enjoying their intimacy. He was thrilled by the way she came apart in his arms. It was too much and not nearly enough all at the same time. Her climax had nearly pushed him to the edge of his control. Darrin hurt, rock-hard with the need to be inside of her. He ached for the release that only she could give. His heart picked up speed at the mere thought of her coming apart while he was deep inside her.

"Sweet," he said, placing a series of kisses across her forehead, down the bridge of her nose to the small tip. Uncertain if he saw moisture in her eyes, he asked, "Sweetheart, are you okay?"

~

Overwhelmed with emotions, Trenna dropped her lids. She managed to nod.

"Good. Now, beautiful, tell me what you like and what you need from me. "

Her eyes went wide realizing that he was serious and expected an answer! Having never been on the receiving end of such sensual attention, she didn't know what to say.

Goodness! She was in shock, trying to process the fact that she had climaxed! It was a first for her. Plus, she was flustered. She was unsure of herself, had no idea what she was feeling. Yet, her body still tingled and craved more. She longed to once again experience that mind-blowing release. Her heart-raced excitement and her body ached when she thought of him deep inside of her.

Darrin cupped her face, then repeated his question.

Instead of answering, she ran her hand down his neck and over his broad shoulders before she smoothed his hair-roughed chest. He was big; his body was long and muscular, his waist lean, his stomach tight, and his buttocks firm. His sex, like the rest of him, was heavy and swollen with desire. Darrin was magnificent, wonderfully made. And she wanted...him.

Pressing open-mouth kisses along the side of his neck and indulging her senses, she luxuriated in his feel and taste. Delighted by his moans of pleasure, she followed the line of his chest hair down to his stomach. She enjoyed touching him until she realized she brushed the heavy crown of his sex.

She froze as thoughts from the past intruded on the moment. She snatched her hand away as she recalled Martin's displeasure. He blamed her when she failed to arouse him. But he had had numerous complaints, ranging from her lack of response to his hard, punishing kisses and his roughness in bed, to him being enraged at her refusal to watch pornography with him and re-enact the scenes. He often voiced his disappointment claiming she was as cold as a dead fish in bed.

"What's wrong?" Darrin whispered as he lavished attention on her throat.

Trenna shivered. She had been studying him through her lashes wondering, if she disappointed him, would he get angry? Would he blame her? Accuse her of teasing him and not being enough?

"Nothing is wrong," she lied.

"Okay, " cradling her face, he whispered against her kiss-swollen mouth. "Trenna...please," he begged, then licked her bottom lip. "Darlin', do it again. I want to feel your hands on me."

The dark blue flame of desire in his eyes was unmistakable. Tentative at first, she caressed his taut stomach, then gradually moved to caress his hard shaft. Eyes closed, he groaned, then he shuddered when she took him in her small hands. He showed her what he liked, strong strokes from the thick base to the broad crest.

By the time he called out her name he was shaking from the pleasure. He caught her hands and kissed the center of each palm. After sharing a series of wildly, seductive kisses, he held her close to his heart.

Trenna was also trembling. And her tremors increased as he caressed her curves. Caught up in a sensuous haze, she automatically opened for him. Finally, he touched her where she longed for most. He cupped her mound and squeezed her softness. Panting from the pleasure of his touch, she was embarrassingly wet, burning with need for his touch. She realized that she wanted him. No, she needed him. And the feelings were so intense she couldn't think.

"Darrin..." she gasped as he caressed the curls covering her sex. She nearly forgot to breathe by the time he parted her folds, opening her to his caresses. He teased, stroked, played while he bent to take her engorged nipple into his mouth and sucked. The combining sensations were intense, the pleasure unlike any she had ever experienced. Her body practically hummed with excitement. All of it was new and she didn't know how to control it, contain it. There was no comparison.

"Trenna…"

"Yes…" she said huskily. She was keenly aware of everything about him. His scent was intoxicating, his taste sinfully enticing, but his touch was utterly sublime. With her eyes closed and her entire focus on him she didn't realize that he was no longer stroking her with his fingers but his shaft. He used the broad crown to tantalize, to tease her moist opening. With thumb, he worried her ultra sensitive nub, repeating the caress until her entire body was shaking. It was when he took her nipple into his mouth and sucked hard, she came apart in his arms.

"Oh! Oh!!!" she gasped as she climaxed. This one was more powerful than the first.

Wrapping her legs and arms around him, she clung to him her heart pounding. Talk about sweet agony! She couldn't remember feeling so feminine, or alive. Every caress of his body against hers, every stroke of his tongue was so unbelievably wonderful that she didn't want it to ever end. As her breathing slowed, she realized he had moved.

"Where are you going?"

He kissed her nose. "Getting condoms."

"Okay." She let him go. Embarrassed because she hadn't thought of protection, plus she was clinging to him. She'd been savoring their closeness, not wanting it to end. The truth was she liked being cradled in his arms, liked that he made her feel special. She still hadn't gotten over what had happened.

Although, he didn't take long, Trenna couldn't relax, not until he was caressing her from nape to hips. She pushed away the questions, the doubts from the past. Instead she concentrated on him and how he made her feel. She ached deep inside for him. Unfamiliar sparks of desire burned from within.

Their kiss was long and deep.

When their lips parted, he said, "Trenna, you feel so good in my arms, so right. Can you feel how badly I want you? Need you?"

"Yes…please, hurry."

He said in her ear in a husky whisper, "I've waited so long to have you like this. But there's no need to rush."

"No! I want you now."

"And I want you. But, sweetheart, you're small. I'm not. I don't want to hurt you."

She shook her head no. "You won't." All she knew was it had to be now…before she lost her nerve. "Hurry…"

Darrin gave a quick nod, before he pressed forward, slowly penetrating her damp heat. Trenna gasped at the unrelenting pressure. He was large and she struggled to accommodate him.

Straining to remain still, he rested his forehead against hers. "I'm hurting you."

"Don't stop," she insisted. But when he pressed forward she winced aloud.

"I am hurting you!"

"I'm fine." She locked her arms and legs around him before he could pull out. She needed this. She was determined to prove to herself that there was nothing wrong with her. She was woman enough to give him pleasure.

Darrin groaned, before he trailed kisses down her cheek, He suckled her earlobe. "Trenna, you're so sweet, so unbelievably tight." He licked her bottom lip before he kissed her again and again. Then he moved down and sponged the sensitive place on the side of her throat.

Overwhelmed by his scent, his muscular frame and his hard, pulsating length deep inside made her tremble.

He husked, "How…long…has…it been?"

Although she heard the question, she could barely think, let alone string coherent sentences together.

"Trenna...how long has it been since..."

Instead of answering, she melted against him stringing kisses across his shoulders and the base of his throat. She tingled when he groaned in response. He felt so good, so right that she wanted him, wanted every inch of him deep inside.

Seduced by the lure of their kisses, she was delighted when he'd dropped his head and licked and then kissed her breast. Uncontrollable tremors shook her as he moved to the other breast. Darrin sampled Trenna's sweetness as if he adored her taste and relished the satiny smoothness of her skin. She was cognizant of him in a way she had never experienced before. It was all so new. His incredible firmness, deep inside made her ache and rock against him. The insistent tug of his mouth on her nipple inflamed her desire until she felt like a throbbing mass of raw nerves.

Darrin groaned heavily as she tightened around him. Cupping and squeezing her hips, his eyes bore urgently into hers. "You're driving me wild, destroying my control."

Following instincts as old as time, she tightened her inner muscles and then released. She did it, again and again, stroking him from the tip to base. They both moaned in response.

"I'm trying not to hurt you."

Frustrated, she leaned over to licked his nipple while rocking her hips against his. He released a husky growl from deep in his throat before he shocked her by rolling onto his back and taking her with him. His strong arms kept her in place.

She was shocked. Not used to being on top, she tucked her face it between his neck and shoulder. Darrin brought her mouth down to his. They shared several tongue-stroking, heart-stopping kisses before he took her breast into his mouth. He tongued and savored it as if the nipple was a rich, sweet drop of chocolate.

Before she could catch her breath, Darrin moved her along his shaft once, twice. Then he allowed her to establish her own rhythm and take as much of him as she liked. At first, her strokes were shallow as she adjusted to his size. He growled and she moaned with mutual pleasure when she took all of him. She marveled at how perfectly they fit together before he began to thrust in earnest. She cried out as he gave them exactly what they craved. She clung to him, riding him hard and fast. There was no holding back for either of them, for they were caught up in the timeless, tantalizing dance of lovemaking.

Mesmerized, Trenna was unable to focus on anything outside of Darrin and the magic they shared. Goosebumps pimpled her skin as he tongued and then gently suckled the tender place on her throat. Shivering, she cried out when he slid a hand down between their bodies to stroke her ultra sensitive nub. He didn't stop until she was screaming his name as she trembled from convulsions. Her release triggered his, thrusting him into a powerful climax.

He caught her when she collapsed on his chest. Even after their heart rates slowed and their breathing returned to normal, he continued to hold her.

STILL IN A DAZE, Trenna's thoughts were all over the place, chaotic and fueled by emotions. She felt as if she had been caught up in a whirlwind. This was not the first time. She had been married, for heaven's sake! She thought she knew all there was to know about what went on between a man and woman. Evidently, she had been mistaken. If what she just experienced with Darrin was sex, then what had she shared with Martin?

Unlike her friends, she didn't enjoy sex. She'd never been tempted to jump into bed with any of the men she'd dated. Long ago, she had accepted her shortcomings. So what had just happened?

She had high hopes of finding true closeness and intimacy when she got married. For years, she had really tried to please her husband. But gradually she had given up, realizing she'd never be the woman Martin wanted. The year before Martin passed, Trenna had given up on them and avoided having sex.

But tonight with Darrin she felt as if she had finally made love. She didn't know what to think or what she was feeling. Goodness! She had not expected and certainly not been prepared for the all-consuming passion and overwhelming pleasure that she discovered in Darrin's arms. It had been pure magic, having his hands, mouth and body all over hers.

Goodness! They had made love. Love? Where had that come from? No! They hadn't! What they had was very good sex. Trenna closed her eyes as if she could block out her thoughts. Love was dangerous, scary. No, it was not love.

How could she have made love with a man she wasn't sure she even liked? Goodness! She really needed to get the "L" word out of her head. Darrin didn't love her and she didn't love him. The only "L" that applied in this situation was lust. Now that that was settled she was able to relax.

Trenna sighed. Her body still tingled from release when Darrin smoothed a soothing hand from her nape down to her spine. When he kissed the tip of her nose she smiled. All too soon, Darrin had Trenna whimpering in frustration as he teased her with feather-light brush of his lips against hers, instead of the deep tongue kisses she now craved. Impatient, she sucked his bottom lip, taking it into her mouth. She was quickly rewarded when he groaned and turned the kiss into a hot, sensual caress. She trembled from the pleasure.

She and Martin had been married for years. Not even once had he been tender, nor had he ever made her body tingle with awareness or her heart pound with excitement. She had never ached for her husband or begged him to come inside her. Was it any wonder she was confused?

She had firsthand knowledge of his impatience and frustration with her. He never bothered to hide his keen disappointment in her. His angry barbs hurt her feelings and destroyed her self-confidence. Every time they had had sex he eroded her self-esteem, and made her feel as if he was using her for his own pleasure.

"Trenna..." Darrin crooned into her ear, "you're so sweet and soft, simply incredible."

She stared at him, wanting to believe his words. His eyes were so dark blue they sparkled like a star-filled sky at midnight. His pleasure in her seemed so real. As her heart was racing at the possibility, she didn't know what to think. She dropped her lids in the hope of concealing her emotions. Tonight had been so special it didn't seem real. Things like this happened to her girlfriends, not her.

Lingering at the base of her throat, Darrin sponged and then peppered kisses there. She shivered, cognizant of his enticing male scent, the firmness of his chest against her breasts and the firm pressure of his erection. Her eyes went wide as she realized he must not have finished. His body was still hard and pulsating with need...

Her disappointment was keen. She had to bit her lip to keep from crying. She had failed...again. Martin had been right about one thing. She wasn't enough.

"What's wrong?"

"Nothing," she said, forcing a smile. She was glad that Darrin knew nothing about her sexual history. He didn't need to know. Tonight was a mistake. So what if, until tonight, she had never climaxed? Her intense response to him was not the issue.

She sighed. The problems in her marriage weren't something she could share with anyone, not even her best friend. No one cared about her personal problems. Talking about it had not changed that she hadn't been enough for her husband.

"Less than a woman." Her late husband's taunt played in her

head again and again. Deeply shamed by her inability, she blinked hard, refusing to cry. But tonight was not about Martin. It was about her. For a short time, she had been euphoric. It ended the moment she realized Darrin was still aroused. Her disappointment overshadowed all that had gone on before.

He kissed her neck and tightened his arms around her. "Finally, I have you where I longed for you to be. I'm sorry that I hurt you. You are awfully quiet. Are you sure okay?"

Although, her body was tender, it wasn't something she was wanted to discuss. Nor did she want to remember the last earth-shaking climax. It hadn't been mutual.

"I'm fine." But Trenna knew she was in trouble when he started those slow, drugging kisses she adored. She was falling under his seductive spell. Instead of caressing the broad expanse of his bare chest and shoulders as she longed to do, she dropped her hands to her sides. She was terribly distracted because she could feel Darrin pulsating deep inside of her. Her breasts were still tender and the nipples hard as shivers of desire raced down her spine. She needed no reminders that with Darrin she had found the most incredible release, not once but twice. Darrin had made her entire body hum with pleasure.

But he had her so confused. It had never been like this... "With Martin..." Trenna gasped, realizing she had spoken her thoughts aloud. Wanting to scream her frustration, she quickly amended, "I'm sorry. I didn't mean to..."

"What?" He clasped her waist and moved from beneath her. "You didn't mean me to know that you were comparing me to Martin?"

Shaking her head firmly, "No! I wasn't!" she insisted, then sighed in regret. "Forget I said anything. It doesn't matter."

She frowned. Did she see hurt in his eyes? Impossible! He just said he had gotten her exactly where he wanted her...in bed. What was a novelty for her was old hat for him. He had just proved he was a master manipulator of women.

Darrin Morgan was an expert—so good that he made her feel as if he actually cared about her. It had taken years but he finally gotten what he wanted from her. Just because he had given her more pleasure than she could have imagined didn't change facts. She was a challenge to him until tonight. Tonight she had given him exactly what he came for: sex. She shuddered at the unvarnished truth.

Darrin drew the quilt over them. "Better?"

"Yes, thank you."

How could a woman her age be so naive? She had slept with the womanizer-of-the-year! Darrin Morgan probably had the trophy on his mantel! It just happened. And she certainly hadn't given a single thought to the consequences. For all she knew he could be involved with ten other women.

What happened to her brain? Had it flown out the window along with her ability to say no? The minute he kissed her she had lost all reason, had been oblivious to everything but how he made her feel.

She tried but failed to convince herself that she had only given him her body, nothing more. Her heart was still whole. She was safe. So why did she feel as if she'd made a terrible mistake? One she was always regretting?

Swinging her legs out from beneath the covers, she grabbed a robe from the back of an armchair and shoved her arms into the velvet sleeves. Her hands were trembling as she tied the belt at her waist. She went to the window, pulled back the drape to look out.

She shivered, but her thoughts weren't on the snow blanketing the streets. The only good she could think of from tonight was that Darrin had cleared up one issue for her. She knew that she was not solely responsible for her lack of enjoyment during sex. Martin had to share a part of the blame. His preferences were a huge turn-off for her.

She had lied. She had been comparing the two men. They were both attorneys. So what if Martin had been in corporate law while

Darrin was a criminal attorney? Clearly, they both were the in-charge type. Right about now she wasn't fond of the trait in either man.

Nor could she deny that for years she had allowed Martin to make decisions for her and to control her. At the time, it was easier than arguing with him constantly. Now here she was with Darrin Morgan, world-class womanizer. Her taste in men stuck.

She kept her back to him when she said, "You should leave. Soon the roads will be impassable."

11

———————

$\mathcal{B}$oth aroused and disheartened, Darrin was scowling when he asked, "Want to tell me what's really going on?"

It was bad enough that she'd compared him to her late husband, now she was acting as if she regretted it already. When he got up to grab his briefs, that's when he looked down and noticed that he'd nearly taken her again wearing a used condom. Upset, he swore.

"Don't swear at me!"

"I'm not..." Darrin stopped abruptly, and went into the bathroom. Instead of giving into his emotions and slam the door, he closed it quietly. Telling himself he had no business feeling hurt, he got rid of the condom and washed up. When he reentered the bedroom it was empty.

He stood, silently in the center of the room taking slow, calming breaths before he reached for his clothes. He found her downstairs?, sitting on the arm of the sofa. The television was on the weather channel, the sound muted.

"Trenna, I don't..."

She interrupted, "The snow has finally stopped. Hopefully, you won't have a problem getting home."

When she didn't look his way, disappointment pierced his heart. He watched her move further away from him. Upset, he struggled to control his emotions. Shoving his hands into his pockets to keep from reaching for her, he said, "Talk to me, honey. Tell me what went wrong."

"Not tonight. It's late."

"Okay. How about dinner tomorrow night? It will be my turn to entertain you."

"No. Please, just go."

Sighing, he dropped his head, massaging his nape. He wasn't one to cut and run from a fight, but his instincts told him an argument would make things worse. Retrieving his jacket and then overcoat, he pulled them on. He reached for his boots rather than for Trenna. He ached for her, wanted to hold her during the night.

Judging by how tightly she held her body and the way she worried her bottom lip, he knew he was fresh out of options. It didn't matter that he didn't want to leave or that he ached to touch her, and to hold her during the night.

It hurt knowing she wanted him to go. For him there was nothing casual about what they'd just shared. It wasn't a game, at least not to him. Boots on, gloves in hand, he said, "I'll call tomor..."

"Don't bother."

Darrin stared at her in disbelief, a muscle jumped in his jaw as he ground his teeth together. She was deliberately pushing him away, skillfully putting barrier after barrier between them. What he still didn't get was why?

Struggling for calm and a level-head, he said, "Spending time with you is hardly a bother. Why are you acting as if we only had a one-night-stand? As if you didn't enjoy our lovemaking as much as I did?"

"It's late," she repeated but wouldn't look at him.

Emotions bubbled inside of him. It was a struggle not to let her see what she was doing to him. "Come lock up. Sleep well." He closed the door quietly behind him.

Darrin stood in the cold until he heard the tumbler engage and knew the deadbolt was in place. Only then did he trudge on. They had shared the most intense pleasure that he had ever experienced. No doubt, she had rocked his world. But that first release had merely taken the edge off. Once hadn't come close to being enough. Even though his body still throbbed with need and his heart ached from disappointment, he kept moving.

The bitter cold couldn't eliminate the desire that burned deep inside of him. They had barely gotten started then it was over. He felt as if he'd been robbed, cheated. They had made love, and already he missed her.

She had acted as if... What? What had he said...done to cause her to change? She had cut him out of her life with ruthless precision. She had lost interest, become almost cold, brutal. He swore.

What was he supposed to think? How was he supposed to go on? Pretend they hadn't made love? Was he to act the way she had, as if they had a one-night-stand and move on? He swore again. He was a lawyer, not an actor! Resentment and bitterness combined and left an acid taste in his mouth.

Despite having been married, he quickly discovered she had a certain naiveté that had charmed him. But as he scraped the windshield free of ice and snow, he told himself none of it mattered. He had given her a ride home, helped a friend out.

Enjoying her body didn't mean he was falling for her. Love didn't happen overnight. Love certainly didn't happen in a vacuum. Love had to be nurtured.

"Love!" he scoffed. He certainly hadn't received anything that even came close to love from Trenna. She had been clear. She didn't have room in her heart for him. That spot was taken. The sooner he accepted that the better.

Blowing on his hands to warm them, he told himself he had

been lucky as he got behind the wheel. He had been lucky, escaped relatively unscarred. His heart was still whole; his hurt came from injured pride. She didn't love him and he didn't love her. Hurt feelings didn't automatically translate into love. What they shared was just plain old lust.

SATURDAY DAWNED COLD AND CRISP. Trenna was sleeping when the phone rang. She frowned. Seven-thirty? She almost didn't answer when she saw Darrin's name on the caller ID. But good manners prevailed. "Good morning."

"Hi," he said softly. "Sounds like I woke you. How did you sleep?"

"I'm fine, and you?" she said politely. She did her best to ignore the way his deep, sexy voice sent shivers racing down her spine.

"I'm better now that I've heard your voice."

Because of him it had taken her hours to get to sleep. Unwilling to pretend, she asked bluntly, "Why are you calling?"

There was a heavy sigh before he said, "The roads are clear. Would you like a ride into town to pick up your car?"

"No thanks."

"What do you mean no thanks?"

"I've ordered a rental car. It should be here around eleven."

"You have time to cancel and save the expense."

"No."

"Trenna…"

"You don't seem like a man who can't accept no for an answer."

"And you're still upset about last night."

"Things got out of hand. We…"

"Out of hand?" Darrin quizzed, "Trenna, we made love."

"It was a mistake that won't be repeated."

"You can't mean that," he persisted. "Darlin', we found pleasure in each other's arms."

"I'm not disputing that you are a skilled lover. It took years, but you got what you wanted last night. Congratulations. I made a mistake when I said yes. It won't happen again. Bye."

After hanging up she told herself that, though he had a right to disagree, she didn't care what he thought. It was over. She was better off without him. She had made a huge mistake. It was a waste of time to think about him or dwell on what happened. With a weary sigh, she assured herself that it was best forgotten. It was over.

～

THE MORGAN TWINS had been racing up and down the racquetball court for the better part of an hour when yet another ball barely missed Douglas' head.

"What's your problem, Dar?"

Darrin didn't respond. Instead, he turned and walked off the court.

Douglas caught up with his twin in the locker room. "You want to tell me what's going on?"

"There's no point," Darrin grumbled. After unlocking his locker, he grabbed his black sweatpants.

Frowning, Douglas opened his own locker and began dressing also. His eyes never left his twin. He managed to reach the door ahead of Darrin and blocked the exit.

"You might as well tell me, because we're not leaving here until you do."

"Leave it alone!" As much as Darrin loved his twin this wasn't something he could talk about…at least not now. Like an open wound, it was raw and painful. Swearing beneath his breath, he didn't even want to think about what happened.

"Move out of the way!"

"Let me help."

"You can't."

With his coat carelessly tossed over one shoulder, his gym bag in the other hand, Darrin pushed past his brother.

"Dar, wait…"

He kept right on going. If this was what a broken heart felt like, he wouldn't recommend it to anyone. What they shared was over before it had really gotten started, and it hurt like hell. Knowing he'd done everything he could didn't take away the pain…or the disappointment.

It didn't matter that his self-control had been stretched to the breaking point. Evidently, being with Trenna, someone he cared about and ached to be with, had taken its toll on him. His brother wanted him to talk. How? He couldn't put his feeling into words.

From the moment he saw Trenna, he had fallen hard and fast for her. The waiting hadn't been easy. But, looking back, he realized it was worth it. He would gladly do it again and again. Spending time with her, being intimate with her last night, had been pure magic. It hadn't been planned; it just happened. He hadn't given much thought to anything, outside of pleasuring her.

Need had taken over, overwhelming all else. Trenna was as sweet as honey, her skin like silk all over her small but curvy frame. How could any man resist such beauty? He had shamelessly indulged his senses and savoring every moment of being with her and inside of her. It wasn't until afterwards that he recognized that one taste of her sweetness was never going to be enough.

But Trenna was so much more than her looks. She was a smart, accomplished, honest woman who was, above all, loyal. There was no doubt that she was a woman with integrity. He knew going in that he cared for her. Since being intimate, his feelings had only intensified.

And he was tired of asking himself if this was love. He had no label to slap on what he felt for her. Besides, what difference would it make? She didn't return his feelings. That fact nagged him.

His twin wanted him to talk, but what was the point? How was talking supposed to help? He couldn't even put his feelings into words. He didn't want to talk about how he felt. It was too painful. Besides, he had blown it with her. She made herself clear. She never wanted to see or talk to him again. He'd ruined his one shot with her. There were no words that could help that kind of devastation.

He swallowed, his throat raw with emotion. Darrin had to blink hard to clear the tears blurring his vision. Trudging halfway across the parking lot, he suddenly stopped remembering he didn't have his car. He had left it at Douglas' place. They'd drove to the club together. He hung his head in abject misery.

Caught up in anger and disappointment, it wasn't until he started to shiver that he noticed the cold. Putting on his down-filled parka, he shoved his hands deep into the pockets rather than look for his gloves.

He had been trained to be an observer, to look at the obvious, to analyze and to sum up a situation quickly. The truth was straightforward. And it didn't change. Yet, he couldn't figure out what was going on in his own head and heart. How long could he continue to ignore the truth, especially when it was smacking him upside the head? It was what he loved about the law.

Unfortunately, for him, Trenna had not bothered to hide her truth. It had been clear, uncomplicated, and there from the start. She would never accept a new man in her life because she was still in love with her late husband. He had been so caught up in his own emotions and his intense response to her that he had not seen what was in front of his face.

The problem was his, not Trenna's. No matter how much it hurt, he did not have a choice. He had to accept her truth, swallow it whole, and pray it did not choke him.

∾

TRENNA WAS ANNOYED with herself for going back to sleep. Now she had to rush to get ready or she was going to be late. She had promised Maureen that she would fill in for her at the Women's Center. She had planned to stop for a quick visit at the hospital first.

Once the rental car had been dropped off at her place, she had no trouble getting into the city. The freeways were clear and salted, and the sun was bright overhead. There was a mountain of dirty snow pushed into the median and the sides the road was littered with abandoned cars. Unfortunately, the snow was not the only reminder of last night.

It was nearly ten by the time she reached her own office building. After a quick call to the rental agency, explaining she had left the key under the floor mat, she attacked the mound of snow covering her car. But it was not until she was inside the car with the heat blasting that she realized she was shaking. She had learned to dress in layers for the Michigan winters. But the bitter cold was not the reason for her tremors.

Even though several hours had passed since his phone call, she was still upset. No, upset was too mild a word to describe her emotions. Her responses to Darrin's lovemaking had been so intense it scared her.

He made her feel things she had never even imagined or expected to feel. He did not suffer from inexperience. Finally, she understood why women were drawn to him like a moth to a flame.

Despite his womanizing ways there were things about him she genuinely admired. She appreciated the way he supported her work. He had gone out of his way to help with her foundation, and even introduced her to a potential sponsor.

After he'd left she had gone back to bed, but had been too restless to sleep. She could not get him out of her head. She had spent hours staring at the muted television. When she had finally settled she had been so exhausted that she was out the moment her head touched the pillow

She had dreamed about Martin. He was fifteen-years older, a friend of the family and her father's lawyer. Because she knew him and she was comfortable with him, she had leaned on him after she lost her parents. As the executor of her father's estate and her guardian, she would come to depend on him. When they married she had not expected their life to be problem-free. She had been a virgin on their wedding night. Unfortunately, she had not enjoyed sex but had learned to tolerate it.

During the first years of marriage she was busy with graduate school. By the time she completed her master's degree, she could not keep up the pretense any longer. As the intimacy between them deteriorated, the verbal abuse increased. Before the accident, Trenna's self-esteem was at its lowest. Her husband had to watch DVD's of other women having sex in order to become aroused. And he expected her to watch with him. Even though their marriage had not worked out the way she would have liked, she had been devastated when Martin died.

After she relocated it had taken her years to rebuild her life, to prove to herself that she was smart and capable. Things were finally going the way she wanted. She did not want to mess up now. One night with Darrin should have convinced her that it was too risky to get involved with him. He made her feel too much... He made her care about him. It was a recipe for disaster.

If she were not very careful, she would fall in love with him. She did not want that. She refused to be beneath another man's thumb. She liked making her own decisions, liked being in control of her business and her personal life. No, love was not for her. She would not repeat past mistakes. Her marriage to Martin had nearly destroyed her.

Why had she let Darrin get so close? She asked herself that question a thousand times and still did not have an answer. It had started with kisses. His kisses were deadly...utter seduction. She had not offered a single objection. His mouth should be a banned as an illegal substance.

Overwhelmed was too mild to describe her reaction when he took her into his arms. Her brain had completely switched off as her body took over. He generated incredible heat, an overwhelming need that she hadn't known existed. Unprepared for his brand of lovemaking was an understatement; she did not have a clue. Lost in a sensuous maze, she was unable to stop while being compelled to move forward to completion. After he left she was certain she did not have feelings for him.

This morning she was unsure. Even for those few moments on the phone with him, her heart raced with excitement. She had not planned any of this. She cared for him. It was the only reason that made sense. How had it happened? She did not want to have feelings for him.

Making love had been a dreadful mistake. It had changed everything. Oh, she was not merely upset about it. She was livid and blamed him for taking advantage of a temporary weakness. What had she been thinking? How quickly she forgot that she was nothing more than a challenge to him.

But even worse, she allowed it to happen. She had said no so often that she unwittingly became a target that he could not resist. How could she have been so foolish and let him use her?

No! She blinked hard, her eyes burned from unshed tears. Never again would she allow a man to take advantage of her. She was never going to be one of those lovesick females who routinely chased after Darrin. She may not be able to change last night's mistake, but it would never be repeated.

Hurrying inside Henry Ford Hospital, Trenna hoped for a private word with Maureen, but was disappointed. After a night in the chair beside her grandmother's bed, Maureen had gone home to shower and get some rest. Trenna only had time for a short visit with Mrs. Hale, Maureen's grandmother, but promised to return.

On the drive to Sheppard's Women's Crisis Center she frowned. She had to stop berating herself about last night. Yes, she made a mistake. That was no reason to feel sorry for herself. She was blessed.

Unlike her friends Jenna, Laura, and Sherri Ann, Trenna had not grown up in foster care. Nor was she like Maureen, who had lost her mother much too soon. Trenna had two wonderful parents who loved each other and her. They had done their best to ensure she knew she was cared for and had provided for her future. Even though there was no special man in her life, she was fine. She was thankful she wasn't one of those women who believed she needed a man to be happy.

It did not take long to reach the Women's Center since it was close to Wayne State University's campus. Although the sun was shining, it was still bitterly cold, and Trenna shivered as she hurried inside.

Glad that she arrived early enough to check the room, Trenna was relieved to find the supplies were in place and the multipurpose room was ready to go. The sewing machines that had been donated for the afternoon by a local vendor were in place. The refreshment table, filled with fresh fruit, snacks, bottled water, and sodas, was also set up. Ever efficient, Maureen had taken care of things ahead of time.

"Hey, stranger," Trenna and Sherri Ann Weber said at the same time then laughed.

Sherri Ann teased, "It's a shame that we both work in the Morgan Building but never see each other except when we're here for mentoring."

The mentoring program had been developed for teen girls, in hopes of promoting high self-esteem and confidence to ensure a successful future. The girls had never been adopted or been successfully placed with a foster family, but had grown up in the foster care system. The teen girls were part of the State's independent living program. Some of the teens lived in rooming homes or apartment buildings that were supervised and licensed by the state.

Trenna quipped, "If you'd joined the Elegant Five, we wouldn't have this problem."

"And when exactly do I have time for a book club meeting or reading anything other than legal briefs?" Sherri Ann was a lawyer, who worked for Morgan and Green. "The partners keep all of us associates on our toes. Speaking of partners, tell me about the rumors I've heard about you and my boss colliding in our lobby."

Trenna sighed. The last person she wanted to talk about was Darrin Morgan. "It's no rumor, it's true. I was not paying attention and got off the elevator on the wrong floor. Unfortunately, I ran into Darrin and nearly bounced off him. Embarrassing, but let's talk about something pleasant. How's Laura?"

Sherri Ann beamed. "She's glowing. Jenna and I saw her last weekend. She could not be happier."

"That's great!" Trenna exclaimed.

Laura Murdock Kramer started the mentoring program when she was a social worker at the Women's Center. Both Maureen and her grandmother had embraced the idea from its concept. They generously offered the use of the Women's Center activity room.

Trenna had always admired Laura. Besides being a former member of the Elegant Five Book Club, Laura was smart, hardworking, and determined to help others. She strongly believed that teen girls needed positive, adult influences in their lives. Two years ago, she had designed the highly successful mentoring program.

Laura, and her two best friends, Sherri Ann and Jenna Gains Hendricks, had grown up in the foster care system. Like the girls they mentored, they had never been adopted. But unlike the teen girls in independent living program, Laura, Sherri Ann, and Jenna were fortunate to have been raised by Mrs. Frances Green, a warm, loving older woman. Early on the three had adopted each other and became foster sisters, and over the years they remained close. All three were well-educated, highly successful women.

When it came time to find mentors, Laura wisely recruited her friends, book club members, as well as the Center's staff. Since its onset, Sherri Ann and Jenna had volunteered. Like Laura, they wanted to give back.

The mentoring sessions were on the first and third Saturday afternoons of the month. Thanks to community support and generous donations, scholarships were established for the girls who would be graduating from high school with plans to further their education.

To everyone's surprised, last year while on a vacation to the Caribbean, Laura met and fell in love with Wilham Kramer, the man of her dreams. Wilham, hotel mogul and artist, swept her off her feet. They married, currently lived in Chicago, and were expecting their first child. As a wedding present, Wilham became the major contributor to their scholarship fund.

Trenna stood in for Maureen and greeted everyone with smile. But as soon as she spotted Grace Brooks, she started to feel guilty even though she knew she'd done her best to help and support Grace emotionally. But it hadn't been enough. Trenna was relieved when Grace gave her warm hug.

Maureen and Trenna had been in the courtroom when Grace had pointed out Todd Marks as her rapist. The three were devastated when the jury came back with the not-guilty verdict. Because of Darrin Morgan's superior skill in the courtroom, Grace's rapist had walked away a free man.

Grace regularly volunteered at the Center, even though Maureen was no longer her rape counselor. Grace often joined Maureen and Trenna for dinner and a movie.

Maureen had kicked off the belt-making project by taking the girls shopping at the fabric store. They excitedly picked out the cloth and notions. Some of the girls had also purchased material for matching skirts. They planned to wear their creations on a supervised outing to the theater. They all seemed to be excited and looking forward to the event.

It was a blessing that Vanessa Grant Prescott, dress designer and bridal shop owner, was a mentor. She showed the girls how to cut out the patterns and use the sewing machines. Vanessa married Ralph Prescott, ex-NBA player and businessman, and was a close friend and fellow book club member.

Trenna took a seat in the back of the room beside Sherri Ann and Jenna. She didn't realize she was tense until she nearly jumped out of her skin when Amber squealed with laughter.

"Look! Look!" she yelled, holding up a nearly finished belt. The other girls were ooohing and aaahing while the mentors clapped enthusiastically.

"You okay?" Jenna whispered.

Sherri Ann interrupted, "Are you worried about Mrs. Hale?"

Trenna shook her head. "Mrs. Hale is doing well. They don't think it's her heart, but she had to stay overnight at the hospital."

"If nothing's wrong, then why are you shaking like a leaf?"

"I'm cold," Trenna said, rubbing her hands up and down the sleeves of her cardigan. "No matter how many layers I put on, I can't get used to your Michigan winters."

"Silk long johns," Sherri Ann said.

"Forget that, you both need what Vanessa and I have," Jenna said. "A husband to snuggle with. There is nothing like it."

Both married ladies giggled as if Jenna had told a joke.

"To each his own poison," Sherri Ann rolled her eyes. Like Trenna, she was also single.

Trenna frowned. Busy pretending last night never happen, she didn't want to think about Darrin. She certainly didn't want to remember the pleasure she found in his arms. She wouldn't be surprised if Sherri Ann had seen her boss in action. Everyone in the building knew about Darrin's reputation as a first-class womanizer. Evidently, Trenna had temporarily lost her mind when she slept with him. She vowed that it was a mistake that she would never repeat.

"Look, Ms. Trenna!".

"It's gorgeous!"

Trenna hadn't hesitated to hire the girl. Tasha was in the first group of girls being mentored to graduate from high school and enter college or a vocational school. Tasha was a hard worker. Trenna was impressed that, in addition to her work at the nursery school, Amber was a full-time student at Wayne State. She was on the dean's list, never late for work, and managed to get everything done. Somehow, she also found time to encourage the younger girls by volunteering at the Women's Center. Most remarkable, she was doing it on her own, without the benefit of parents or family to fall back on.

That first group of successes had strengthened Maureen and Laura's dedication to the mentoring project. Determined to expand, the two had met several times during the summer and in the autumn. Neither was going to let a little thing like living in different states keep them from reaching as many teen girls as possible through the independent living program.

Vanessa, Jenna, Sherri Ann, and Trenna had gone with Maureen to meet Laura for a ladies weekend of shopping and fun in the Windy City.

"Mine is the prettiest!" Ginger Langston boasted.

"No mine!" someone else shouted.

The excitement was contagious, judging by the way the normally reserved Grace was beaming. It was good to see. Grace had been through so much and had worked hard to get her life back on track.

It might not make sense to anyone else, but Trenna couldn't help resenting Darrin for his part in getting Marks off. Nor could she stop feeling guilty for what she had done: sleeping with the enemy. She'd made a huge mistake! Seeing Grace made her feel like a traitor. She should have never gotten involved with Darrin Morgan!

Grace was Trenna's friend and she was bound to be upset when she learned the truth. Darrin had done his job, but there was no denying that he was the reason Todd Marks was walking the streets. Because Marks was a free man, Grace no longer felt safe in her own home and had been forced to move.

Trenna sighed. Why had Darrin taken the case? He was already very successful. He didn't need the notoriety or the money. So why? Was it because Marks came from wealth? Or was Marks an old friend? Maybe it had been about ego, and Darrin had set out to prove he was smarter than the head prosecutor on the case was.

"Your turn, Vanessa!" Grace prompted.

Vanessa nodded, then went up to the front to show the girls samples of beadwork that had been done on lace, denim, and leather that might be added to a neckline, hem, or cuff.

Trenna frowned, upset with herself. Instead of being involved with the girls, she was wasting time thinking about Darrin. Why couldn't she forget? Her response to him was intense, unlike anything she had ever experienced. She hated admitting that she wanted him. Only it had been a huge mistake.

Full of remorse, her conscience nagged at her, a reminder that she was God's child and must do the right thing. Lying by omission served no purpose and changed nothing. She needed to speak to Grace and be honest.

12

---

*D*arrin was shivering from the cold by the time his twin left the gym. What he couldn't figure out was how he had fallen so fast and hard for the one woman in the entire metropolitan area who wanted nothing to do with him.

"Okay, babe," Douglas said into his phone. "I'll see you at seven. Yeah, I will. Love you, bye." Using the keyless entry, he started the motor and disengaged the locks to let them both inside. They tossed their bags on the backseat.

Darrin silently waited, bracing himself for a ribbing from his brother. Instead, Douglas complained, "Man, the cold is not letting up today. I hoped we'd at least get into the twenties. At least the seat warmers are doing their thing. It's the best feature in this model."

"You're not going to say anything?" Darrin asked with a frown.

"About you being a jackass? No point. We're not too far from your favorite pizza place. Hungry? Want me to stop?"

The combination of a heavy heart and dark thoughts pushed food from Darrin's mind. "No thanks."

He didn't think he could feel any worse but he soon discovered he was wrong. He felt like a heel when Douglas said, "Whenever you're ready, I'll listen,"

He immediately blurted out, "I blew it with Trenna last night. I still can't believe how badly I messed up. I gave her a ride home. She invited me to dinner. One thing led to another. Instead of following my instincts and taking things slow I rushed ahead like a lovesick kid. It all blew up in my face, Doug."

"Did you say Trenna?"

"Yeah, you know how I feel about her."

"I do," Douglas nodded. "Back up. Take it from the beginning."

Darrin told his twin about the call from Maureen. Eager to spend time with Trenna, he hadn't given the weather a thought. It had been about her. He admitted that they'd made love and it had been pure magic for him. He left it at that.

He didn't say that, given half a chance, he would have made love to her again and again. But something had gone terribly wrong for her. While he had no regrets, she had a boatload. But he couldn't forget her heated responses to his lovemaking.

He surmised, "I thought the pleasure was mutual, but evidently I was wrong. Trenna asked me to leave. She acted as if I took advantage of her, seduced her, and she resented me for it."

Thoughtful for a moment, Doug eventually said, "Give her some time. She'll come around."

"No, she won't. Look, you didn't see her face when she asked me to leave."

"Come on, bro. You didn't force yourself on her!"

Darrin winced. "Yeah. I know. But you didn't see her face. It was how she looked at me during Todd Marks' trial. She made no secret of the fact she resents me for getting him off."

"Bro, you're a damn good attorney, period. Plus it was business, not personal. As for the other, there is certainly nothing wrong with a man making love to the woman he loves. If that was the case, we'd all be behind bars."

"Wait! I never said the 'L' word."

"You don't have to. You've been chasing her down since the day you two met. Or did you think I didn't notice that you haven't been involved with anyone else?"

"Okay, I'm guilty," he confessed. "I want her. She's gorgeous."

"It's a lot more than that and we both know it," his twin snapped.

Darrin sighed heavily. "Having feelings for her has turned out to be a huge mistake. I was a fool to believe that once she got to know me things would be different." He snarled with frustration, "She can't have feelings for me. She's still in love with her dead husband!"

"Say what?" Douglas took his eyes off the road for a second.

"You heard correctly."

"You think..." Douglas stopped and then asked, "Did she come right out and say that...?"

"Not exactly."

"Then how can you be so sure? Her husband has been gone... What? Over four years?"

"Yeah."

When Darrin said nothing more Douglas prompted, "We're talking about Trenna McAdams. Yeah, she's a book-club-reading, bible-toting, and churching-going lady, but like you said she's also beautiful, and like Maureen she owns her own business and has no shortage of dates."

Darrin frowned. "So?"

"Hear me out! In looks, Trenna and Maureen, are like ebony and ivory, but in personality they could be two peas in the same pod. Maureen also dates frequently and likes to have fun, but doesn't sleep around."

"Your point?"

They had stopped at a traffic light. Douglas glared at his twin, "Dar, evidently you were asleep when Dad told us the difference between a good girl and a skank. You have got it all wrong. Trenna..."

Darrin interrupted, "You're the one not listening? I'm not one to kiss and tell, but I suspect I was the first in a very long time. I wouldn't be surprised if she hasn't been sexually active since her husband died. Trenna's special. I would never treat her like a..."

"Well, you did something wrong! Figure it out, so you can fix it, knuckle-head."

"Dating frequently can't change the facts. She buried Martin McAdams, but her heart still belongs to him." Darrin scowled. He knew how hard it had been on him to pick up the pieces and move on after their father passed. He still couldn't talk about it after more than a year with his sibling or mother. "She can't give away what she no longer has," he ended with a heavy sigh.

"Did she say she was still in love with him?"

Outraged, he practically shouted, "I didn't ask!"

"Then you can't be sure. Maybe you're too close the situation to be objective?"

"Have you considered that you're a jack-ass and don't know what in the hell you're talking about?"

Douglas warned, "Hey! Watch your mouth!"

Frustrated, Darrin snapped, "Or what? You'll tell Mom, you big baby!"

Douglas was still chuckling when they pulled into his circular drive. He stopped beside his brother's jeep and then smacked Darrin on the back.

"Just because it has taken Trenna a while to see your finer points doesn't mean she buried her heart with her late husband. Maureen has known her for years and has never even hinted at that possibility. I wouldn't be surprised if she wasn't using the Marks case to keep you at bay. Cheer up! If you asked me, things have changed for the better. Besides if she was still in love with her husband, why did she hop into bed with you?"

"I seduced her."

Douglas chuckled. "You may have been born with your share

of the Morgan charm, but even you aren't that good. You need to talk to her and find out her reason for saying yes."

Although he scowled, Darrin's heart raced at the possibility. He was unsure if he was ready to hear why she had said yes. He knew the truth was always better than a lie, but he also knew the unvarnished truth could do some serious damage. "Considering how badly the evening ended, I'm not sure I can trust her to tell me the truth."

"Which means you haven't told her how you feel about her, right?" Douglas shook his head. "I shouldn't have to remind you that women view these things vastly different than we do. You slept with her, but did you say a word about having any feelings for her? For all she knows, you got what you came to the party for and that's the end of story. Only it's not over for you and it might not be over for her."

"She asked me to leave."

Douglas advised, "Do yourself a favor, bro, and put a label on your feelings for Trenna."

Looking into eyes identical to his own, Darrin asked in earnest, "How did you know what you felt for Megan was love?"

"I didn't...not at first. It wasn't until I accepted that I couldn't live without her that it began to make sense to me. More importantly, I didn't want to live without her. Megan owns my heart."

Darrin nodded. "Thanks."

"No problem. It's nothing considering what you did for me. Do you remember when Megan got in my face? She called me a spoiled brat, said she had no use for or respect for men like me, who never had to work for anything in their lives. I was livid when she said, as far as she was concerned, everything I had, including my fancy law degree and my job, had all been handed to me on a silver platter by wealthy parents." Doug sighed, "I was crushed. No one had ever spoken to me that way. I was this close"—he held up nearly touching thumb and forefinger—"to walking away and never looking back."

"Yeah, I remember."

"It wasn't until you and I talked that I was able to calm down and start using my head. Bro, you gave me hope, helped me get beyond the hurt feelings and bruised ego. That was when I realized she was deliberately pushing me away and I had to figure out why. Because of you, I was able to pull myself together...to start thinking and stop reacting. Attacking me was her way of protecting herself and keeping me away."

Darrin shrugged. "All we did was talk."

"You gave me another perspective. Megan and I owe you." Doug affectionately squeezed his brother's nape. "Hey, I'm sure we wouldn't be getting married, if not for you. No matter how much self-pity and trash talk I dished out, you always listened."

Darrin grinned. "I'm happy for you, little bro. There's no doubt that you two love each other. You're blessed to have what Mom and Dad had. That's rare."

"Agreed, but who said you can't have it?"

"I can't compete against a dead man. It's too late for me," Darrin ended dejectedly.

"That's a truck load of manure! You're here and can still win the brass ring."

"Stop! "

"He has won, if you're going to give up and play dead! From where I'm sitting you're alive and virile. He can no longer romance her with moonlit walks and late-night phone calls. Stop me if I'm wrong, but you can call her, take her out to dinner, or out dancing. Every time you take her into your arms and hold her, kiss her and caress her, you will be reminding her that she's still very much alive. She has needs you can satisfy."

Darrin was silent for so long that Doug prompted, "What? You're not up to the challenge?"

"I just need to be sure."

Douglas laughed, "Megan sure had me jumping through hoops, trying to prove my feelings were genuine. Now, it's your turn." He hesitated, before he went on, "Could be that the difficulty isn't love? If you have doubts that she's worthy of your trust, then she's not the one. Dad always said trust and love go hand in hand"—he spelled out the last word—"a-l-w-a-y-s. Without trust there can be no love. It's right up there with great sex."

Darrin was quiet, thoughtful.

"Think about it, bro. Consider how you feel when you're with Trenna. Maybe speaking to Maureen might help? Whatever you decide, remember Mama took us to Sunday school and church for a reason. Even if you haven't been going lately, you're still God's child. Pray, ask for God's guidance. There's no better way to find out if Trenna is genuine and worth fighting for."

"You okay?" Grace Brooks was seated across the table from Trenna. "Is something wrong with your salad? You're staring at it, but not eating."

"Sorry, it's been a long day." Trenna admitted, "What did you say?"

"I was telling you how thrilled I was that the girls liked their belts. I'm considering doing another sewing project with them. Have any ideas?"

Trenna shook her head. "Not one clue."

"I'm just glad Maureen convinced me to get involved."

Trenna teased, "Don't you mean she talked you into it?"

They laughed.

"Yes, and she was right."

"Don't tell her that or we will never hear the end of it." Trenna smiled. "Grace, you are very talented and creative. Your belts are beautiful."

Grace blushed. "I was so fortunate that Vanessa went to the craft fair where I had my display. She liked my designs. I'm thrilled to see them in her shop."

"Vanessa has good taste. I surprised you aren't selling online. But I'm sure your belts will go quickly, especially if you pair them with evening bags."

"Really? I haven't thought of doing evening bags."

"Absolutely. How many has Maureen bought?"

"Three," Grace blushed. "And you own two. Until recently it has only been a hobby. Something I enjoy doing in the evenings while watching TV."

"Hobby? I wouldn't be surprised if Vanessa keeps you so busy with orders from her shop that you won't have time to volunteer. Who knows, maybe you will add embellished hats, pillbox, or even newsboy styles."

"Goodness!" Grace gushed. "Thank you."

"Another week and we can mark this project off as a huge hit." Trenna laughed. "When Vanessa introduced the sewing machines the girls were skeptical, called it dated, old-fashion. I don't think they realized that sewing is a skill they can use for a lifetime. Now most of them are planning to make either evening slacks or maxi skirts for the outing."

Nodding, Grace agreed. "It was fun. Until recently most of my time at the Center has been devoted to helping in the rape counseling group sessions."

"From what I understand, you've done a wonderful job." Trenna smiled. "Believe me when I say, I know how hard it is to say 'no' to Maureen. I've been trying without much success for years."

"How long have you two been friends?"

"Since we were roommates our freshman year in college. We had a lot in common, were only children and became close, like family. We graduated together. Maureen was my maid of honor at my wedding. Even though when we lived in different states, we remained close. After my husband passed, I moved to the Detroit area to be near her. It feels like we've been friends forever."

Grace said candidly, "I envy your friendship. It's rare to find someone you can trust with your secrets, willing to stick by you when life gets hard." Grace said, "I'm surprised she didn't come today, even though you were willing to step in for her."

Trenna smiled, "Me, too. But I'm glad she decided to be sensible. She hasn't gotten much sleep since her grandmother has been ill."

"How is Mrs. Hale?"

"I dropped in to see her earlier. She was feeling much better. But, honestly, I'm glad they kept her overnight, forced her to rest. She had chest pains. I'm thankful it wasn't a heart attack. Maureen and her grandmother haven't had a vacation in years, since they opened the Women's Center," Trenna revealed.

"But Mrs. Hale must be in her seventies."

"Yes, and Maureen loves her so much that she has a hard time telling her to sit down. That will probably change after this health scare," Trenna said.

"I hope so. Both Maureen and Mrs. Hale are such good people, so kind and accepting of all the women who come into the Center. They are blessed to still have each other."

"I agree. What about you, Grace? Do you have family in the area?"

She shook her head. "There are a few distant cousins out there somewhere, but no close family. Maureen didn't tell you?"

Trenna laughed. "No, nothing. The girl would make an excellent CIA agent. She'd cut out her tongue before breaking a confidence, professional or otherwise."

Just then the waiter arrived with their orders, grilled whiting for Grace and shrimp scampi for Trenna.

Grace surprised Trenna when she said, "I'm so grateful that Maureen was the one who came to see me in the hospital after the rape. She has helped me tremendously. I couldn't have gotten through the therapy or the trial without her." Then she reached and squeezed Trenna's hand before she added, "I'm grateful that you were also there and are a great friend to me.

Thank you for including me in your outings with Maureen and your friends."

"It's no hardship." Trenna's heart had immediately gone out to Grace when Maureen introduced them. She had no trouble recalling the day she met Grace. It was after a counseling session at Maureen's office and she still bore the scars from being battered.

Maureen encouraged all of her clients to attend the group sessions and volunteer at the Women Center's in some capacity. There were self-defense classes to help build confidence.

"I can't tell you enough how much I appreciate your support during the trial."

"I did what any friend would do," Trenna said as she twisted the napkin in her lap. The mention of the trial brought Darrin to mind and memories of the intimacy they shared.

"What is it?"

"I need to be candid with you, but I'm not sure how to do this." Trenna said, then surprised them both by asking, "Do you have room for desert?"

Grace blinked. "Now I'm really curious."

Trenna shook her head. "You have been through enough. The last thing I want to do is upset you."

Grace said, "Trenna, just say it."

Trenna shook her head. "Now for dessert. The chocolate…"

In an urgent whisper, Grace asked, "You haven't been raped—?"

"No! Nothing like that!" She sighed before blurting out, "I slept with Darrin Morgan. I know it is crazy considering he represented Todd Marks during the trial." She confessed that she'd had avoided him, then he had gone out of his way to help her. He had called an old friend, who turned out to be a potential backer for her foundation. "It just happened. Last night, he'd given me a lift home and one thing led to another."

Grace surprised her when she said, "It sounds to me as if your resentment toward Darrin has gone on for so long that it became a bad habit. Evidently, you saw him in a new way. That's a good thing, right?"

Trenna frowned, wondering if Grace was right. Had she been so caught up in the old resentment that she hadn't questioned it? Had she been unfair? Only since his help with her foundation had she started to see another side of him, and had begun to trust him. He had been kind, thoughtful even. There was no doubt he was a generous lover. Goodness! Was she was starting to care about him? No! No!

It was the darn charm. He had so much of it that it practically oozed from the man's pores. Women fell like dominoes for that Morgan charm. It was disgusting. Unfortunately, last night he turned it her way and she had fallen faster than a house of cards.

With him, she had felt things she had never before experienced. She couldn't explain why she had wanted him. His kisses were irresistible, and being in his arms was pure magic. There could be only one word to describe his love-making: incredible. He was that and so much more. Her response to him was unbelievable. She thought she knew all there was to know about what happened between a man and a woman, after all she'd been married. But she'd been wrong. Darrin was nothing like Martin. And Darrin's lovemaking had shaken her to the core.

Goodness! She'd been so caught up in him she'd forgotten the anger, the resentment...everything! She had no idea why her brain had switched off, for she'd stopped thinking, and merely felt. The feelings had been so intense.

No! It should have never happened. She knew about his reputation with women! Talk about asking for trouble. Sleeping with him was utterly stupid.

"Now that you've gotten to know him, what do you think?"

Instead of answering, Trenna said, "Doesn't it bother you that I'm involved with him?"

"Bother?" Grace laughed, "Darrin Morgan's a very attractive man."

Trenna's eyes went wide. Giving up all pretense of eating, she put down her fork. "It looks as if I was upset enough for the both of us. I couldn't forget that during the trial, Darrin was merciless. When you were on the stand, he treated you as if you were the criminal, not his own low-life client. He can be so annoying, especially the way he kept asking me out and refused to take no for an answer. For so long, I had to make myself be polite and speak to him."

Grace shook her head. "I'm surprised he didn't give up on you."

Trenna had wondered the same thing. Darrin Morgan was a brilliant lawyer and a very attractive man. He had his pick of females, eager to be seen on his arm and hop into his bed. Yet, he continued to go after her. Why had he been so persistent?

"I can't help but see red every time I think about what Todd Marks did. The man raped you! If I live to be hundred, I'll never understand why such a high-powered lawyer as Darrin would work for that low-life. Was it because Marks came from money?" Worried she had said too much, Trenna quickly added, "Grace, I'm so sorry. I didn't mean to upset you."

"You have no reason to apologize."

"But I do. I shouldn't have brought the subject up. Let's talk about something pleasant. Didn't Amber do a great job on her belt?"

Grace nodded, "She's very talented and has a good eye for color." Then she hesitated before she said earnestly, "This is hard for me to admit, but Darrin Morgan did both me and Todd Marks a huge favor when he him got off."

"What?"

"I should have told you when you first mentioned the trial." Grace frowned, then confessed, "Even after talking about this in group sessions with other rape victims, it's still not easy for me to talk about the rape. Recently, I realized I had made a horrible mistake."

Confused, Trenna said, "I don't understand."

"I know." Grace paused before she said, "I'm trying to find a way to tell you that Todd Marks didn't rape me." Grace sighed. "I wish Maureen had told you."

13

---

*T*renna was so rattled that instead of going home she drove to the Henry Ford Hospital. She was surprised to find that Mrs. Hale wasn't in bed but seated in the padded armchair near Maureen. Though she was covered with blankets and propped up by pillows, she looked stronger than she had that morning.

"Hi, you two," she said. "It's good to see you out of bed, Ms. H. What are you two arguing about? I could hear you in the hall."

"Trenna, you're back."

"That's right. How are you feeling?"

"Much better. Told this one to go on home, she's being stubborn."

Maureen laughed. "Hi, Trenna, did you hear her calling me stubborn? Wonder who I got it from?"

Trenna giggled. "I think, she has you there, Ms. H."

Maureen and her grandmother were very close. Mrs. Hale had practically raised her, even before Maureen's mother died. The older woman had been blessed with elegance, charm, and a keen intellect. What was most important to Trenna was Mrs. Hale's kindness. From day one Mrs. Hale had treated her like family.

"How was the mentoring session?" Maureen wanted to know.

"Yes, dear, did it go well?"

As Trenna filled them in, she noticed that Mrs. Hale was tiring. Once she was back in bed with her dinner tray, she shooed Trenna and Maureen out the door, insisting she'd see them tomorrow.

They were nearing the bank of elevators when Trenna said, "I'm glad you decided to be sensible and not stay over another night."

Maureen sighed, "I didn't have a choice. You heard how she reacted when I mentioned canceling the dinner/dance tonight. She practically threw me out of her room. How am I supposed to concentrate on business with her in the hospital?"

Trenna squeezed Maureen's hand. "I was just so happy to see that she's better. Try not to worry. There is much to be thankful for, Maureen."

"I agree, it's hard to concentrate on anything with her in here. And I really don't want to go tonight," Maureen complained.

"You heard her. You're going, so you might as well stop complaining. Who's your date?"

"Steve Manning."

They giggled. Steve was a childhood friend who lived a few doors away. Like the Morgan twins, the four had grown up attending the same schools and church.

Trenna smiled. They had few secrets. When they were sophomores at Spellman they both were engaged. Maureen fell in love with a law school student while Trenna loved a long-time family friend. Things went badly for Maureen when her fiancé was arrested and then convicted of rape. Maureen was crushed but had the good sense to break off her engagement. Trenna went ahead and married Martin anyway.

It took years before Trenna learned there was a difference between love and being in love. Both relationships ended badly, and they both suffered keen disappointments. The friends continued to be there for each other and learned how to cope with life and regrets.

As the years passed, although they still hoped to find love and have children, neither of them was counting on it. There was always a reason not to let things progress beyond a certain level of intimacy. That was until last night.

Maureen broke into Trenna's thoughts when she said, "We've both been so busy that it seems like forever since we last talked." Linking arms as they stepped out of the elevator, Maureen asked, "How are you? How was your dinner with Darrin? Did you have fun? You did feed him, didn't you?"

"Not only did I feed him, but I also went to bed with him."

"Did you say…". Maureen stopped abruptly.

"Yes." With a heavy heart, she admitted, "I still can't believe what happened. If that wasn't bad enough, at dinner with Grace, I learned Todd Marks didn't rape her. She identified the wrong man."

"Come." Maureen pulled her arm, steering her to an isolated group of armchairs in the corner of the lobby. They found two seats away from the others. "Okay, tell me about you and Darrin. And start with the ride to your place."

Sighing, Trenna told her nearly everything, including her strong reaction to Darrin. The only thing Trenna left out was the intimate details of their lovemaking. She ended with having asked him to leave.

"Wow, I didn't expect that," Maureen exclaimed.

"Neither did I. It started with a single kiss and I still don't know how it got out of hand. But I'm glad it's over." Her friend stared at her without speaking for so long that Trenna said, "You look as if you're in shock."

"Yeah!"

"Get over it, because I need advice."

Maureen said with a frown, "On what?"

"Grace's confession. She said that she only recently realized she'd picked the wrong man out of the lineup. Todd Marks didn't rape her. It never occurred to me that she might have doubts."

"Nor did it occur to her. But I'm glad she told you. Trust's a big issue for most rape victims. Grace has come a long way."

"I'm glad but she probably only told me because I was feeling guilty for getting involved with Darrin."

"That's not true. Trenna, Grace trusts you and knows you care about her. Now, let's talk about you and Darrin."

"There nothing to talk about." She blushed as she recalled the intense pleasure she discovered in his arms. "Darrin was right all this time and I was wrong. When I think…" Her voice trailed away. "It's embarrassing! I practically called him everything except a child of God for taking that horrible man's case and then getting him off. On top of that I'm not sure I ever showed my appreciation for his help with my school. Because of him, I may have a major investor for my foundation, someone who is willing to pay for the children's college education, if they graduate from high school."

"I have my fingers crossed that it will go through. But you have to stop beating yourself up over what happened," Maureen scolded. "Grace just realized herself that she identified the wrong guy. She has been heart-sick about it since she discovered her error."

"You're right."

"All three of us resented Darrin's skill in the courtroom. He got Todd Marks off. He's an excellent lawyer, the best, which is why the Marks hired him to defend their son." She squeezed Trenna's hand. "I feel as if I owe you an apology. I really wasn't match-making when I called Darrin to ask him to take you home."

"No one's accusing you of anything."

"I know but I hate to see you upset like this. To me, Darrin's family but that does not mean he's the one for you. I should not have asked for his help the night of the storm. I'm sorry."

"Don't be."

"I'm on your side, girlfriend. Why are you frowning?"

"Not important."

Maureen insisted, "Something more is going on here. What is it?"

"It doesn't matter."

"It matters. And I won't not going asking questions until you explain why you went to bed with Darrin, a man you can't stand. And don't give me some bologna about his kisses."

There was more, but Trenna wasn't ready to get into it. She was having enough trouble admitting she might have feelings for Darrin. There was no label to place on her emotions. All she knew was that her feelings were all over the place. Her reaction to him was intense, so unnerving that she didn't know how to handle it. It was easier to push him away than examine her feelings too closely.

Plus, she couldn't stop wondering if she had seen hurt in his eyes when she asked him to leave. Was it in his voice when he called the next morning and she refused his help? She was letting her imagination get the best of her. She must not forget that above all else, Darrin Morgan was a first-class womanizer.

But what if it were true? It could mean he changed…that he genuinely cared. The mere possibility had her blinking back tears. Goodness! It didn't matter to her. It didn't!

Life could change swiftly. Almost overnight, she had gone from being someone's daughter to being someone's wife. She had spent years trying to make him happy and failed miserably. After losing Martin, her life had changed again. She had something to prove to herself. For the first time in her life, she had no father, no husband to lean on. She had learned to stand on her own two feet.

She was proud of what she had accomplished on her own. She discovered she liked being her own woman, liked making her own decisions. She refused to go backward.

When Darrin entered her life, she had made a serious blunder by sharing her body with him. She risked letting him into her heart. It was foolish to care about...

"Trenna..."

"It just happened."

There was no logical explanation, any more than there was a reason for how he made her feel. Pleasure and passion mixed with urgent need, and she'd lost control. Why couldn't she forget how it felt when she came apart in his arms? It had been raw, explosive, and wrong!

"Nothing just happens."

"It did this time!"

"Try again."

"I am not one of your clients, Maureen Hale Sheppard! Leave it alone."

"Do you remember when you first moved to Detroit? We agreed to leave our past mistakes in the past. You didn't want to talk about Martin any more than I wanted to remember my broken engagement. We both decided to get out there, to date and have fun. We stuck to the plan: have male friends while not repeating mistakes. But last night something changed. Let's talk about that change."

Annoyed, Trenna demanded, "Don't you have to get ready for that dinner/dance?"

"So I'll be a little late. Stop trying to distract me. The last time we talked you couldn't be in the same room with Darrin without getting into an argument. After years of saying no to every guy that you've ever gone out with, you suddenly say yes to Darrin. Why?"

Trenna's failure to respond did not stop Maureen from saying, "Something was different about last night. Think about it and while you're thinking maybe you can figure out what has you so upset. Do you feel as if you were being disloyal to Martin? Maybe you realize you have feelings for Darrin? It could be that the possibility of getting hurt scares you?"

"Honesty, Maureen, there are times when you get on my last nerve! Why are you bringing Martin into this? This has nothing to do with him."

"Okay. Explain why you slept with Darrin and I'll drop it."

"Goodness! I don't know why I even brought it up. It's bad enough knowing I made a stupid mistake."

"You think you made a mistake? Is that why you asked him to leave?"

Trenna jumped to her feet, saying, "Maureen, as much as I love you, I cannot talk about this!" She grabbed her purse and headed out the door.

IT WAS FRIDAY NIGHT. Her staff had rushed out, eager to get the weekend underway. Trenna had turned down an invitation to have dinner with her book club friends. She wasn't in the mood to smile and pretend all was well.

As Trenna paced the length of her office, she didn't so much as glance at the twinkling light on the small tabletop or the Christmas tree in the center of the credenza. Nor did she take notice of the festive greenery and holiday lights decorating the landscape outsides her office window.

She'd barely noticed the bustling sounds of activity in the building had gradually ebbed. Weeks had passed since the night she slept with Darrin. Thanksgiving had come and gone, and Christmas was fast approaching. She hadn't seen or spoken to him.

True, she had asked him not call, to keep his distance. She hadn't wanted to see him, hadn't wanted to remember what they shared. Nor did she want to be the subject of the building's gossip mill.

She frowned. So why wasn't she grateful that he respected her wishes? Because it hurt! Darrin didn't seem to be having any trouble avoiding her.

She lost count of the number of times she told herself it was for the best that she hadn't caught so much as a glimpse of him. She appreciated that Maureen had lightened up on her and let the subject drop. She still couldn't talk about that night. Her reasons for sleeping with him and then asking him to leave were too painful to examine.

She was glad that her days were busy. But it didn't help that she was having trouble sleeping and the nights seemed endless. She had tried everything she could think of to keep the thoughts at bay…nothing worked. She couldn't just let it go.

She woke each morning exhausted from tossing and turning until the wee hours. And when sleep finally claimed her, she dreamed about him. She knew she couldn't go on like this. She had to find a way to let it go, to stop reliving every detail of that night. What difference did it make now? It wasn't as if she could change what happened. Heck, she still didn't know why she said yes in the first place. What she needed was answers.

For a time, Darrin acted as if he genuinely cared about her. And she believed him. She needed to know if it was real. Did he care? Making love with him had affected her so profoundly. She wasn't a naive or inexperienced young girl. Nor was she a fool or foolish. She had no illusions about marriage or men. She had been married to Martin for years.

With Darrin… She sighed. Making love with Darrin had been vastly different from being with her late husband. Darrin made her feel things that she hadn't even come close to feeling before. She had gone over it again and again. She told herself she had made too much of it, blowing it out of proportion.

It was so confusing. Responding to Darrin didn't mean she hadn't cared about Martin. There was no doubt in her mind that she had once loved her husband. Or that she had tried her best to please him and had also failed, time and time again.

Her self-esteem had taken a hard hit when she had also failed to satisfy Darrin. Her success rate with men was abysmal. Yet, there was no doubt she had responded to Darrin's lovemaking. She had thought she had pleased him until she realized he had still been aroused. She had been devastated, which was why she asked him to go.

There was no doubt that when it came to the female body, he knew what he was about. He was the master at that game. She was the one to lose control. He had proven beyond all doubt that he was an experienced lover, a master with women. He knew more about the machinations of a woman's body than she did.

Yet, it was his tenderness that had become endearing to her, important to her. He had been wonderful. She had tried, but was unable to forget how he made her feel. She told herself that it was sex...only sex. But Darrin's touch had been gentle, almost loving. Loving? No way!

She closed her eyes trying not to recall the look in his eyes when she asked him to leave. No, it hadn't been anger. There had been no sign of rage, no sharpness, or any fury on his face. He had seemed disappointed, almost sad.

Trenna's eyes went wide and her heart began to pound. Doubt warred with hope as she struggled to put a label on what she seen in his eyes. Had she been wrong? What if he did care? Did it matter? Her heart pounded with dread as she realized it mattered.

Crossing to the desk, Trenna picked up the phone, and then quickly replaced it. No! She was overreacting. They had sex...not made love. It was not as if he had taken something she hadn't been willing give. She had wanted him as she had never believed it possible to want a man.

Darrin had not rushed. He had taken his time. Was there an inch of her body that he hadn't caressed or kissed? She shook head no. Then, she sighed recalling his kisses. It was amazing the way those kisses had gone from being sweet and tender but had then gradually heated until they were sizzling hot. He had been warm, so caring in a way that made her feel special.

She covered her face as if she could hide from the truth. The pleasure had not been mutual. It was one-sided. No, he hadn't complained or degraded her for her failure. She bit her lip to keep from crying as she accepted that Darrin had turned out to be a generous lover and a real friend. Trenna was ashamed that she had not called to tell him that the contracts were signed and to thank him for his help.

He didn't have to introduce her to the Murrays, who had agreed to be generous sponsors of her scholarship fund. She had tried but she couldn't overlook such kindness. Starting next fall, Murrays would be making it possible for so many children to have brighter futures.

There was no doubt about it—she owed him. The night of the storm, instead of going home to wait it out, Darrin had volunteered to give her a ride home. It was her decision to invite him to dinner and then to stay with her. He was prepared to leave, but she had stopped him.

Releasing a heavy sigh, Trenna knew she had to apologize. He had gone out of his way to help her, on more than one occasion. She had let fear keep her from doing what was right. So how could she fix this? Would he let her?

She had no answers. But she had to make an attempt, didn't she? Was she a woman or a coward? She picked up the receiver and punched in his office number. It rang and rang before going to voicemail.

"Too late, he's gone," she muttered aloud. Disappointed, she covered her face with her hands. She sighed heavily and then began to wander around the room. She ended up at the window and studied the darkening sky.

The parking lot was nearly empty. It was getting late, and she should go home. Only her empty house held little appeal. There were only few cars left. One of them was Darrin's jeep.

Looking up from his laptop, Darrin rubbed tired eyes. He rotated his head from side to side, hoping to ease the stiffness in his neck and shoulders. He didn't need to glance at the clock or listen to his empty stomach to know it was time to call it a day.

As he looked at the pages of notes he'd jotted on the legal pad in front of him, he smiled imagining how his dad would have teased him, insisting that he should have been a doctor since his handwriting resembled chicken scratch. He sighed. Even after all this time, he still missed his dad. Time didn't heal every wound.

He was glad that his assistant was good at deciphering his handwriting, but this might even be a stretch for her. He had just started on the last brief when his stomach grumbled loudly, reminding him that he'd skipped lunch.

There was no point in looking in the compact refrigerator in his office. It was empty, just like his refrigerator at home. It had been a while since he'd gone to the market. Tonight, like most nights, he'd end up calling one of the nearby restaurants and place a takeout order that he'd pick up on the way home.

Sighing heavily, he knew his stomach wasn't the problem. Work, go home, and sleep were all he had done lately. Thanksgiving had been disappointing for him. The holidays were difficult without his dad. Having Megan, Douglas' fiancée, join them helped both his mother and Douglas. But missing his dad wasn't the sole reason for Darrin's funky mood.

He couldn't remember what he ate. But then, food was near the bottom on his list of priorities. Not that he couldn't recall the last time he'd enjoyed a meal. No, that wasn't true. He recalled the date, the day of the week, and the time of night when his life had gone south.

Had he ever experienced such an overwhelming sense of hopelessness and despair? He was normally an upbeat kind of guy. He was blessed and knew he had a great deal to be grateful. He was healthy, his mind was sharp, but most importantly, he was part of a loving family. Then his attitude toward life had spiraled downward. It started the night Trenna rejected him and pushed him out of her life.

The wanting started the moment his eyes met hers across the crowded restaurant. He knew she was special. The attraction was strong and immediate. His pursuit of her had been packed with hurdles. Like an Olympic champion, he didn't shy away from a challenge. Determination and drive were no mystery to him. He grew up with parents who believed anything worthwhile didn't come easily.

Silently, he mouthed Trenna's name, unable to get the feel of her dark, beautiful skin out of his mind. She was so incredibly soft and her lush mouth unbelievable sweet. He adored the way she tasted. Who was he kidding? He loved everything about her. A single night with her didn't come close to being enough. He couldn't stop wanting her. He swore beneath his breath.

Considering how badly the evening ended, it was unlikely he'd ever have more time with her. Being with her, holding her in his arms had been remarkable. There was no comparison. For so long he'd imagined what it would be like to be with her. Nothing had prepared him for her sweetness. Being with her had been unforgettable.

He'd lost count of the number of times he grabbed his phone. He longed to hear her voice, only to be brought up short. She had hurt him, rejected him, compared him to her another man, and then asked him to leave. She couldn't have been clearer when she said she wanted nothing to do with him.

Time and time again, he tried but failed to push all thoughts of her from his mind. Work had become his solace and made the daylight hours tolerable. Unable to sleep, his nights were unbearably long. And when he finally managed to sleep, he dreamed about Trenna.

He detested those dreams. They were hot and steamy, brimming from his longing and hunger for her. The dreams were proof that he could no more control his need for her any more than he could sprout wings and fly. The dreams invariably left him hard, aching for her and dripping with sweat. And he woke alone, his arms empty and his heart aching.

Hearing Trenna's name was enough to set him on edge. He found it highly irritating that nearly everyone in the building had something good to say about her. The cleaning crew would mention how thoughtful she was, or one of the security guards, on duty at the front desk, would brag about her delicious, home-made cookies or breads. He needed no reminders that she was warm, generous, and special. Or that she was beautiful on the inside and outside. He was unlikely to forget Trenna didn't want anything to do with him.

Even his assistant had gotten in on the chatter. Because her little nephew was enrolled in the nursery school, she frequently boasted that Trenna was particular about her staff and she truly loved the children. Darrin almost told her to shut up. He didn't bother to ask himself why should he care, Trenna hired people who genuinely cared about the children. He ground his teeth in frustration. If he did not know better he'd assumed that Trenna had paid them to rave about her.

He muttered aloud, "You would think everyone around here loved her as much as I do."

Love? Where had that come from? Love? Was this love? If this was what being in love felt like then he'd pass. He flatly refused to love a woman who didn't want him.

The problem wasn't with him. Despite what she claimed, Trenna wasn't really free. Even though she no longer wore Martin McAdams' wedding band, she still used his name. And she used his name because her heart belonged to him... her dead husband.

For weeks, he had been blind to the truth. He wrongly assumed she understood how he felt about losing his father. He'd only been partly correct. She understood because of her own loss:

those of her parents and then that of the love of her life. Only he hadn't realized how she felt until they'd made love.

It had taken a while but finally he was able to piece it all together. Why she was unwilling to go out with him, give him a real chance, and why she had no room in her heart for him. She still grieved for Martin because she was still very much in love with him.

But the absolute worst for him was when she slipped up and said "...with Martin." Clearly, she had been comparing the two of them. And there was no doubt in his mind that he was the one who came up lacking. That pain had been devastating.

Why had she bothered to say yes? Evidently, for a short time, desire had gotten the best of her. What other reason could she have for letting him make love to her? Well, she had certainly recovered her equilibrium quick enough. After a single love-making session, she had turned her back on him and what they shared.

He ground his teeth in mute frustration. No way! What he felt for her couldn't be love. How could it when this felt like he'd descended into hell? And to make matters worse, the longer he was forced to go without seeing her or hearing her voice was pure torment.

What was he supposed to do? How much longer could he ignore her, pretend he hadn't sampled her sweetness? He was already on edge; his temper was razor-sharp these days. He knew that being around him was no picnic. Most days, it was all he could do not to bellow his disappointment like a wounded bear.

Despite his brother's attempts to encourage him, Darrin knew there was no fixing it. He needed to face that there was no relationship to repair. All they had ever had was a one-night-stand. He had tried but couldn't get it through his brother's thick head that he was neither like his twin nor was Trenna like Megan. He was so sick of Douglas offering to talk to Trenna for him that he'd threatened to punch him in the face if he didn't leave it alone.

Unfortunately their mother had overheard their conversation, and began asking questions and giving him advice. It was just his rotten luck that she adored Trenna. His mother had told him in no uncertain terms to get his act together. She wanted grandbabies.

Darrin had no trouble recalling every intimate detail of being wrapped in Trenna's arms. The memory was so vivid it filled his dreams, every kiss, every caress, and every delicious detail. He knew exactly what he had said to her and done to her. Her sweet response to his lovemaking was seared inside his head. There was no doubt that she climaxed several times. Her last climax was so intense it triggered his. And the force of his release had been so powerful that he suspected he'd lost consciousness for a few seconds. Being inside of her, a part of her had blown his mind. He could never forget the magic of her sweet heat stroking him from base to tip.

Incredible! He was amazed by how badly he wanted her again. In record time, she had him rock hard and ready for more. No woman had ever pleasured him and affected him so deeply. Once hadn't come close to being enough for him. Had he ever been in more need? He didn't think so.

He had it bad, so much so that he forgot about everything, including the used condom he had been wearing. She had stared at his erection as if in shock, and very upset. Had she been sore and believed he was taking advantage? Did she think he was being careless, putting her at risk?

But that one time with Trenna had messed with him. He hadn't been with another woman since that night. And he was a virile man with a strong sex drive. He wasn't cut out to live like a monk. It had been that way since she had refused to go out with him, then made love, and rejected him. She had broken his heart and turned his life inside out.

Enough with this brooding about her! He still had work to finish.

14

*H*er heart rate drummed in her ears as her high heels sank into the hall's plush carpeting outside of Darrin's office. His name was etched in bold black lettering on the frosted glass-panel. The door was partially opened. Her hands were unsteady when she knocked.

"Hi," Trenna called, "do you have a minute?"

Floor to ceiling oak shelves lined three walls of the spacious interior. Adjacent to the massive oak desk was a picture window. Twin taupe leather chairs sat front of the desk.

When Darrin looked up from the notes he was making, his pen slipped from his fingers and rolled across the surface of the desk. He didn't say anything, but his dark blue eyes moved over her curvy figure. His gaze lingered on her small features before he looked away.

He quirked a dark brow. "Get off on the wrong floor again?"

"Not this time, I'd hoped we could talk." Nervously, she smoothed the collar of her pale-pink turtleneck sweater that she'd teamed with a burgundy wool pant suit. Hoping to hide the jitters attacking her stomach, she lifted her chin. "I was getting ready to leave when I noticed your car in the lot…" Her voice trailed off.

She had to clear her throat, before she said, "You didn't answer my question. Do you have a minute?"

He nodded, as he rose to his feet, gesturing to the formal seating area where a large bronze, sectional leather sofa was positioned on a beautiful russet oriental area rug.

Trenna did her best not to notice the way his tailor-made navy suit followed the lines of his long, muscular frame or the way the top two buttons of his pale-blue silk shirt were undone. The material emphasized the width of his wide chest and his trim mid-section. A red, dark blue, and white striped tie had been flung over his suit coat, which hung on the back of his chair. He looked good.

Looking at him brought back memories of their love-making and caused her heart to pick up speed. She had tried, but nothing stopped her from thinking about him, caring about him, and wanting him. The longing was essential, as natural as her next breath.

A muscle jumped in his cheek as if he were gritting his teeth, but his voice was even when he asked, "Care for something to drink?" He indicated the single-serve coffeemaker. "There's gourmet coffee, tea, hot chocolate, hot cider, and bottled water. What would you like?"

"Nothing." Because her legs were shaking, Trenna sat down. "Very nice. Your mother does excellent job of decorating."

"Thanks." He seemed surprised that she remembered.

Hoping to fill the tense silence, she asked, "Did she decorate your brother's office as well?"

"Yes and our lobby." Frowning, he got straight to the point. "Trenna, why are you here? The last time we spoke you couldn't get rid of me fast enough. Something change?"

"You're still angry."

"I'm confused. You're here but you won't look me in the eye. And you haven't answered my question. What changed?"

She looked at him when she said, "Me. I owe you an apology."

Darrin arched an eyebrow, but didn't comment. Instead he got up and crossed to the bookshelf that held a liquor tray. He reached for two squat crystal tumblers and poured. He held a glass out to her.

"No thanks. Darrin, I'm not sure I even thanked you for introducing me to your friends, the—"

He interrupted, "I don't know what game you're playing but I don't find it amusing."

"I'm not playing at anything." She insisted, "I'm trying to apologize."

"For what?" He put the glass down without taking a sip. "Inviting me into your bed? Or kicking me out after you came?" He shrugged broad showers, "We had sex. It's over and best forgotten."

Shocked by his candor, she repeated, "Forgotten?" It was a struggle to control her emotions. Reluctantly, she admitted, "I've tried to pretend nothing happened, but it hasn't worked." Unable to remain still, she jumped up and began to move restlessly around the room. She stood in front of the window staring out at the city lights before she said, "I came here tonight hoping we could talk, that I could make you understand.

"What happened between us was totally unexpected. I didn't have time to process it, make sense of it. It was easier to put the blame for it on you rather than where it belonged...on me. I felt guilty because I let things go too far."

She didn't turn around, but took a breath before confessing, "It was a shock to me because until that night I had only been with one man...my husband. I wasn't prepared and was quickly overwhelmed. After..." Trenna stopped, unable to find the right words.

"After..." Darrin prompted.

She sighed, "Afterwards, I was very upset," she forced herself to say. "I honestly didn't know how I felt and that scared me. You were never the problem, I was. I should have told you about

Martin instead of asking you to leave. I'm sorry I handled things poorly."

Frowning, he said, "Pretty speech. I might have believed it, if you made eye contact, but you never looked at me. It's over and I'd rather forget that night ever happened." He glanced at his watch. "I was on my way out."

Although hurt by his cool demeanor, she slowly turned to face him. "What's the hurry? Do you have a date?"

"Why ask? Trenna, you were clear when you said you don't care what I do or who I see, as long as it's not you."

"That's not true!"

"Since when? How many times have you accused me of being a player? I believe you said a no-good womanizer. And you say you're not playing games?" He paused, running a hand over his close-cut natural before he reluctantly admitted, "No, I don't have a date." He chuckled, "If I didn't know better, I'd think you were jealous."

"It's not funny!"

"As long as I'm not sleeping with you, you don't care."

"If I didn't have feelings for you, I wouldn't have slept with you."

His entire body tensed from fury. "You threw me out of your house! Now you're telling me you care?" He scoffed, "Get real, Trenna! How many times have I asked you out? Too many to count. Every single time you told me you weren't interested. Seems to me, you should be celebrating that I finally got the message and have left you alone." "Just like that"—he snapped his fingers—"problem solved."

"Darrin, I said I was sorry! I never suspected that you might—"

"Suspected what?" he interrupted. "That you might hurt me? That I might actually have feelings for you? Not that it still matters, since we both know it's over. You can relax, I won't bother you again."

Trenna stared at him, feeling as if her heart was breaking.

Darrin was the first to break the silence. "But there was only one thing left to clear up. Since the storm, we've managed to avoid each other. Yet, tonight you show up here acting as if I don't know what's really going on. I know, Trenna."

"Know what?" she said calmly, but her hands were clenched so tightly her nails bit painfully into her palms.

"But what I don't understand was why? Why did you do it? First you invite me into your home and then you ask me to stay. You let me kiss you, touch you, and hold you. Why did you make me believe I had a chance with you when I never had a hope or a prayer?" He growled impatiently, "But then how could I when there was another man in your life? Why couldn't you just have been honest with me?"

"I never lied to you!"

Ignoring the comment, he glanced at his watch. Then he said impatiently, "It's late and I've had about as much of this game of yours as I can take."

Trenna watched as he grabbed his suit jacket from the back of his chair and pulled it on. He tossed in his laptop, along with legal pad and files into his briefcase then slammed it closed. He straightened with the briefcase in hard.

Stunned by the accusations, Trenna was unaware that Darrin was ready to leave.

"After you," he motioned for her to proceed.

She blinked, then shook her head. "No, I'm not leaving until we've finished. I don't know where you get the idea that there's someone else. Darrin, I'm not the one who sleeps around. And since we're being frank, why not admit to being involved with more than half the women in this building at one time or another? Even some of married ones have chased after you."

"Really? Have you ever seen me out socially with any of the women in this building?" Darrin didn't give her a chance to respond. After dropping his briefcase on the desk, he kept coming until he stood directly in front of her. His large frame towered

BETTE FORD

over hers as he glared at her. "Have you? The correct answer
would be no! The correct word would be celibate. I haven't been
with anyone in a very long time. I've been attracted to you from
day one.

"You may not have noticed, but my friends and family
certainly have. I was coping until the night you came by the house
after my Dad passed. Since then, the wanting has intensified. I feel
like an idiot admitting that I've been celibate. The instant I saw
you, I knew you were the one I'd been waiting for...the only one
for me."

She confessed, "I had no idea—"

He interrupted, "My mistake was falling in love with a woman,
who's in love with a dead man!"

Her eyes went wide and she began to shake as she wondered if
she heard correctly. Had he said he loved her? Loved her? A
sudden rush of elation came with the crushing weight of anguish
and slammed into her with dual forces. No way! He couldn't claim
to be in love with her, and then in the very next breath accuse her
of still being in love with Martin!

Instead of screaming at him, she said quietly, "You're wrong.
I'm not in love with Martin." Trenna swallowed down her keen
disappointment. "My life with Martin's over."

When she moved to Detroit, she had permanently left her
troubled past and painful marriage behind her. Determined to
make a fresh start and a new life for herself, she had succeeded
beyond her wildest dreams. She had worked tirelessly to make her
nursery school into something she could be proud of. Her home
was hers alone. She had bought and decorated it to suit her taste.
In the years she'd been on her own, she had become independent
and confident.

Never again would she repeat the mistakes of getting involved
with a controlling man. It had been her experience that lawyers in
particular had that tendency. She had wasted enough years trying
to please a man. When she started to date she felt safe going out

with male friends. She was working hard plus having fun. It had taken a few years, but she felt as if her life was back on track.

When she met Darrin, the attraction was strong and immediate, so much that it unnerved her. He was too much, too male, too good-looking, and too self-assured. Alarmed, Trenna had run in the opposite direction. She didn't want to get involved with him; she wasn't interested in a relationship and had no intensions of ever remarrying. Once was enough. She needed no reminders of past mistakes or her inadequacy.

Strong, confident, and intense, Darrin, in her estimation, had the qualities that were synonymous with controlling and demanding. Determined to protect herself, she had done an excellent job of keeping her distance.

Unfortunately for her, Darrin refused to accept no for an answer. Giving up was not part of his personality. Over time she had come to secretly admire him. Unlike Martin, Darrin was not insecure. Strong and confident in his own right, he didn't need to belittle her to make himself feel like a man.

She struggled to understand why when she was with him she felt incredibly feminine, almost beautiful. The night of the storm when he took her in his arms, her defenses had shattered. The instant he kissed her she stopped thinking. Mesmerized, she quickly learned he didn't make love with the same determination and expertise he exhibited in the courtroom. His focus was on her. Because he had been such an incredible lover, all her defenses had crumbled, tumbling like a tower of toy blocks.

After weeks trying, she could not stop thinking him. She couldn't forget that night and what they shared. Nor could she overlook what she might have seen in his eyes. She needed to know what it was. Had she hurt him when she asked him to leave? She couldn't explain: not without going into her horrible past failures.

She came tonight to apologize, and it had backfired. He was too angry to listen. She had never seen him this way, so closed off, unapproachable. Yet, despite the anger she was not afraid of him. He didn't frighten her. Even if he had not said it, deep down she knew he cared about her...just as she cared about him.

Yes, Darrin had said the three most highly coveted words on Earth. The question was if he meant them. And why had he said them? Trenna's heart ached because there was no doubt in her mind that the only man who had ever said those words to her and had meant them was her father.

She sighed, having no idea how to handle this. Love? Her heart had nearly stopped when he said it. Unable to come up with response she'd stared at him like a heart-sick fool. Was this some kind of mind game? He sounded angry, resentful.

With her hands curled into smell fists at her side, Trenna knew how frightening it was to be in love. The intensity and vulnerability was unbearable painful, especially if it was one-sided. Love had never worked for her. And judging by the look on his face it wasn't doing much for him either.

The instant he said L-word the atmosphere in the room changed. Just because the secret part of her had longed to be loved didn't make it true. Unfortunately, she had learned the hard way that to be in love and be loved in return was nothing more than a girlhood fairytale. She was a grownup and had left that romantic fantasy behind. Thank goodness, her common sense prevailed. Her eyes nearly filled as she accepted that whatever she and Darrin might have had was over...before it had ever really begun.

Trenna said firmly, "No, Darrin." She was practically wringing her hands in frustration when she added, "I am not in love with my late husband. What I felt for him has been over for a very long time."

"I'm not wrong!" Darrin snapped. "Trenna, give me some credit. I've been reading body language for years. Any good attorney will tell you it's essential, in order to tell if a client or witness has been lying. It's not over for you."

"No!" It was all she could do not to stomp her feet in frustration.

"Then tell me why you said 'with Martin'? Why won't you admit you were comparing us?"

"How many times must…"

"Trenna, I was there. I saw your face."

"That's crazy! He's gone. Believe me, I'm not likely to forget that since I was behind the wheel when the car slid on the icy road and crashed. I made the funeral arrangements. And I was the one who had to listen to his daughters accuse me of deliberately killing their father. Do you honestly think I could forget any of that when I was responsible?"

Darrin frowned, "We're talking about two different things. We both know that accident wasn't your fault. Martin was the one who insisted on traveling late at night on an icy road. And he was the one who refused to wear a seatbelt. You did your best in unfortunate circumstances."

Trenna whispered, "Yes, but I will always feel responsible. But, Darrin, that doesn't mean I'm still in love with him." She didn't add she thought she knew what love was until she met him. Since that night she has been an emotional mess.

"I know what I saw. There was shock in your eyes, maybe even confusion after we finished. You looked as if you couldn't believe you were with me and not him. Then you said 'with Martin.' We both knew you were comparing the two of us and I was the one who didn't measure up. Can you imagine how I felt?"

Close to tears, she shook her head vehemently. "I'm sorry! It just came out! You two are nothing alike!"

How could she explain about Martin? Their relationship had been complicated. He had to be in control. And he was fond of showing her off like a trophy. He actually enjoyed having a much younger wife, one who was totally dependent on him. She wanted a career and a child. He said no. When she realized he was not going to change, instead of constantly fighting, she chose to concentrate on finishing her schooling and being active in her church.

After several years of doing things his way, including giving into his sexual demands, she realized she had changed. She wasn't the same young girl he'd married. What she thought of as love was gone. She resented him for his need to always be in control. She had matured and was ready to make her own decisions. She wanted to use her education and her family's wealth for good. Disillusioned about love and marriage, she finally stood up for herself. Unfortunately for her, Martin's rude and crude comments escalated into full scale verbal abuse.

"Trenna, talk to me. I'm struggling here to understand. You said..."

"I know what I said! I wish you would just drop it! Why can't you see our night together was never about my late husband? I don't enjoy talking about my past. I've moved on..."

"Moved on?" He quirked a brow as if he had serious doubts. "If that's true, then you shouldn't have a problem telling me what went wrong between us. We had a nice dinner. We talked, we kissed. When I put on my coat to leave you invited me to stay. We went up to your bedroom, we kissed, we got undressed and then we made love. Until then, I was under the impression that you were enjoying being with me as much as I was being with you. Then you said his name.

"Suddenly, you went cold. You couldn't get me out of your place fast enough. From my viewpoint, no man can ever measure up to that lofty pedestal you've hoisted old Martin up on!" He didn't give her chance to respond. "Trenna, since you're not going to be honest with me, at least be honest with yourself. Admit it! You're still in love with your late husband."

"No, Darrin! How many times do I have to tell you this wasn't about—"

Frustrated, he interrupted, "The truth. That's all I want!" He ran an impatient hand over his dark, wavy hair. "You refused to see my side of it. Did you ever stop and think how it made me feel, knowing the entire time I was inside of you, doing my best to pleasure you that you were thinking about him? Did you?"

"It was never like that!"

Until that night she hadn't known true intimacy. All she'd ever had with Martin was sex. And she hated it! Darrin had changed all that. With him, she had felt cherished, had experienced tenderness. He had quickly replaced all her preconceived notions about what happened between two people who cared about each other.

In his arms, for the first time in her adult life, Trenna felt as if she was special. He made her feel as if she was finally where she belonged. How quickly she lost control. Maybe if he hadn't been so gorgeous, so darn sexy she would have been able to resist him? After those incredible kisses, instead of resisting, she could barely keep her hands off him.

Darrin went on as it she hadn't spoken. "You taught me a hard lesson that night, Trenna, one that I'm not likely to ever forget." He shook his head as if to clear it. "I can't deny I was needy. I wanted you so badly that I convinced myself that you were with me, all the way." Then, he said with a scowl, "I'm fortunate that you didn't call me by his name when you climaxed."

She gasped, "How can you say that? I care about you!"

"Really?" His voice vibrated with bitterness. "Man, I thought it was bad when you insisted I leave after what we had just shared. Now you are suddenly claiming to have feelings for me? What's next?"

"It's true!" Close to tears, she said, "Why are you making this so difficult?"

"Because it doesn't add up! Trenna, you were warm and responsive in bed, open to me and what we shared. Everything was good...really good between us...until you climaxed. Afterwards, I don't know what changed, but something sure did. What was it?"

"It doesn't matter." Trenna's heart began to pound with dread.

"It does to me. You acted as if you felt guilty about finding pleasure with me instead of him."

The deep hurt in his midnight blue eyes was unmistakable. Troubled, she took a step toward him, but Darrin held up a hand as if to ward for her off. Crushed, she couldn't hold back the tears that slipped past her lashes and ran down her cheeks.

Hands clenched, she insisted, "I don't feel guilty about Martin. He's gone. Yes, it was the first time for me since he passed. But this is not about him!"

"If that's true, then, why are you crying?"

"If…" She tried but failed to collect the moisture with her fingers.

"Here," he pulled the handkerchief from his lapel pocket and gave it to her.

"I can't, it's silk."

"Use it, damn it!"

"Don't swear at me!" Trenna bristled, blotting her cheeks. "Are you done telling me how I feel? Or are you going to shut up and listen to me?" As if suddenly recalling the lady-like manners her mother had drills into her, she tacked on, "…Please."

Nodding, he folded his arms over his chest.

She took a deep breath. "Let's back up. I'm not denying that I've made plenty of mistakes. I overreacted when you took the Todd Marks case. I apologize for blaming you. I was upset and treated you as if you did something wrong when you were only doing your job. Only recently, I had dinner with Grace Brooks and found out from her that you have been right all along about Todd Marks. He didn't rape her."

"Say what?"

"You heard correctly. She honestly believed it was him. She started having nightmares, reliving the rape. In one of the dreams she saw his face clearly. It was not Todd Marks. She was horrified that she'd been wrong and the harm it has caused."

"Frequently, eyewitness testimony has been proven to be incorrect," he said matter-of-factly.

"You're awfully calm."

"If Todd Marks had gone to jail I'd feel differently."

"I'm sorry that..."

"We've both made mistakes, Trenna."

"What do you mean?"

"Judging by your respond to making love, you weren't ready. Maybe it was because it was the first time for you since Martin? Or maybe it was the grief? I don't know. But clearly, I rushed you into it. Losing my father has made me realized that grief can not only be painful, but debilitating. We don't all grieve the same way. No one can predict how they might be affected by loss. "

"That's true, partly. Naturally, after losing my parents, I was devastated. I felt so alone. I had no idea how to move on with my life." She paused before she said, "Martin was a friend of our family and became my legal guardian after I lost my folks. I will always be grateful that Martin was there for me when I needed him the most. He helped me get past the worst of it. When we married I thought I was in love, but I was wrong. Toward the end, I had no choice but to accept what Martin and I had wasn't love.

"And then I met you. Darrin, I didn't know what to think. I tried but couldn't control my response to you. I did my best to ignore it and avoid you. On the night of the storm I couldn't say no. You shocked me tonight when you told me how you felt about me. It forced me into acknowledging the feelings I have for you."

Darrin cupped her shoulders, so quickly she would have fallen if he hadn't been holding her. "You aren't in love with Martin?"

"No! I believed I loved him when we married. But I've never..."

"Never what?"

"Never felt for him what I feel for you. I love you," she confessed, breathing deeply.

He stared into her eyes. "Are you're sure you're not..."

"I'm positive—"

Before she could finish his mouth covered hers. Shivers raced along her nerve endings as he gave her one of the slow, drugging sweet kisses she adored. Her entire body sizzled like a cold pat of butter in a searing hot skillet. Desire inflamed her senses.

When he lifted his head, he said, "But when we were together you said..."

"I know..." She stopped abruptly, biting her bottom lip. When she felt his lips brush her forehead she found the courage to look up and press her mouth against his. "I love you. Let me finish. It's important that you understand."

The heat in his gaze told her she had his undivided attention. Darrin nodded. "Okay, but remember, I love you, too. Go ahead. I'm listening."

Overcome by tender emotions, Trenna nodded and blinked to clear the tears clouding her vision. All this time, she'd been too afraid to hope for his love. His confession had floored her, but she could not make herself believe he meant it. Once she had seen the truth in his eyes her heart pounded with a combination of relief, joy, and fear with the force of dozen steel drums.

"I hated the way things were between us. Tonight when I saw your car in the lot I had to come, even though I was afraid to face you."

"I'm glad you came." His smile was tender, his kiss even more so. "I adore you." His eyes were suspiciously moist. "Go ahead. Say what you need to say."

Although nervous, she told herself the worst was behind her. It was important that he understood...all of it. "I married the day I graduated from college. It wasn't until afterwards that I realized I had married for the wrong reasons." She sighed, "I'm sorry... I'm going too fast.

"I was barely eighteen, had just graduated from high school when the boating accident happened. Being an only child of only children made losing them really difficult. My parents trusted Martin, had arranged for him to be my guardian if something ever happened to them. I was so thankful he made the funeral arrangements. He was there for me during the service and I came to depend on him.

"He managed my trust fund, took care of my tuition and all my expenses. He also took over the managing of my parents' businesses. In addition to his law practice, he was raising his twin daughters alone, after losing his first wife to cancer. "

Darrin asked, "How old were you when you became involved with him romantically?"

"I was twenty, in my second year of college, the first time Martin asked me to marry him. I was shocked and quickly refused. You see, I was just getting over the loss enough to start dating. I wanted to be like everyone else on campus; I wanted to have fun. Martin was furious with me, so much that he stopped taking my calls. I was devastated. It felt as if I had lost the only family member I had left."

"How old was he?"

"Forty-two when we wed. Please, let me finish."

"Go ahead."

She said, "I was so upset that I flew home during the break to talk to him. That was when I realized he had romantic feelings for me. He was jealous of the guys I was dating on campus." Trenna shrugged. "I suppose I was flattered, but also torn. I never thought of him that way. I got to know him since I lost my folks and thought of him as family. I was so unsure of myself and him. I knew I loved him, but marriage? I went back to college with a heavy heart. I didn't know what to do.

"When I told Maureen she was against me marrying him. She believed he was too old for me, and that he was trying to rush me into a decision I wasn't ready for. After several weeks without hearing from him, I was crushed. I caved in and agreed to marry him. We got engaged, but I insisted on waiting until after my graduation."

"And after the wedding were you happy?"

Trenna nodded. "I thought so. It was a huge adjustment for me. I wanted to be a good wife to Martin and to be good to his girls. But the twins were only a few years younger than I was. They resented me, believed I wanted to take their mother's place. So I concentrated on making him happy."

"You were young. I imagine it was a big chance. Were you involved in your family business?"

"No. Martin handled the businesses and since they were thriving I didn't interfere. I wanted to teach but he wanted me to be a full-time wife. To compromise, I went to grad school to work on my master's and then doctorate.

"Like all couples, Martin and I had our problems." Trenna took a breath before she confessed, "I never told anyone, not even Maureen, that I wasn't very good at sex. I didn't enjoy it and avoided it whenever possible. He was so frustrated with my lack of response that he turned to porn. He insisted I watch those films with him."

"And how did you feel about it?"

"I hated it. It wasn't about love! Or even me! As time went on Martin needed more and more graphic pornography to become aroused, claiming I wasn't enough. Things were so bad between us that I refused to watch and avoided having sex. Even though he was furious, I didn't back down."

"So brave." Tenderly, Darrin brushed his lips over her forehead.

Trenna sighed in relief, grateful to finally have the truth out in the open. She lifted her face and pressed her lips against his, needing his love and support. He encircled her waist, holding her close.

"Do you see that I never consciously compared the two of you? It was never a competition, because if it was then he'd lose hands down. I'm in love with you, Darrin... Only you."

15

'*S*he loves me!' Darrin silently repeated to himself. His heart raced. He felt as if he had just won some mega sweepstakes and all his dreams had finally come true. He was in shock! He had not seen this coming. He didn't have a clue her marriage had been a nightmare or that she had suffered because of it. No, he wasn't proud that he'd been so jealous of a dead man. Most of all, he was deeply touched by her candor.

"Thank you for telling me. That had to be hard for you. You don't have to say more. I'm beginning to understand." For years he'd assumed her marriage had been a happy one. He'd been wrong.

Trenna shook her head. "But I need to tell you…all of it."

Although he didn't enjoy seeing her hurting, he nodded. "Go ahead."

"On the night of the accident, we had gone to a formal affair at a local hotel. I begged to stay at the hotel because the weather was so bad, but Martin refused. He was already angry with me because I'd moved out of our bedroom at home. We hadn't had sex in months. So he wouldn't listen to me." She sighed heavily. "You know about the accident and that I was behind the wheel."

Darrin was content to just hold her. "Yes, and I'm so sorry, sweetheart. You didn't ask for any of this. You never let on that your marriage had been troubled. Nor did Maureen."

"She doesn't know," Trenna confessed. "I tried, but I couldn't talk about it. It was too painful and I'm ashamed that I had ignored her warnings. Maureen tried to stop me from marrying Martin, but I wouldn't listen. And then it all blew up in my face. She'd been right."

"Thank you for being straight with me. But, my love, you've done nothing to be ashamed of. None of it was your fault." He gave her a gentle squeeze. "Trenna, you were young and inexperienced. All these years, I'm amazed that you were able to cope with this on your own."

"It hasn't been easy," she admitted, and then confessed, "It's important to me that you understand I didn't confuse you and Martin. How could I? The two of you are not alike. While you're strong and confident, Martin was the exact opposite. He liked to boast and was fond of showing me off to his friends like was a trophy. He enjoyed having a much younger wife. He wanted me to be totally dependent on him."

She sighed heavily. "He did everything he could to keep me from having a career. Everything I wanted to do turned into a battle. He tried, but he didn't control everything. He couldn't stop me from finishing my education. Thanks to my trust fund from my maternal grandmother, I had the means, plus the grades to enroll in grad school. After I started working on my master's degree there was no holding me back.

"Once I had my degree, I was fed up. For years of doing nearly everything his way, I didn't have a career. I rebelled by working toward a doctorate." She sighed heavily, "I promised myself that one day I'd have my nursery school and a career.

"But intimacy was a big problem for us. Eventually things deteriorated to where I couldn't bear his touch. I felt as if what we shared wasn't about us. By then what love and respect I thought I had for him had vanished. I could not contain my resentment toward him or take his need to control me any longer. I came from a line of strong independent women. Both my mother and grandmother were business women."

"What about your inheritance from your parents?"

"The way the will was set up Martin controlled nearly everything except my trust fund. It became important to me that he understand I was no longer a young girl. I needed to make my own decisions and my own mistakes. I was tired of dreaming about owning a nursery school. Martin said no. He was determined to keep things the way they were when we first married. He enjoyed being in control of the boutiques around the country, the factory and me.

"It was important to me that I use my education and wealth for good. Because I was upset, and frustrate I refused to back down. We had a huge fight and I stood up to him. That was the first time I refused to have sex with him. He was livid! He had a vicious tongue and was not above being mean or cruel to get his way. His favorite pastime was belittling or insulting me.

"When I complained about his temper, he claimed it was my fault. He insisted that my refusal to sleep with him caused his temper to flair. He warned me that things wouldn't get better until I start acting like a real wife."

Clearly outraged, Darrin snarled, "Was he physically abusive? Did he ever hurt you?"

She shook her head. "No, he never hit me. He was just verbally." Then she added, "But I quickly learned that verbal abuse can be just as painful and destructive. I always believed that marriage was forever. There was no such thing as divorce in my family. And I refused to be the first. I had to keep reminding myself how fortunate I was to have grown up in the home of two loving parents who were in love. They didn't always agree. Sometimes, they argued but there was never any doubt they didn't adore each other and me. They raised me to believe in love and marriage."

Darrin nodded. "I get it. That's the way it was with my folks also."

She reluctantly admitted, "The love was gone. And I was barely holding on by a thread the night of the ice storm. I had begged him for weeks to consider marriage counseling. He flatly refused. You know what happened. After the accident, I was a mess. I couldn't get pass the guilt. It was devastating knowing I was the one behind the wheel and Martin was dead. I had resented him, but I never, ever wished him dead."

"I know. Sweetheart, you're not that kind of a person. It was a horrible accident."

Trenna sighed, "Yes. From day one Martin's twin girls resented me. After the accident they hated me. They accused me of marrying him for the insurance money, of cheating on him with other men, and deliberately causing the accident. His twins weren't interested in anything I had to say."

He kissed her forehead, "If need be I will remind you every day it was an accident."

"Thank you."

"You moved to Michigan because of Maureen, right?"

"Partly, I wanted a fresh start. Plus, I had something to prove to myself. I started the nursery school, developed the curriculum, and hired the best staff I could find. Running Little Hearts, and giving back to those in need, has been a huge blessing for me." She smiled. "It was important to me that everything I did benefited all of our students and addressed their individual needs. There were no shortcuts. It took a lot of hard work, but thanks to God, I was able to get it done. I don't mean to sound vain, but can't help being proud of myself."

Caressing her cheek, he said, "You've shown everyone that you're a strong and capable woman. No one can ever take that from you. I'm very proud of you. But what matters most to me was getting to know you." He brushed her lips with his. "You're as lovely on the inside as you're on the outside."

"Thank you," Trenna said softy. She was deeply touched by Darrin's sincerity and faith in her. She was forced to wipe the tears that slipped past her lashes. She briefly pressed her lips against his. "That means so much to me."

"Just as you mean so much to me." He cradled her face in his wide palm. Darrin said in a voice husky with emotion, "Trenna, I meant it when I said I loved you."

Her heart began to pound. "I know you said that but…"

"I mean it. I've waited years for you to realize that I care for you."

Struggling to take it all in, she said, "Years? Surely not."

"It's true. Why don't you believe me?"

She frowned. It was painful to admit, but she was determined to put it all out there. She forced herself to say, "When we were together I wasn't enough to satisfy you."

"That's not true."

"I was there."

"And so was I."

"But you didn't…" Too embarrassed to meet his gaze, she dropped her lids and said in a painful whisper, "…finish."

He stared at her as if in disbelief. And then he chuckled, his laugh turned deep and throaty.

She was crushed. It was all she could do not to wail. She hissed, "It's not funny!"

Darrin grabbed Trenna around the waist and pulled her down on the sofa. She ended up in his lap. She averted her face so his kisses missed her mouth instead landed on her cheeks.

"Sweetheart, listen to me." He lifted her chin until their gaze locked. "Beautiful, sexy and so sweet, you more than satisfied me. Don't you know that you're everything I could ever want or need in a woman? I've waited years to be with you. I was so hungry for you…in so much need that once didn't even come close to being enough for me. Your body fit mine like a satin-lined glove. You may not have been aware that I came inside of you because mine followed yours."

He suckled her bottom lip before he confessed, "Trenna, you were so incredible that it didn't take me long before I was hard and ready for more. I should have gotten rid of the old condom. But, baby, you felt so good that I couldn't make myself move." He kissed her before he teased, "Unlike you females it's impossible for man to hide his desire."

She studied his eyes. "Are you saying all this to make—?"

"To make you feel better?"

She nodded, afraid to hope. "You gave me such pleasure. And I disappointed you."

"That's not how I felt. Sweetheart, Trenna, for so long you have owned my heart. Do you remember that old song *You're All I Need to Get by*? That's how I feel about you." He moved a caressing hand down her back. "You're perfect for me in every way. I adore you. Your curves are so unbelievably soft, your skin so smooth, you made me wild for you."

Darrin placed a lingering kiss on the side of her throat. "Mmm, you're more than enough to keep me coming back night after night, week after week, month after month and year after year. But despite your beauty, it was your warmth and kindness to everyone that stole my heart."

His kisses were slow, filled with need and longing. When they came up for air she moaned with pleasure. "Baby, your lips are so soft and enticing I can't help wanting to kiss you again and again."

"Oh, Darrin," she sighed. "Whenever you kiss me, sweet man, I melt like a pat of butter on a hot griddle. From our first meeting I was attracted to you. And it scared me, so much that I fought my feelings for you. The mere thought of being vulnerable to another man was terrifying. I put up a wall to protect myself and keep you out." She sighed. "And you were the talk of the building, handsome and successful. I hated the gossip about you, the speculation about who you were dating and sleeping with. All of it gave me reason to keep a wall between us. Only you, stubborn man, *refused* to give up on me."

He shook his head. "No way, no how."

They smiled at each other.

"I couldn't figure you out, couldn't believe you wanted to help with my foundation. You introduced me to your friends, looking to invest. The most shocking was that you didn't expect anything in return. My defenses started to crumble. I honestly did not know what to think, how I felt about you. It was a struggle to keep you at a distance. It became a losing battle.

"The day of the snow storm I was preparing to spend the night at my school when you called. I couldn't believe you were willing to take me home in that blizzard. To me storms were something to avoid at all costs." She laughed, "I should have known I was in deep trouble, because despite my fear of getting involved, you managed to make me feel safe. I don't know how you did it, but I trusted you." She caressed his cheeks enjoying the feel of his hair-roughed skin.

He whispered huskily, "I like having your hands on me."

Flattered, she admitted, "I'm glad. I hadn't planned to invite you inside, but I did. It was important that I repay your kindness. Deep down, I wanted you to stay. I enjoyed spending time with you. Things were fine until you kissed me." Thrilled by the warmth in his eyes, she crooned into his ear, "I had no idea your kisses would be so dangerous, seductive. That entire evening with you was special to me. Even though, I was shocked by my response to your kisses, I didn't want you to ever stop."

"And I didn't want to stop," he said in her ear before he tongued her earlobe.

Shivers of delight raced along her spine as she said, "You don't understand. It wasn't until I was with you that I understood that Martin and I just had had sex. But what you and I had was vastly different... We made love. The difference was you. You made it special...magical for me.

"Most important, you made me feel beautiful for the first time in my life. I'd never known such tenderness, never even imagined it could be that way. When we made love, you, sweet man, made sure I was with you every step of the way." Trenna paused before she revealed, "I couldn't get over that you were more concerned about me and my needs than your own. You set out to pleasure me, and you were very successful. I lost control and came apart in your arms. That had never happened before...not ever. Goodness, you made me feel so much and so deeply that it terrified me. I was afraid of giving you power over me."

"I didn't want to control you. I wanted to love you."

"It took me a while to realize that." She dropped her lids, unable to meet his gaze, then said, "You were right. I did compare you and Martin. I couldn't help it. I was in shock. You made me feel sexy, beautiful, and cherished. I had been married for years, but never even had come close to climaxing. I wasn't exaggerating when I said I hated having sex with Martin. It hurt. And I didn't sleep around."

"But I thought..." He stopped, then said with a frown, "You were dating."

She lifted a brow. "To me dating means having fun, not having sex. They are two different things. I've been celibate for a long time. So now you can understand why I was totally unprepared for you and your special brand of lovemaking." She smoothed a hand over his shoulder and down his chest. "You, sweet man, were incredible, tender yet unbelievably sexy. It was a major turn on for me."

Darrin grinned but didn't interrupt. Perhaps he sensed how important it was for her to finish, to get it all out, and to put the past behind her?

Locking her arms around his neck, she moved until they were

chest-to-chest. She pressed her lips against his cheek, his chin, then lingered in the hollow of his throat.

"Being with you opened my eyes. Because of you, I discovered that certain things I believed were factual about men and women, lust and love were false, myths. After we made love I didn't know how to handle what happened between us or how it made me feel.

"When I realized that you were still aroused, I was devastated. I thought I failed, again. That I wasn't enough. For a few moments, I thought it would different. And then it wasn't. Upset and confused, I couldn't handle another failure. I was replaying in my head, all the mean things he'd said about me. I pushed you away, asked you to leave." She shook her head before saying, "Even though I cared about you, I wasn't ready to admit it, not even to myself. I was such an emotional basket case. I could not label my feelings. All I knew for sure was that my emotions were raw, new and so deep they terrified me."

"Why are you saying these things? Is this some kind of game?"

"No!" Shaking her head, she whispered, "I'm sorry it took so long for me to figure it all out." Then she revealed, "It didn't help that you were avoiding me. I hated not being able to see you or talk to you. It was horrible. I couldn't stop thinking about you. I kept remembering how you helped me when you didn't have to. I couldn't figure out why.

"Darrin, I tried and tried, but I couldn't get you out of my head. Tonight, when I saw that your car was still in the lot, I knew I had to talk to you. I came because I owed you an apology. I came even though I knew you probably would not want to see me. I don't know why, but it all came together for me."

He stared at her.

"I realized I was taking huge risk. But I had to tell you all of it. You deserved the truth and so much more. I didn't want there to be any more secrets between us. I love you, Darrin Morgan."

"Don't play with me," he growled.

"I'm not…"

He said nothing more, just stared at her. Finally, he asked, "Are you absolutely sure that..."

"That I love you?" Trenna nodded. "I'm positive."

He slowly released a deep breath before he said, "Thank you."

Before she could take her next breath, she was in his arms and he was kissing her. Slow, deep, and incredibly tender caresses that left her shaking.

She whispered against his lips those all-important words to him. "I love you, love only you. I'm so sorry that I asked you to leave."

He pressed his hand against her kiss swollen lips. "You don't owe me an apology, you owe me nothing." Then he placed a kiss in the center of each of her palms. "But you have my heart."

"And you have mine."

"Trenna...sweetheart," Darrin's voice was gruff with emotion when he repeated her name. He claimed her lips, this time taking a series of hot and hungry kisses. When they parted, they were both breathing hard.

"I feel as if I've waited forever to have you like this, warm and responsive in my arms. How could you not know that you're my world? Trenna McAdams. I love you and I need you."

Startled dark brown eyes stared into dark blue ones. The love she saw there was unmistakable. It meant everything to her. This was no dream. It was real. With her heart pounding like a steel drum, Trenna bit her bottom lip. She took a deep breath and then slowly let it out. "Darrin, I love you. I suck at relationships."

"That's because you married the wrong man. You didn't marry me."

She couldn't help smiling. "Darrin...I'm just getting used to the idea of being in love. Don't get me wrong, I'm so thankful that you, sweet man, didn't give up on me. You believed in us when I was too scared to try. We're here together, like this, because of you. Darrin, you've been so patient with me. The memory of your tenderness gave me hope. But trust doesn't come easily to me."

"Sweetheart," Darrin husked, reclaiming her lips, but the sound of the vacuum outside his office intruded. He sighed, "Let's get out of here."

"And go where?"

"It doesn't matter as long as we're together."

16

On their way to her home they stopped at a Chinese restaurant and picked up take-out. But instead of eating they cuddled on her sofa.

"Say it again," Darrin begged, his mouth caressing her kiss swollen lips.

"Love you," Trenna repeated, still tingling from the intensity of his kisses. Her head was on his shoulder. There was no doubt that this was love. She had never felt more cared about or cherished. She was happy and couldn't contain her smile.

Raining kissing down her forehead and cheeks, he said, "Good. Because I will never get tired of hearing you say it. Say it again."

Giggling, she could barely get the words out. Blushing, she said, "You're staring. Stop it!"

"I can't help myself. You're gorgeous," Darrin murmured between kisses. "…And perfect for me."

Just then her stomach grumbled and they both laughed.

"Excuse me." She glanced at the clock. "Is it eleven?"

"I'm afraid so. Let's eat."

After sharing a meal of shrimp fried rice, pepper steak, and steamed vegetables, once again they were seated side by side on the couch, their feet propped up on the padded ottoman.

With her head resting on his chest, he stroked her hair. "I'm still trying to wrap my head around us being together like this. I'd lost hope. I left that night believing you were still in love with Martin, that you wanted him and not me. I was eaten alive with jealousy after you said his name."

"Darrin, I'm sorry I hurt you. Until we were together I believed him. I believed there was something wrong with me. That it was my fault that he needed more and more stimulation to become aroused."

Squeezing his hand, she said, "Finally the blinders were off. You were the one who came out favorably, not Martin. You and I had made love. For the first time I understood the difference. I found no enjoyment with Martin. I was floored by my reaction to you and was very confused."

When she saw his wide grin she punched him arm.

He chuckled, "Hey, I didn't say a word!" Still grinning, he said, "I like being alone like this, just the two of us." He admitted, "For weeks, I kept hoping you'd change your mind, that you would realize how much you meant to me. You ordered me to stay away. I respected that, but I was miserable."

He brushed her lips with his. "Since I met you, there was no one else for me. No women had ever told me no. I thought you were grieving so I tried to honor that. The day when you got off on my floor and bumped into me, I nearly lost it. My heart pounded with excitement at the possibility that you had come to see me."

"I don't understand why you hadn't given up. It would have been so much easier on both of us if you had walked away."

"I couldn't do that. Heaven knows you gave me reasons to never look your way again. I don't know. Maybe I was just too stubborn to walk away from the woman I believed that I'd waited a lifetime to find? Trenna, I had no doubt that you were it for me. Unfortunately, I just couldn't convince you. It wasn't until weeks later that I lost hope. I was a wreck after being with you and knowing your sweetness. I could not handle you not wanting to see me or even talk to me. That was the worst for me."

"I'm sorry. I was a mess. I had all these feelings for you but I was also terrified of being hurt. Plus there were always other women. The office building was full of them."

"After meeting you, I didn't want anyone else." He kissed his way down the side of her throat to the scented hollow. He tongued the soft skin there. "No one else can satisfy the ache I have for you. Deep inside, I knew from the beginning that you were the one for me. Sweetheart, you're my love…my heart."

"How can you be sure?" she asked in an urgent whisper.

Somber, he stared into her eyes. "It started with attraction and as I got to know you it grew into respect, admiration and eventually to love. I'm very sure about my feelings for you, Trenna McAdams. You can believe, I tried so many times to convince myself to get over you. I told myself to walk away, save myself from the endless heartache. I went out with other women, hoping to get past these feelings for you. But it didn't work, nothing worked. I couldn't get you out of my head."

"I'm sorry."

"Don't be. Early on, my brother recognized the signs and knew I was a goner. Even at my lowest point, Doug kept encouraging me. Lately, he was the only one who still believed because I nearly lost hope. He understood because he had been through something similar with Megan."

Trenna smiled, "Remind me to thank your brother. I'm surprised you didn't guess that the attraction between us has always been mutual."

He chuckled. "I can appreciate the humor now. Darlin', you've done an excellent job of keeping it a secret."

She cupped his cheek. "All I knew about love was what I had with Martin." Shuddering at the painful memories, she confessed, "I couldn't put myself back in a position of vulnerability. I was terrified of losing control of my life again. So I kept coming up with reasons not to get involved with you, not to feel anything at all for you. But it never worked." He was silent for so long that she looked at him expectantly. "What?"

"I'm just trying to understand it all. How did you move past the verbal abuse? How did you find the courage to do it on your own, without counseling?"

"Courage? Hardly!" she scoffed.

He reminded, "You're strong and fiery."

Although touched by the compliments, she said, "I don't know how you can say that. I was a coward. I should have left him." She dropped her head not wanting him to see her shame. "I call that weak not strong." Wiping away a tear, she admitted, "I'm ashamed that I stayed so long, that I allowed Martin to control me, bully me and force me to look at those awful movies with him. I told him yes when I wanted to say no. It was horrible! And when I finally put my foot down, Martin was furious. He tormented me, called me names and belittled me. I took it for too long. Unfortunately, I couldn't talk about it to anyone, not even Maureen. That has been the hardest part for me, finding a way to forgive myself for staying."

Darrin put a finger under her chin, but she refused to lift her lids. He urged, "Look at me, Sweetheart. I need you to look into my eyes, to see and hear the truth in my words." He waited until she met his gaze. "You were a victim. Yet, you were strong enough to do what you thought was the right thing to do. Despite the hurt and berating you had to endure, you chose to stay and keep the vows you made. I respect you for keeping your word. I repeat you were a victim. Say it!"

"I was a victim. But…"

"Trenna, there are no buts about it."

She shrugged. "I'm still working on not blaming myself. I slip up. Having a best friend, who specializes in abuse cases at a Women's Center was been a huge bonus. Maureen helped me without realizing it. And I will be forever grateful that I was raised in the church.

"I allowed Martin to keep me from going to church. But he could not control my faith in God. That faith has helped tremendously. He could not keep me from praying or reading my Bible. I gained such strength from God's Word."

"What was the straw that pushed you to the edge?"

"Church. He had no right. I said no and meant it. I moved out of our bedroom."

Darrin hugged her.

She sighed, "I know my way of handling the abuse was unusual. I should have sought counseling or gotten a divorce but I couldn't. So I endured it. When Martin passed, all I felt was relief and so much guilt."

He kissed her cheek. "I'm glad you moved to Michigan."

"Me, too. I was able to pick up the pieces and move on with my life. I'm grateful that God took the overwhelming pain and most of the shame away. I'm not saying that I'm perfect or that my way would be best for anyone else. But it's working for me. God's gave me the courage to fight."

He kissed her forehead. "I believe God helped you persevere. Just as God helps everyone who believes. I hate to speak ill of the dead, but Martin McAdams was a class-A jerk. He didn't realize what a sweet treasure he had in you." Darrin cradled Trenna against him, her cheek rested over his heart. He surprised her when he asked, "Was the trouble in your marriage the reason you waited to have kids? I ask because you clearly love children and would make a wonderful mother."

She sighed heavily. "Martin was the reason. He said no. He already had twin girls from his first marriage and they're a few years older than I am. He had raised his kids and didn't want to be a father again."

"How did you handle that?"

"I understood. I would be lying if I didn't admit I was very disappointed. But I had no choice but to accept it. I kept busy with grad school."

"Are you saying you just gave up on ever having kids?"

She nodded.

"I'm so sorry. Everyone knows you were born to be a mother."

"Thanks, but no one gets everything they want in life. I've been blessed to have had such wonderful parents. I grew up in a home surrounded by love. Now that I have my own school, and thanks to you, am able to expand my foundation, I've accomplished all my professional dreams." She smiled up at him when she said, "Now I'm grateful to have you in my life. For so long I was alone."

"You're not alone any more. You have me. And I love you."

Before she could respond Darrin tilted her face up until he could reach her mouth. He devoured her lips as if they were coated with honey. She quivered, not expecting the sudden rush of pleasure. He tasted her, moving slowly down her throat, and when he reached the valleys between her breasts, Darrin lingered.

Trenna moaned, unable to contain her enjoyment. Her entire body felt as if it were on fire from direct rays of the sun. It wasn't long before she ached from deep inside. Her feminine center moistened, became dewy with need. Goodness, how she wanted him...wanted his hands all over her...wanted his body to be a part of hers.

That realization was unsettling. Her thoughts flew back to their last time together. Thoughts of intimacy brought back the old fears and doubts about her ability to please a man. They quickly overwhelmed her and swiftly replaced her desire for him. She needed no reminders that her history with the opposite sex was abysmal. How could this be happening to her?

Fighting back tears, she hid her face against the base of his throat. She whispered, "You have no idea how much I wish I'd met you first."

"Me, too. But we can't change the past. Now that we're together, I plan to show you every single day how much I love you. Trenna, I'm not like Martin. I have no need to dominate you or control you. I like just the way you are, strong and feisty. But most of all I want you to be happy."

Trenna smiled: there was that word again. Strong. He kept calling her strong because he believed it. He meant every word, and he meant the world to her. Darrin was such an accomplished man, confident in his manhood, and not in the least bit intimidated by her success. "Thank you."

"You are welcome."

She whispered, "You deserve better."

"How? You are the best."

She blushed. "You were always smooth-talking, charming, and too good-looking for your own good. I told myself not to believe anything that came out of your mouth."

He arched a brow. "You certainly never bothered to hide your animosity."

"Trust was beyond me." Wrapping her arms around his neck, she clung to him. "I'm so sorry, about a lot of things, especially the way I treated you. I was afraid of how you made me feel, so I kept pushing you out of my life. The past few weeks apart have been hard. What I didn't expect was to miss you so much."

She hesitated before adding, "I was miserable without you, hated the way things were between us. I didn't know how to fix things. I was shaking when I came to see you. I had no idea what I was going to say. But I had to try to make things right." She caressed his cheek before she admitted, "I've said it before but I'm truly thankful that you didn't give up on me. I'm in love with you and I pray that you won't regret tonight."

Darrin stared into her eyes, and then studied Trenna's small, rich brown features. As his gaze moved down her curvy figure, the hunger in his dark eyes was unmistakable. The way he looked at her caused her heart pick up speed, made her knees shake, and she felt as if she were the most beautiful, desirable woman on the planet.

"No regrets. And now that we know the feelings are mutual, my first inclination would be to hold on to you with both hands. For me, that means flying to Vegas and sealing the deal. Because of the way feel about you, I won't rush you into doing anything that you are not ready for. Love means I want what's best for you...always."

Overcome by emotion, her eyes filled with tears.

"Why are you crying? "

Forced to swallow a lump in her throat, she laughed. "I'm happy! And for the first time since I lost my parents, I'm my own person. I'm truly free from the past." She giggled when he gave her a tight squeeze. "It feels good knowing my heart's no longer weighed down by anger or resentment. I prayed for this day. And with God's help, I can honestly say that I've let it go and forgiven Martin."

"That's incredible! What a blessing. But I'm not surprised because God's able. He took the grief and pain of losing my father from me. There is nothing God can't do."

"I'm glad you feel they way. I've noticed for the last few weeks you have been sitting in the back of the church during service. I didn't know what it meant."

"I'm growing in my faith." He smiled. "It's our time, Trenna. From now on you and I are going to do this love thing the right way."

Puzzled, she asked, "What does that mean?"

"It means we aren't doing it my way or your way, but God's way. That's the only way we can be assured what we have will last for a lifetime." Darrin cradled her face in his palms. "I want you to be my wife. I want to marry you, Trenna McAdams."

"You're serious?"

He nodded.

Although her heart pounded with excitement, she held back. Instead of answering she quizzed, "Right way? What do you mean?"

"We've both grown up in the AME church. And we share similar beliefs and faith in God. I'd like to honor that."

"Are you saying that we're not going..." She stopped unable to get the words pass the lump in her throat.

"To make love? Oh yeah, we are." He grinned. "But not until we're man and wife."

Shock and disappointment battled with a deep sense of relief. She loved him, more than she thought it was possible. Even more surprising, she wanted to be with him.

But she also knew herself well enough to know she needed time to get used to the idea. She smiled at him and firmly pushed the doubts always. They loved and cherished each other and wanted to be together. That was all that really mattered. Trenna teased, "I haven't said yes."

"I'm aware."

She was somber when she asked, "What if I can't make you happy? Remember, my track record with marriage is not good."

"You married the wrong guy."

"I'm serious! What if I mess this up? How can I say yes? Second chances are rare in life. I don't want to disappoint either one of us."

"I know, love. And I don't expect it to be easy. Nothing worth having comes easily. I have enough faith in God and in you to believe we can make it work. The only thing I'm absolutely certain of is that I love you and that you love me. That's enough for me. The big question is, is it enough for you? We both know that all we really have is today. Only God knows the future." He squeezed her hand. "Well, is our love enough?"

There was no hesitation when Trenna said, "Yes, Darrin. I will marry you. When?"

Darrin threw his head back and laughed. When he sobered he kissed her tenderly. "Sweetheart, you decide. I will be there whether it's tomorrow, next week, next month, or next year. It is up to you."

17

$\mathcal{I}$t was Valentine's Day. That Saturday morning dawned bright and sunny, without a cloud in the winter sky. It was also cold and crisp, perfect for their wedding. Unable to sleep, Trenna was up at six.

She admired the four-carat pink fluorite engagement ring that Darrin had surprised her with on Christmas Eve. She couldn't control the tremors in her hands as she moved the ring to her right hand for the ceremony or the butterflies in her stomach. 'Just nerves,' she assured herself, 'nothing to worry about.'

"A perfect day for a wedding," Mrs. Hale echoed, hours later from an armchair in the church's lounge.

Both Maureen and her grandmother were both elegantly dressed in shades of pink. Maureen was in a pale pink, knee-length lace dress, and Mrs. Hale was in a deep rose silk suit.

Trenna peeked out the window at the long line of cars parked along the curve of the church's drive. Bells chimed as a sleek, steel-gray limousine came to a stop at the entrance.

"Oh, no you don't!" Maureen scolded as she pulled Trenna away from the window.

"I was only checking to see if the florist was back with my

bouquet. I can't believe she forgot it! What if she got the colors or the flowers wrong?"

Maureen said, "Not likely, Shanna is a pro. The sanctuary looks beautiful. Don't worry, she will be back soon."

"I hope so. I can't get married without it!" Trenna complained.

"Nonsense," Mrs. Hale laughed. "Your groom's here, that's what matters. Darrin arrived before you did. He's waiting with Douglas in Pastor's study."

Maureen, still at the window, reported, "That's Mrs. Morgan and Megan. I'm sure the florist will be here very soon." She came over and took Trenna's hands. "You're trembling."

"I'll be fine once my bouquet arrives."

"You look beautiful," Maureen gushed.

Mrs. Hale beamed, "Maureen's correct. You're a gorgeous bride."

Trenna smiled. "Thank you both." She smoothed her hand over her pale pink satin dress. Blinking away sentimental tears, she said, "I love this dress and the matching coat. Vanessa did a wonderful job. I'm so pleased with the way it turned out. My mother would have been so happy that I'm wearing one of her designs. It was so kind of Vanessa to make it for me. And Grace's bead work on the hem and cuffs are exquisite."

A sparkling pillbox hat was perched on her head with a wispy veil. In her ears, she wore her mother's pearl and diamond earrings, around her neck was the strand of pink pearls that her father had given her the day she had graduated from high school.

"Vanessa has become an incredible designer in her own right but using your mother's designs was brilliant." Maureen said.

"She was impressed by my mother's designs and interested in using some of them in her bridal boutique."

"I'm not surprised," Mrs. Hale said. "Your mother was a true artist. Her styles are elegant, classic, and have stood the test of time. She reminds me of a designer that I saw while Paris as a girl."

"Thank you." Trenna brushed away tears. Her wedding day. She sighed,

trying to ignore the way her hand shook as she smoothed the slim lines of the knee- length design.

Maureen whispered, "Trenna, tell me you're not comparing today with…"

"My first wedding?" She frowned. "Absolutely not, that's part of my past. Today is about me and Darrin. I love him with all my heart. And I can't wait to start my life with him."

Maureen hugged her. "I'm so glad you told me told me about your past. And you are right, today is just the beginning of a bright future filled with promise. I'm so happy for you and Darrin."

Trenna clung to her best friend for a long moment. "Thank you. I'm so glad that both you and Mrs. Hale are here to share this with me."

"Me too. Now, tell me why you're still shaking."

Before she could admit that she was nervous about tonight there was a knock on the door. Trenna loved Darrin so much that last thing she wanted was to disappoint him. They'd only made love once, and it ended badly. Their wedding night had to be perfect.

"Come in," Maureen called.

Shanna Carter, the florist, brought in the elaborate spray of tiny rosebuds ranging from blush pink to deep crimson. "I'm so very sorry, Ms. McAdams, that I held up your wedding. I checked and double-checked to make sure I had everything and have no idea how it was left behind."

Trenna smiled, relieved. "It's okay. Thank you, they're gorgeous. Aren't they, Maureen?"

"Yes, absolutely gorgeous."

A message was sent to the pastor. After that, things seemed to move swiftly. All too soon Maureen was arranging Trenna's veil. As she looked in the mirror, she was confident she had never looked better. Unfortunately, it didn't ease the butterflies in her stomach. She was unaware of the way she clenched the ribbon-covered stems of her bouquet.

"You're perfect." Maureen nodded, and then said to her grandmother, "Nana, will you please tell them we're coming?"

Once the friends were alone, Maureen squeezed Trenna's hand. "What is it? Are you having doubts?"

Trenna shook her head. "Nerves, that's all. Before we go I want to take a moment to thank you for your love and support. Lucky for me, you're such an excellent counselor. You helped me deal with so many lingering issues without even being aware. I'm sorry I kept it a secret."

The two hugged. Maureen said, "I do understand. Any time you need to talk I'm here for you."

Trenna smiled. "I know. But that goes both ways."

Maureen laughed. "Agreed. Now let's get you married."

When she entered the sanctuary and her eyes met Darrin's, Trenna was radiantly happy. She saw his love for her and acceptance. Instantly, her fears fled as she made her way down the aisle accompanied by Mrs. Hale.

"Did I tell you how beautiful you are?" Darrin whispered in her ear as they stood in the back of the hotel's crowded elevator. They were heading to the penthouse suite on the top floor.

Blushing, she said, "So many times I've lost count."

"Good." He grinned.

Unfortunately for her the nerves were back with a vengeance. The unease started the moment they left the banquet room where their reception was still in full swing.

Over and over, she assured herself that she was okay and that this was her 'second chance' at happiness. It didn't soothe the fears. She wasn't likely to forget that this was her last chance at love. If she messed things up tonight there would be no more chances.

She sighed, feelings woefully inadequate.

"Tired?" Darrin quizzed.

"Oh, no you don't!" she teased. "Stop trying to distract me. You're stalling. Now tell me where you're taking me on our honeymoon."

He grinned. "It's a surprise. You will find out in the morning when we get on the plane."

"Sure hope you're taking me some place warm because I packed shorts, sundresses, and bathing suits. If there's ski lifts and snow, you're going to have to buy me a whole new wardrobe!"

He chuckled. "I can't believe I will have you all to myself for three weeks." He squeezed her waist, keeping her close.

"I can't believe it either. I actually let you talk me into closing the school for that long. I will be lucky if we have any students when the break is over."

"Sweetheart, you haven't had a vacation since you opened. You're entitled to some rest and relaxation."

The elevator slowly emptied as it climbed. When it reached top floor, he leaned down to place a kiss on the side of her throat. "We should have eloped. It has been hours since I put that ring on your hand. I can't wait to make you mine, Mrs. Morgan."

Trenna shivered at the huskiness of his voice as the doors slid open. Before she could blink, Darrin swung her off her feet and up into his arms. She wrapped her arms around his neck as he moved purposefully toward the double doors at the end of the corridor.

Her nerves were on full alert by the time he unlocked the door and carried her inside. He held her close as he released her legs, allowing her to slide down his body. She took a quick step away. Since dawn she had blamed her unease on bridal jitters. The truth was staring her in the face.

She was acutely aware that she married a good man. But a very attractive man with the same needs as any other. How long before her wedding finery would be stripped away, leaving all her insecurities bare and on full display?

Even though she shared his beliefs, secretly, she had been relieved when Darrin had suggested they wait to make love. He had married her, despite knowing about her limitations. Instead of being reassured, she was afraid. She blinked away tears, alarmed by the extent of her selfishness.

She loved him so much that she'd gone ahead and married him. She convinced herself they could find happiness together. And, now that the harsh reality of what she had set into motion was staring her in the face, she was terrified that she'd made a horrible mistake.

How long before she messed up? How soon before she disappointed him? How could she have been so reckless? She shouldn't have married him knowing full well that deep inside she was the one with the problem, not him. She was the weak link. He deserved the best. He deserved to be happy.

Evidently, she hadn't been thinking. Talk about being blinded by love! Goodness, she wasn't likely to ever forget how badly their one and only night together had ended! What made her think their wedding tonight would be different? She was still the weak—

"What do you think?" Darrin asked from behind her, his hands on her small shoulders. They were in the center of a luxuriously appointed suite, thick, bronze carpet underfoot. Massive twin cream sofas faced each other. The cream and bronze patterned drapes had been left open, the cream-sheer lace curtains covered the floor-to-ceiling windows, veiling the fabulous view of Detroit's riverfront. Lights from Windsor Canada shimmered in the distance.

"How lovely." Trenna worried her bottom lip, struggling for calm. Her knees were shaking so badly that she quickly moved to the table behind the sofa. She was grateful for the support and space it put between them. Everything in the room was perfect.

Darrin was expertly tailored in a black tuxedo that fit the long, muscular lines of his body to perfection. He certainly looked at home. She was the one who was out of place.

She inhaled the sweet scent of artfully arranged wildflowers displayed in a heavy crystal vase. They were her favorites. She didn't need to read the card to know who they were from. Darrin had gone out of his way to make this day special for her.

"Flowers, too? I don't know if I can take another surprise. I nearly fainted during the ceremony when you placed that pink fluorite infinity wedding band on my hand. I've never seen anything so beautiful." She couldn't help gushing. "Sweet man, you're spoiling me."

"It's called loving you." Darrin turned her but he didn't kiss or take her into his arms, but looked into her eyes. "What's wrong, love?"

"Noth—" she stopped abruptly. What was she doing? She'd nearly told a lie to the man she loved with her whole heart. He was her husband. But she didn't want to think about, let alone talk about her insecurities. Not now...not yet. This fear wasn't welcome—it was an intrusion into what was supposed to be their special day.

The fear had been there all day but eased the moment her eyes met his in the church. His love had gotten her down the aisle. Since leaving the reception the fear felt as if had formed into a tight knot and settled in her stomach. Refusing to give into tears, she said, "I-I-I..." She stopped, unable to find the right words.

Cupping her face, Darrin brushed his lips over her forehead, her cheeks. "Whatever it is, we can work it out...together."

She watched him remove his jacket and toss it over an armchair. He slid her coat off her shoulders, unpinned her hat and placed both on the same chair Then taking her hand, he led her around to the sofa and pulled his bride down beside him. He kneaded the muscled in her neck and then her shoulders, until she was limp with relief. She had no idea when it happened but she was in his lap, her cheek on his chest.

She placed a kiss in the center of his palm "You have the most incredible hands, strong and capable."

"Thank you. Did I happen to mention how beautiful you…"

She laughed.

"If you can still laugh it can't be so bad."

"You're right, I know you're right. But it's just that…" Trenna hesitated. Unable to meet his gaze, she stared at pink gel-coated nails. "I'm sorry, so sorry. Tonight was supposed to be perfect and I'm ruining it."

"You haven't ruined anything." He kissed her nose, her cheek, before he kissed her lips tenderly. "Lean back, Trenna. Now take slow, deep breaths. That's right."

She nodded, kicking her heels off.

After several minutes, he asked, "Better?"

"Yes, thank you."

"Don't stop. Slow, deep breaths."

Eyes closed, she rested against him with her head on his shoulder and concentrated on her breathing. Gradually, she was able to relax and savor Darrin's warmth while enjoying his scent and their closeness.

"This is what I needed…time alone with you. I love you, Darrin Morgan."

"And I love you, Trenna Morgan." He cradled her against him, and held her hands in his. "Okay?" When she nodded, he said smiled. "Good. Are you ready to talk about it?"

"Yes, the wedding and reception were perfect. I was nervous when I got up this morning. I told myself it was bridal jitters. Everything went exactly as planned. But in the elevator on our way up here I started to panic. I felt selfish for marrying you. As if I took advantage of you. And when we got here, everything in the suite seemed perfect, including you. I was the one who didn't belong here with you." Trenna impatiently wiped away a trickle of tears.

"If everything today seemed perfect, then I'm glad because it's the way you planned it, sweetheart. All I cared about was marrying you and making you happy. We could have eloped and that would have been fine with me. I've got what's important to me... You. I wanted to be your husband."

Watching her closely, Darrin asked with a troubled frown, "Don't belong? Trenna Morgan, which part of 'I love you' didn't you get? You're my heart, my life, my blessing from God. And I thank Him every day for you."

He sighed heavily. "I really thought we had dealt with the trust issue and put it behind us for good. Evidently, I was wrong. When we got into the elevator I sensed something was on your mind but it wasn't until we reached the suite I could see that you were upset." The light and laughter had gone from his eyes when he said, "Finally, we're together and alone, but you still haven't told me what's wrong. Trenna, I want a marriage where we can tell each other everything and anything...where there are no secrets."

Alarmed by the hurt she saw in his eyes, her eyes were instantly flooded by tears that trickled onto her cheeks. It was her fault. She had married him and then let her fears get the best of her. Filled with shame, her natural instinct was to hide her insecurities, but she couldn't. She didn't want hide anything from him. She wanted what he wanted... no secrets only truth, trust and love. He deserved her complete honesty.

"I'm sorry." Lifting her hand to cup his cheek, she kissed his chin and then pressed her lips against his. "I trust you. Darrin, you have to believe that. You aren't the problem. It's me. I'm scared." She sighed. "This isn't easy for me. This is my last chance and I don't want to mess it up."

"What are you more afraid of? Being married to me? Or having to sleep with me because I might be like Mar—"

"No! You are not like him!" Trenna interrupted. "We've settled that. How can you think even for one minute that I might still be comparing—?"

"Then what?" Darrin quizzed as he ran a hand over his close-cut natural. "It's not that we haven't done the deed?."

"Me. I'm the problem. We've kissed, caressed, but we haven't made love, not since the night of the storm. I tried but I can't forget how badly it ended." She closed her eyes and took a deep breath, then admitted, "I have been on a rollercoaster of euphoria since you told me you loved me and proposed. It lasted until this morning. I decided it was bridal jitters and then the ceremony was delayed, which didn't help. But I was holding it together until we left the reception, that's when the fears resurfaced and seemed to mushroom."

"Trenna, we agreed to wait."

"I know. I realize the waiting has been especially hard for you. But today…" She frowned, "I can't turn off my thoughts or forget how upset I was upset that night. Or that you left, angry and disappointed. What if history repeats itself? Like you, I want our marriage to work. Tonight is our wedding night. What if I disappoint you again?"

"Not possible. The only way you can disappointment me, Trenna Morgan, would be if you stopped loving me." Again and again, he brushed her lips with his each pass slower than the one before. "If we had gone ahead, and made love, then you would know how good it's going to be between us. Because of our faith, we chose to do what was right for us and honor God. Putting God first has never been easy. Believe me, it has been torture, not being able to make you mine. Today, finally, you're my wife. Never forget that I love you, Trenna Morgan, with my whole heart and body."

She sighed with relief as her heart rate picked up speed. "Sweet man, you know I feel the same way about you. You're my husband, my heart. I can't explain how important it is for me to please you. I want to please you."

He smiled. "You have nothing to be afraid of. I'll make you a promise. I will never ask anything of you sexually that you aren't comfortable with. To prove it, I'll tell you exactly what I've fantasized about tonight."

Trenna's eyes went wide. "Fantasized?"

"Oh yeah," he drawled, "Detailed fantasies about making love to you, sweetheart."

Curiosity got the better of her, and she blurted out, "Tell me!"

He quirked a brow, his eyes twinkled like a deep blue flame. His voice was husky when he said, "There's an old Otis Redding song that sums up how I feel. *These Arms of Mine.*" Darrin started by humming the melody and then he sang in a deep, sexy baritone, as they swayed to together.

Trenna released a long sigh. Her entire body trembled when she gushed, "Oh my, that was amazing." Cupping, his face she kissed his jaw, his cheek and then lingered on his firm lips. She said in a whisper, "That was wonderful. Thank you, sweet, sweet man."

He dropped his head, licked her lips before pulling back. When she leaned forward he opened to her, allowing her access to his mouth. Unable to resist, she eagerly took what was offered. She shivered, as they shared a lengthy but tender exchange.

She was tingling all over when she said, "Tell me about this fantasy, and don't leave out a single detail."

He laughed so hard that it was a few moments before he sobered enough to say, "You already know that I think you're incredibly sexy." He paused, his gaze locked with hers. His voice dropped to an even richer baritone when he said, "I only have to look at you to want to be a part of you. I've had a lot of time to think about making love to you. In my fantasy, you are not in a wedding dress."

18

"No?"

He shook his head. "You're wearing nothing except for one of my dress shirts and a pair of those very high heels you prefer. I get hard every time I think about loving you that way."

"No lace or see-through nightgown?" she teased.

"Nope."

"Is there more?" she prompted.

"Oh, yeah." He grinned. "I envision slowly opening the shirt while kissing you, starting at your neck baring more and more of your beautiful brown skin. Then I lick every sweet inch...until you are screaming my name. But it doesn't stop there. I imagine that you're wet, ready for me. Since it's my fantasy, I have super control and I wait until you beg me to come deep inside. Once I'm there you tighten around me, urging me to hurry. But it's a slow burn."

"Slow burn?"

Darrin nodded. "So slow that we won't stop until we're both burning with need."

Her eyes went wide when she said, "But..."

"No but's sweetheart. We love each other. It will be any way you want me, babe, quick and hard, or easy and slow. And there's nothing to keep us apart. Trenna, you have no idea how badly I want you, baby. Or how hard it has been to wait to make love to you. Watching you walk down aisle, all I could think about was how much you mean to me, how much I love you," Darrin said in a rough whisper, then asked, "Have I shocked you?"

Trenna whispered, "No," and she meant it. "Darrin, I love you so much." Her heart was full and raced with excitement. She wanted everything he wanted, but before she could formulate the words he rose from the sofa with her in his arms. He carried her as if she weighed next to nothing.

"I can walk."

"Why bother? Remember, we took vows this morning. It's my job to keep a smile on your pretty face and your job to do the same for me." He kissed her brows, the tip of her nose, her small chin, before he focused on the sensitive spot below her ear. When she shivered, he chuckled, "My beautiful bride, my love. When-ever you're in need of some loving, I say bring it on."

When he had placed her on the side of the bed she saw the love in his dark blue gaze. She also saw complete and total acceptance. Suddenly overcome with emotion, she didn't speak... She couldn't. Her heart was full, brimming with the most incredible love. It was like a dream come true, and she welcomed it with profound gratitude.

It seemed fitting that tonight, their wedding night, she was finally able to accept her personal truth. For the first time in her life she felt truly loved, despite her faults. Darrin was the man she had been waiting all these years for, her heart, her husband...her one true love.

And now that they were finally together that knowledge chased away any lingering fears or doubts. Those fears didn't belong to her anymore and served no more purpose than snowflakes in sunlight on a warm spring day.

Darrin slowly undressed her and then quickly himself, her heart began to pound. When she saw the awe on his face, she didn't waste another thought on her imperfections.

"Trenna…" he husked.

Her breath caught in her throat when he knelt on the floor in front of her. She felt no embarrassment when he looked at her, for he gazed at her as if she was a rare, priceless jewel.

His voice was deep, thick with need, when he lifted her left hand to kiss her soft palm and then her wedding ring. "When I put this on your hand I didn't think you could be more beautiful. I realize now, Mrs. Morgan, that I was wrong. Tonight, you're even more beautiful, and all mine, Trenna Morgan. Let me…" he kissed the sensitive spot behind her ear, "…make love to you."

Before Trenna could do more than nod, Darrin rained kisses down her throat. She sighed as he tongued the hollow at the base of her throat. He lingered there, before placing kiss after heated kiss in the valley between her small, plump breasts. She moaned when he peppered the swell of each curve with more kisses.

Dark blue flames of desire lit his eyes as he took a hard, ebony peak into his mouth. He took his time, leisurely tasting her, savoring her as if he were sampling a drop of rich chocolate. By the time Darrin moved to the other breast Trenna felt as if she were on fire from the scorching heat of his hungry mouth. She practically sizzled from the inside out.

Unaware of her soft moans, she clung to him. He felt so good, so right against her. As she inhaled his scent, she fully accepted her love for him. He was strong and capable but also kind and tender. Most important, he was all hers. Suddenly, she wanted to touch him, longed to caress him.

She began by caressing the column of his throat, and then ran her hands over the broad lines of his shoulders and his chest before she moved to stroke his muscular arms.

"Goodness!" she whispered. What was he doing to her? While burning for him, she was eager to give and receive pleasure. As she caressed him she could not help but marvel at his keen response to her touch. Trenna kissed a path down his throat down, tongued his small, rigid nipple as thoroughly as he had laved hers.

His groans of enjoyment were like a full concert to her ears. Her heart swelled with joy. Knowing she was able to pleasure him thrilled her to her very core. In that instant, her past inadequacy no longer mattered. All she could think about was loving him. When Trenna lifted her head, Darrin was breathing hard, uneven.

"Sweetheart," he husked, "you were not supposed to do that."

Eyes wide with apprehension, she asked, "No?"

He confessed, "It feels too good. What are you trying to do to me, love? Drive me out of my mind? Or make me completely lose control?"

She laughed in delight. "Absolutely!" She dipped her head to repeat the action. Darrin moaned, and then lifted her until he could cover her lips with his. This kiss was even deeper than the last, urgent with need. And her response was immediate and spontaneous. She didn't weigh or analyze her reaction.

Like a dew-kissed rose, blooming in the morning light, Trenna opened herself to him. She matched him kiss for hot, hungry kiss. She needed him now, craved the full force of Darrin's love. She was breathless by the time he raised his head. Her lips were swollen from his kisses. Darrin cupped Trenna's breasts.

"Beautiful," he murmured before he thoroughly laved each nipple in turn. He dropped back on his haunches and kissed his way down her ribcage to her stomach, then licked her belly button.

Gasping she fell back on the bed. Before she could catch her breath, he kissed the soft curls covering her mound. With shivers racing along her nerve endings, she leaned up onto her elbow in order to watch as Darrin placed a trail of damp kisses along the inside of her left thigh.

"No!" she exclaimed. Although shocked at the level of intimacy, Trenna couldn't stop shaking from the sheer pleasure of his mouth on her skin. And he had accused her of driving him out of his mind. She was the one losing control of her senses.

"No?" He paused, and looked up, into her eyes. "You want me to stop?" He didn't wait for a verbal response, instead, he licked the length of her right thigh.

Gasping from the pleasure, she covered mound. Darrin lingered on the tiny mole at the top of her thigh. He laved it slowly.

"Darrin…"

"What, my love? Am I hurting you? Or just making you uncomfortable?"

Unable to swallow a soft moan, she managed to get out, "You know you aren't hur…"

"I love you and you love me, but do you trust me?" When she quickly nodded, he said in a husky whisper, "Then, let me love you."

Trenna was shaking with desire when she removed her hand. Darrin's large fingers, tenderly parted her damp folds, and slowly caressing her. He didn't stop until Trenna was dewy and soft. She called out when he dipped his head and leisurely tasted her. This time, he was the one who moaned, as if he were savoring a drop of chocolate. Trenna was sizzling hot, as flames of desire surged throughout her entire system. Overcome by the intensity of the pleasure, she screamed his name as she climaxed. When she came back to herself, she realized they were in the center of the king-size bed. The top sheet, blanket and comforter had been shoved to the foot of the bed. Darrin was wearing a huge grin.

"Don't gloat. It's unbecoming," she teased, as she smoothed her hands over his hair-roughed chest. "Besides, it's my turn."

Quirking a dark brow, he drawled, "Should I ask what you plan to do, Mrs. Morgan?"

"Well, Mr. Morgan, I plan to make love to you until you holler for mercy."

Darrin said one word—"Hurry"—then leaned back against the pillows with his hands laced behind his head.

Trenna's heart was full of love as she digested the knowledge that she had his heart. She was so giddy with the excitement of having full access to his beautiful, muscular body that her mind raced from all the possibilities.

She caressed Darrin as boldly as he had done to her earlier. Like him, she didn't rush, taking her time as she made her way down his chest, first caressing, and then licking her way down to his flat stomach. He bolstered her confidence when he husked her name.

She loved the texture of his skin. He was deliciously toned and muscular, yet smooth in some places and hair-roughed in others. "Goodness! You're so..." she hesitated.

"Needy? Hard?"

She laughed. There was no doubting the strength of his desire for her. It was there in the smoldering, heat of his gaze. But most important to her, she knew this was more than desire and pent-up longing. Despite his own needs, he had waited for her. This realization proved beyond all doubt that he genuinely loved her and assured her he would always put her first. She was deeply touched.

"Trenna..." he husked out when she touched him. He was rock-hard, his skin both hot and soft, like velvet over hard steel. He took her hands and showed her how to stroke along his entire length from thick root to the broad tip. She was thrilled by his deep guttural groans of pleasure. She was just getting into it when he caught her hands and held them still.

She frowned. "But I want to please you like..."

"Like what, baby? What I did to you?"

At her nod Darrin's dark eyes heated. "I'd like that, but another time. I need to be inside of you. Okay?"

"Yes." She'd barely got the word out when he swung his legs over the side of the bed. "Where are you going?"

"Condoms." He reached for his duffle bag.

"Don't." Her gaze locked with his when she said, "We don't need them." He hesitated, but before he could speak she rushed ahead to say, "I don't want to wait. I love you and want your babies."

"Are you sure?"

"Yes, I'm ready. How about you?" She didn't realize she was holding her breath until she saw his grin. She gasped for air. There was a rush of relief and happiness the instant he crossed over to her and gave her a hard, hungry kiss. Stroking his back, his shoulders, his chest, she hugged him close.

She asked in a nervous whisper, "You don't mind...not waiting?"

He chuckled, moving against her. "I'm more than ready to do my part."

She giggled until his mouth settled over hers. His kisses were hot and urgent, brimming with need. She opened her mouth for him, deepening the kiss, and opened her body, wrapping her arms around his neck and her legs around his waist. There was no hesitation on her part as Trenna welcomed Darrin.

"Sweet," he said close to her ear as his stroking fingers found she was wet, ready for him. He took care to keep most of his weight off her, by resting on his forearms. He caressed her, using his hair-roughed chest to tease her soft breasts, and then he licked each taut peak in turn. While she moaned her pleasure, he rubbed the hard crown of his sex against her mound.

She shivered, enjoying the feel of him along her entire length.

"Love me..." she urged.

"My sweet Trenna ... My love," he groaned as she instinctively tightened around him. With a deep, throaty growl, he surged forward, slowly filling her emptiness.

"Ooh! Darrin," she gasped.

Finally, they were one. She pressed her lips against his as they connected on every level. Goodness... It felt right, better than she remembered. And this time there was no pain as she eagerly accepted his entire hard length. She welcomed him into both her body and her heart. There was no holding back or any doubts. There was only deep hunger, burgeoning need...and so much love.

She felt his desire for her. It was raw, in the most basic form. Yet, Trenna was unafraid because of the love they shared. All her adult life she had hoped for, even dreamed about, such intimacy. What they shared surpassed even her wildest dreams. Her senses soared as she felt the strength and power of their connection... their commitment. Without even realizing it, that love had become as essential to her well-being as any of her major organs. She needed this...needed him. Knowing he was hers alone was exhilarating.

Her breathing quickened and her heart pounded with excitement when he dropped his head and took a hard peak deep into his mouth to suckle while he thrust into her. She cried out as the pleasure spiraled. He didn't stop there. Darrin cupped Trenna's hips, silently urging her to open even more for him. And she did. She couldn't hold anything back from him. She gave him her all and was richly rewarded by his deep groans. She clung to him, even managed to keep up with his relentless pace. He was moving hard and fast.

When he thrust even deeper, he stroked her ultra-sensitive knob. She trembled uncontrollably as he repeated the move, but he didn't slow, didn't stop. He increased his pace until she was quivering all over like a willow in a windstorm.

She nearly asked him to stop but soon realized that was the last thing she wanted. It was incredible. No, he was incredible, and she told him so. Then she gasped, "Darrin. Yes. Oh, yes!" She tongued then sucked his earlobe.

He shuddered. "Love me," he chanted.

"Yes." He was hers and she was his. They were bombarded with the most intense sensations. Her entire body tingled. She was achingly close…on the edge but couldn't seem to get there on her own. He quickened his pace, giving her the hard, firm strokes she craved.

"Don't stop!"

He didn't stop, but reached between them to caress her taut, ultra-sensitive, button of nerve-endings. Trenna screamed his name as she climaxed and Darrin issued a hoarse shout. They convulsed in the same instant, soaring as if they were hurled through time and space. Together they experienced the ultimate pinnacle, just as they intended to go on throughout their lives… Partners and lovers… Sharing everything. Lost in a mind-numbing daze the pleasure seemed to go on and on. Gradually their heart rates slowed and their bodies cooled.

Darrin was the first to speak. "You okay, love?" He rolled onto his side, bringing Trenna against him.

"I'm better than okay," Trenna nearly purred. She rested with her head on Darrin's chest, her arm around his waist. "Have you no shame?" she teased.

Chuckling, he quipped, "None when it comes to making love to you," then sobered. "Did I hurt you?"

"No!"

He released a pent-up sigh. "I was so hungry for you that I lost it. For weeks, all I thought about was making love to you. Since I put my ring on your finger, the need has been relentless. Should I apologize? I hope I didn't upset or shock you. I'm not like Mar—"

She pressed her fingers against his mouth to stop him. "I know that. Tonight was about you and me, no one else. Nothing we shared reminded me of Martin." She cupped his face. "Thank you for making our wedding night special."

"No, thank you, my love. I'm glad you're not upset. Tonight was magical, just as our wedding was perfect."

She smiled then said candidly, "I wish I could change my past, but I can't. The good and the bad, the ugly, it all happened."

"True, but why not focus on being glad it's finally over?" He moved a caressing hand down her back and over her shoulder.

"This feels so good. I've waited forever to finally have you all to myself like this."

"But we agreed to wait."

"I know. I'm not saying I have any regrets. The wait wasn't easy," he admitted. "And I'm relieved it's behind us. "

"It wasn't easy for me either," she confessed. "You were so sweet to share your fantasy with me, let me know what to expect. Because of your candor, fear was the furthest thing from my mind."

"Good. You deserve to be happy."

She kissed the base of his throat, savoring his scent. "All I thought about was you, my sweet husband, my lover, and my heart. Married one day and already you've made me feel so loved and appreciated. Will it always be like this, so..." She struggled to find the word.

"Incredible?" he supplied. "It was that way for me."

"Really?" she beamed.

"Yes. Get used to it, my love," he crooned into her ear, "because I hope to make love to you often."

"Next time I'll wear your shirt?" Trenna giggled at the size of his grin.

But Darrin was serious when he said, "I got the impression that you married Martin when you were the most vulnerable and in need of a friend, not a lover."

"True. When we married I believed we loved each other. It was years before I understood the difference between loving someone and being in love. What we had wasn't enough to make what was wrong between us right. It's taken a good deal of time and prayer for me to accept that it's okay. I've learned from it.

"Most important, I've gotten to the point where I've been able forgive Martin and myself. We both made mistakes." She lifted up so she could look into his eyes. "I'm glad it's finally over and I have moved on. I have so much to be grateful for. And I'm so thankful that God has given me a second chance at love and marriage. This time I intend to get it right."

Trenna's stomach growled loudly. They both laughed.

"Sweetheart, we'd better feed you. I didn't see you do more than nibble at the reception." Brushing his lips against hers, he said, "Come on. Let's grab a shower and get something to eat. Our flight leaves early."

"How early?" she quizzed as he ushered her into the bathroom.

"Eight."

"You still haven't told me where we are going."

He just grinned but didn't answer.

THEY PUT on robes and ordered an elaborate array of cheeses, fruit, and finger sandwiches. Trenna couldn't stop laughing when Darrin wheeled the food chart into the bedroom.

"What are you doing?"

"Exactly what it looks like," he grinned and stacked pillows against the headboard. He patted the place beside him. "Come on, sugar. Let's eat."

Settling in, she surmised, "Not worried about crumbs."

"That's right."

As she watched her new husband bow his head to give thanks for the meal it hit home that she was truly blessed. She had never dreamed it was possible to be this happy. Overcome by emotions, tears suddenly filled her eyes. She tried to quickly wipe them away.

"Trenna..." Darrin put down the plate he'd been filling. "What's wrong, baby?"

She laughed. "Not one thing. I'm so happy." And it was absolutely true. For the first time since her parents passed she didn't fear the future. No matter what might be ahead, she knew beyond all doubt that together they would find a way to get through it.

"You, my love, are a very special man. I'm sorry it took me so long for me to really see you and even longer to trust you. I'm so grateful for how patient you've been with me. It would have been so easy for you to give up and walk away from me." She blinked back fresh tears. "Despite all the mess I threw your way, you never gave up on me. Tell me why?"

"After you take a bit of this."

She nibbled on a turkey and cheese sandwich. "Okay. Now, tell me. It was the challenge, right?"

"No. It was always you. For a long time, I assumed you were grieving and were still in love with Martin. I kept telling myself to be patient, give you the time you needed." He paused, taking a swallow of bottled water, then admitted, "It was tough. As a distraction, I dated as many women as I could, hoping to get over you. It didn't work, nothing worked. It felt like a kick in the teeth when you accused me of being a player, of sleeping with every woman in the building. No matter what I said or did you refused to have anything to do with me. "

"You know why." She fed him a chocolate-covered strawberry.

"Mmm," he said. "You can believe I wasn't laughing then. It really got to me. So I kept reminding myself that I was a Morgan and we don't run from battle. But there was no getting around it. I wanted you. When we met I knew there was something special about you, something that spoke to my heart. I needed you in my life. No matter what you threw at me or how often you said no, I kept coming back. I couldn't walk away."

He chuckled. "You made my day when you got off on the wrong floor. I was convinced you were weakening and were too stubborn to admit there was something between us. But you quickly shot me down. I called myself all kinds of bad names because instead of walking away I came back for more of the same."

He kissed her hard and she wrapped her arms around his neck. She whispered, "I'm glad."

He grinned. "Me too. I was drawn to you from the first moment I saw you. Somehow, I knew you were the one for me. Heck, I liked everything about you. You're feisty, intelligent, hardworking, talented, and so incredibly sexy that it was tough to keep my hands off you. I made no secret that I wanted you, Trenna McAdams."

She teased, "It's Trenna Morgan."

Darrin grinned. "I forgot. It won't happen again." His kiss was slow and tender. "I'm so proud of you. You had to be strong, and determined in order to make your school successful. And you did it! I was so impressed by your determination to give back. I had to find a way to help you."

"I didn't know what to think when you invited me out to dinner to meet your friends. It shook me up, forced me to notice you."

"Good." He smiled as they shared a flute of pink champagne. "Despite that hard-shell you showed the world, I sensed your vulnerability. Talk about a puzzle, you, my love, are that in spades." Laughing, he said, "And you're right. You challenged me, intrigued me. Mostly, you infuriated me when you wouldn't give an inch. I lost count of the number of times you told me no. But what bugged me the most, you were dating men I knew, some even worked in the building."

"Dating, not sleeping with," she reminded.

"And I knew that how?"

"I didn't want you to know."

"Yeah. I suspected you were hiding something because you were so guarded, practically had 'no trespassing' stamped all over you. It's a good thing I'm stubborn, because I tried everything I could think of to change your mind. Then you shocked me when you came over and helped when we lost dad. I was touched by your candor and kindness. Afterwards, I started to wonder why.

"I hated the way things were between us. So when Maureen called and said you needed a ride home, I was all ears."

She cuddled close, giving him a bite of her strawberry. "And I was stuck. I had to say yes. But I found you highly annoying. I didn't want to spend time with you, certainly didn't want you to be nice to me. Mostly, I didn't want to care about you. My awareness of you was so strong it scared me silly. That night changed everything. I fed you, even though every single time you were near I felt things I didn't want to feel." Trenna giggled, "I couldn't decide who I was angrier with you or Maureen but, because her grandmother was ill, you won."

"Won? Hardly. That night I reached my limit. After we made love and you pushed me away, I was sure I was done." He chuckled, "I didn't realize you had wormed your way into my heart."

"Wormed!" she challenged.

"Yeah."

"Darrin, I will always regret the way that night ended. I hurt you and couldn't bear it. I remember how nervous I was when I came to your office. I expected you to throw me out. It was what I deserved. But I needed to see you. Somehow, I had to tell you how I felt about you. I couldn't keep it inside, any longer.

"Sweet man, I love you so much," she whispered, then kissed him. "You listened to me, which means so much. You're the one I have been waiting for, even when I didn't realize I was waiting. I was convinced I didn't need or want a man in my life. Oh, honey, you were so patient with me, and you kept loving me. You accepted me despite my endless flaws and hang-ups."

"Trenna, none of us are perfect, least of all me. It tore me apart when you blamed me for taking Todd Marks' case, for getting him off, and subsequently hurting your friend."

"I was wrong. You were doing your job."

He said, "It was a tough time for us. Yet, you were there when I needed you the most. Losing my father left me angry, bitter, and feeling broken inside. Both my brother and my mother tried to reach me, but couldn't. You came over, you sat with me, stayed until I understood you knew the pain of loss because you'd lived it. Because of you I was able to open up and talk.

"I think that was when I realized what I felt was more than desire." Darrin said tenderly, "I knew I was in love with you. You reminded me that I still had a heavenly Father and He had not turned his back on me. Thank you, my love."

Smiling, Trenna shook her head. "I should be the one thanking you. You allowed us to start our new life together in this very special way. By honoring God our marriage will be blessed for it. Even though the waiting was harder for you than for me because of my fears, it was important and meant so much to me. I am so grateful because you put your love for me on full display. All my doubts about remarrying are gone."

He studied her eyes before he asked, "What about the fears?

She shrugged. "Gone, thanks to you."

They exchanged a deeply, passionate kiss.

Snuggling against him, she said, "Darrin, thank you for giving me a second chance at love. I can almost see a future, filled with love and babies."

"You're welcome. Our marriage may feel like a second chance, but it's okay if you need a third or fourth, even. The door to my heart is open to as many chances as you need. God's love lasts forever and I pray our love will last just as long. As long as we remain honest and open with each other, there is nothing to stop us."

She nodded because her throat was closed by tears of joy. As she pressed her lips his, she vowed, "I promise no more secrets."

"Me, too."

"Good. That means you can tell me where we're going tomorrow morning on our honeymoon."

"Alaska!" Darrin laughed when she shuddered with dread. "No, I'm just teasing. We're going to our vacation home in Honolulu, Hawaii."

"We have a home in…?"

He nodded. "We do now. Years ago my father bought it as an anniversary surprise for my mother. She hasn't been back since he passed. She gave me the keys and the deed to the property before the ceremony...our wedding gift from her and Dad."

"Wow!"

She remembered to give thanks to her God for His goodness, and then she wrapped her arms around her husband's neck to bring his mouth down to hers.

ALSO BY BETTE FORD

Mrs. Green's Girls Series

Can't Get Enough of You

Can't Stop Loving You

The Prescott Series

Unforgettable

An Everlasting Love

Can't Say No

Malcolm-X Community Center Series

For Always

Forever After

After Dark

One of a Kind

Single Title Romances

Mama's Pearl

All the Love

Island Magic

When a Man Loves a Woman

ABOUT THE AUTHOR

Bette Ford grew up in Saginaw Michigan, where she continues to live. She obtained her bachelor's degree from Central State University in Wilberforce, Ohio. Bette began her teaching career in Detroit and completed a master's degree at Wayne State University. She has taught in the Detroit Public School HEAD-START Project for many years. She is now writing full time.

She has received several awards, including the Romantic Times Reviewers Choice Award for Best Multicultural Romance, as well as the Romantic Times Career Achievement Award.

She is the author of eleven books including, UNFORGET-TABLE, AN EVERLASTING LOVE and CAN'T SAY NO. She truly enjoys hearing from readers.

Please connect with Bette on her website or Facebook!

CPSIA information can be obtained
at www.ICGtesting.com
Printed in the USA
LVHW081320240219
608548LV00007BA/64/P